Red Rose and Tiger Lily

L. T. Meade

Contents

RED ROSE AND TIGER LILY

BY

L. T. Meade

CHAPTER I.
NAN'S GOLDEN MANE.

It was a perfect summer's evening. The sun had just set, and purple, gold, violet, rose colour still filled the sky in the west. There was a tender new moon, looking like a silver bow, also to be seen; before long the evening star would be visible.

Hester Thornton stepped out of the drawing-room at the Grange, and, walking a little way down the broad gravel sweep, began to listen intently. Hester was about seventeen--a slender girl for her age. Her eyes were dark, her eyebrows somewhat strongly marked, her abundant hair, of a much lighter shade of brown, was coiled in close folds round her well-shaped head. Her lips were slightly compressed, her chin showed determination. Hester had not been beautiful as a child, and she was not beautiful as a girl, but her face was pleasant to look at, very bright when animated, very steadfast and sweet when in repose. The air was like nectar to her cheeks. She was naturally a pale girl, but a faint rose colour was now discernible in her complexion, and the look of expectation in her dark eyes made them charming.

A step was heard on the gravel behind, and she turned quickly.

"Is that you, father?" she exclaimed.

"Yes. Are not you very imprudent to come out at this hour in your thin house shoes, and with nothing on your head? There is a very heavy dew falling."

"Oh, I never take cold," replied Hester with a smile, which showed her even and pretty white teeth; "and I certainly shan't to-night," she continued, "for I am feeling far too excited."

Sir John Thornton was considered by most of his acquaintances (he could boast of scarcely any friends) as a reserved and almost repellent person, but now, as his eyes rested on his young daughter, something seemed to soften their expression; he took her slight hand and drew it affectionately through his arm.

"It takes a small thing to excite you, my love," he said; "but you always were of a turbulent disposition--just your poor mother over again."

Hester sighed faintly when Sir John spoke of his wife, then she quickly cheered up and said in an eager voice--

"You don't call it a little thing, father, to know that in a minute or two I shall welcome Nan back from school? Nan comes to-night--Annie Forest to-morrow. It would be difficult for any girl to want more to make her perfectly happy."

Sir John raised his brows.

"I only know Miss Forest by hearsay," he said, "so I will reserve my judgment upon her; but I do know Nan. She will upset the entire *regime* of the house. I like order, and she likes disorder. I like quiet meals, she likes uproarious ones. I hate shocks and she adores them. I am glad, of course, to welcome the child home, but at the same time I dread her arrival. I cannot possibly understand how it is that Mrs. Willis, who is supposed to be such a splendid instructor of youth, should not have brought Nan a little better into control. Now, you, my dear Hetty, are very different. You have passions and feelings--no one has them more strongly--but you keep them in check. Your reticence and your reserve please me much. In short, Hester, no father could have a more admirable daughter to live with him. I am pleased with you, my dear; the experiment of having you home from school to look after my house has turned out well. There is nothing I would not do to please you, and while your friend Miss Forest is here, I will do my best to render her visit a success. The only discordant element will be Nan. I cannot understand why Mrs. Willis has not got Nan into the same control she had you in."

"You forget," said Hester, "that I am seventeen and Nan only eight. No one ever yet could say 'No' to Nan. Father, don't you hear the carriage wheels? She is coming--I know she is coming. Please forgive me, I must run to meet her."

Sir John released his daughter's hand, and Hester flew with the speed of an arrow from a bow up the long avenue. She was not mistaken. Her keen ears had detected the smooth roll of wheels. A landau drawn by a pair of horses had even now entered the lodge gates. Hester, looking up, heard some gay voices, some childish laughter. Then an imperious voice shouted to the coachman to pull up the horses and Nan Thornton and another girl sprang out of the carriage and ran to Hester's side.

Confused utterances, sundry embraces, the quick intermingling of ejaculations, kisses, commands, explanatory remarks--all rose on the sweet night air.

"Hetty, you look quite grown up. Please, Jenkins, you can drive on to the house. I'm not getting in again. Aren't you glad to see me, Het? I have come back a greater tease and torment than ever."

"Yes, Nan, delighted--more than delighted. Oh! you sweet, how nice it is to feel you kissing me! Why, Annie, how did you happen to come to-night? I didn't expect you until to-morrow. I was wondering how I could endure the next twenty-four hours of expectation, even with Nan to keep me company, and now you are here. Oh, how very, very glad I am."

"Kiss me, Hester," said Annie. "Nan and I concocted this little plan. We thought we'd take you by surprise. Oh dear, oh dear, I feel so wild and excited that I'm sure I shall be just as troublesome as I used to be before you tamed me down at school. Now then, Nan, you are not to have all the kisses. Hester, dear, how sweet and gracious and prim and lady-of-the-manorish you do look!"

"I don't care what I look like, I only know what I feel," replied Hester: "about the happiest girl in England. But don't let us stand here talking any longer, or father will take it into his head that I am catching cold in the night air. Here, Nan, take my arm. Annie, my other side is at your disposal. Now, do let us come to the house."

The girls began to move slowly down the long winding avenue. Nan had the pretty, soft dark eyes which used to characterise her as a little child. Her abundant fluffy golden hair hung below her waist. Her baby lips and sweet little face looked as charming as of old. She was a very pretty child, and promised to be a beautiful woman by-and-by. Her beauty, however, was nothing at all beside the radiant sort of loveliness which Annie Forest possessed. She was a creature all moods, all expression, all life, all movement. She had early given promise of remarkable beauty, and this had been more than fulfilled. Hester glanced at her now and again in the most loving admiration.

"It is good to have you back, Nan," she said, "and it is delightful to know that you have come at last to pay your long, long promised visit," she continued, looking at Annie. "Well, here we are at home. Nan, you must go up and show yourself to nurse this minute. Annie, let me take you to your room."

"Dear old nursey," said Nan; she rushed up the stairs, shouting her old nurse's name as she went; her quick footsteps flew down the long corridor, she pushed open the baize door which separated the nurseries from the rest of the house, and in a moment found herself in the old room.

Nan's nurse was a cherry-cheeked old woman of between sixty and seventy years of age.

"Eh, my darling, and how did you get back without me hearing the sound of the carriage wheels!" she exclaimed. "Eh dear, eh dear, I meant to be down on the front steps to greet you, Miss Nan. Eh, but you look bonny, and let me examine your hair, dear--I hope they cut the points regular. If they don't, it will break away and not keep even."

"Oh, don't bother about my hair now," said Nan. "What does hair signify when a child has just got home, and when she wants a kiss more than anything else in the world? Now, nursey, sit down in that low armchair and let us have a real hug. *That's* better; and how are you? You look as jolly as ever."

"So I am, my pet; I'm as happy as the day is long since Miss Hetty has come home and took the housekeeping over. I was in a mortal fret before, with her at school and you at school, but now I think the danger is past."

"What danger?" asked Nan; "you always were a dear old croak, you know, nurse."

"Yes, pet, perhaps so; but I didn't fret without reason, you may be quite sure of that."

"Well, what were you afraid of? You know I'm an awfully curious girl, so you must tell me."

"It's a sin to be too curious, Miss Nan--it leads people into untold mischief. Curiosity was the sin of Eve, and it's best to nip it in the bud while you're young. Now let me brush out your hair, my darling, and get you ready for supper."

"Yes, in a minute," said Nan. She pushed back the shady hat in which she had traveled, and seated herself afresh on her nurse's knee.

"How do my kisses feel?" she asked, breathing a very soft one on each of the old woman's cheeks.

"Eh, dear," said the nurse, "they're like fresh cream and strawberries."

"Well, you shall have six more if you tell me what your fears were."

Nurse looked admiringly back at Nan.

"You're just the audacious, contrary, troublesome bit of a thing you always were," she said; "but somehow I can't resist you. There's no fear now of anything happening, so you needn't be in a taking; but what did put me out was this: I thought your father, Sir John, might be bringing a new mistress here."

"What! a new mistress?--A housekeeper, do you mean?" Nan's brown eyes were open at their widest.

"No, dearie, no, a wife--someone to take the head of the house. Men like Sir John must have their comforts, and a house without a mistress isn't as it ought to be. But there, Miss Hetty is here now, and that makes everything right."

"But a new mistress," repeated Nan--"a new wife for father. Why, she--she'd be a *stepmother*. Oh, how I'd hate her."

"Well, darling, there's not going to be any such person; it was only an idle fear of your poor old nurse's that will never come to anything. Forget that I said it to you, Miss Nan. Oh, my word! and there's the gong, so supper is ready, and Sir John won't like to be kept waiting. Let me brush out your hair, I won't be a minute. Now, there's my pretty. It's good to have you back again, Miss Nancy. Only I misdoubt me that you'll turn the house topsy-turvy, as you always and ever did."

While nurse was speaking, she was deftly and quickly changing Nan's travel-stained frock for a white one, and was tying a coral pink sash round her waist.

"Now you're ready," she said, giving the little figure a final pat.

Nan shook out her golden mane and went demurely downstairs--more demurely than was her wont. The dawning of possible trouble filled her sweet eyes. A new wife--a possible stepmother! Oh, no, by no possibility could such a horror be coming; nevertheless, her full cup of happiness was vaguely troubled by the thought.

CHAPTER II.
CRUSHED.

Sir John Thornton could be a very pleasant host. He was a reserved man with a really cold nature. He disliked fuss and what he called "ebullitions of affection;" he hated kissing and fondling. He liked to treat even his nearest and dearest with ceremony, but he was a perfect host--the little attentions, the small politenesses which the *role* of host requires, suited his character exactly. Hester and Nan, his only children, were his opposites in every respect. It is true that Hester inherited some of his pride, and a good deal of his reserve, but the fire underneath her calm, the passionate love which she could give so warmly to her chosen friends, she inherited from her mother, not from her father. Nan had never yet shown reserve to anyone. As far as any creature could be said to be without false pride, Nan was that individual--she was also absolutely devoid of fear. She believed that all the world loved her. Why not? She was perfectly willing to love all the world back again. If it chose to hate her, she could and would hate it in return with interest; but, then, why should it? The world was a good place to Nan Thornton up to the present.

Now, Sir John dreaded his impulsive younger daughter more than words can say. Perhaps somewhere in his heart he had a certain fatherly admiration for her, but if so it did not show itself in the usual fatherly way. Annie Forest was at the present moment absorbing his attention.

Annie was between sixteen and seventeen years of age; she was still, of course, quite a child in Sir John's eyes, but she was undoubtedly very pretty--she had winning ways and bright glances. Her little speeches were full of wit and repartee, and she was naturally so full of tact that she knew when a word would hurt, and therefore seldom said it.

When Nan entered the room in which a hasty supper had been prepared for the hungry travellers, she found her father and Annie talking pleasantly to one another at one end of the table, while Hester presided over the tea equipage at the other.

"Here you are, little whirlwind," said Sir John, slipping his arm round his younger daughter's waist and drawing her for a moment to his side.

Nan looked at him soberly. She gazed into his eyes and examined the curves of his lips, and noted with satisfaction the wrinkles on his brow, the crows' feet at the corner of each eye, and some strong lines which betokened the advance of years in the lower part of his face.

"You're too old," she said, in a contemplative voice. "I'm so glad--you're much too old."

She stroked his deepest wrinkle affectionately as she spoke.

Now Sir John hated being considered old, and an angry wave of colour mounted to his forehead.

"As usual, you are a most impolite little girl," he said. "I do not trouble myself to inquire what your sage remark means, nor why you rejoice in the fact of my possessing the infirmities of years; but I wish to repeat to you a proverb which I hope you will bear in mind, at least, when in *my* presence during the holidays, 'Little girls should be seen and not heard.' Now go to your seat."

Sir John released his hold of Nan's broad waist and turned to Annie.

"Yes, a good deal of the country is flat," he said, "but we have some pretty drives. Are you fond of riding?"

"I should be if I had a chance," replied Annie; "but the fact is, I never was on horseback since I was five years old, so I cannot be said to know much about it."

"I am sure you could quickly learn," said Sir John. "Hester has a very quiet pony which she can lend you while you are here. By the way, Hester, Squire Lorrimer called to-day. I said you would go to the Towers to-morrow morning--you can take Miss Forest with you. The Lorrimers are a very lively household, and it will amuse her to know them."

"I should think they are lively," burst from Nan at the far end of the table. "How is Kitty Lorrimer, and how is Boris? And have they got as many pets as ever? Oh, *can* you tell me, please, father, if the dormouse has awakened yet? It was fast asleep when I was home at Christmas, and Boris said it mightn't wake again until May. Boris was so sorry it wasn't quite dead, because he wanted to stuff it; but he couldn't if it was alive, could he? That would be cruel, wouldn't it? Father, can you tell me if the dormouse is awake?"

Sir John fixed a cold eye upon Nan.

"I am unacquainted with the state of the dormouse's health," he said--"disgusting little beasts," he added, turning for sympathy to Annie, whose bright dark eyes danced with fun as she watched him.

"They're not disgusting; they're perfectly heavenly little darlings," came from Nan in an indignant voice. "Oh, and what about the white rats? Boris had four in a box when I went last to the Towers, and Kitty had one all to herself, and Boris and Kitty were always fighting as to which were the most beautiful--the one rat or the four. Did you ever see a white rat, Annie? They *are* pets, with long tails like worms."

"Hester," exclaimed Sir John, "will you induce Nan to hold her tongue and eat her supper in peace?"

Hester bent forward and whispered something to Nan, who shrugged her shoulders indignantly. Her face grew crimson.

"I can't learn that proverb," she said, after a pause. "I can't obey it, its no use trying. Father, do you hear? I can't be one of those seen-and-not-heard girls. Do you hear me, father?"

"I do, Nan. If we have finished supper, shall we go into the drawing-room?" he added, turning to Annie.

Nan lingered behind. She slipped her hand through her sister's arm and dragged her on to the terrace.

"I feel so wicked that I think I'll burst," she exclaimed. "Why is father always throwing a damp cloth over me?"

"Nan, dear, you irritate him a good deal. Why do you talk in that silly way when you know he cannot bear it?"

"Because I'm Nan," answered the child, pouting her lips.

"But Nan can learn wisdom," said Hester, in her sweet elder-sisterly tone. "Even though you are the liveliest, merriest, dearest little girl in the world, and though it is delicious to have you back"--here there came an ecstatic hug--"you need not say things that you know will hurt. For instance, you are perfectly well aware that father does not like his age commented on."

"Oh, *that*," said Nan, some of the trouble which nurse's words had caused coming back to her eyes. "Oh, but I really said what I *meant*, then--it was not mischief. I was so glad to see that he is old. I love those wrinkles of his--I adore them."

"What can you mean, you queer little thing?"

"Why, you see, Hetty, he won't be attractive, and there'll be no fear."

"No fear of what?"

"Nurse said that perhaps he'd be having a wife, and giving us a stepmother."

"Oh, what nonsense!" said Hester, in a vexed tone. "What a silly thing for nurse to say. I am quite surprised at her. As far as I can tell our father has no intention of marrying again; but if he did?"

"If he did," repeated Nancy, "nurse says that you wouldn't be mistress of the Grange any longer."

A wistful sort of look, half of pain, half of suppressed longing, filled Hester's dark eyes for a moment.

"I might go out into the world," she said, "and have my heart's desire."

"But aren't you happy here?"

"Yes, oh yes! I am talking nonsense. My duty lies here, at least at present. Mrs. Willis has taught me always to put duty first. Now, Nan, let us forget what is not likely to happen. It is nearly time for you to go to bed; you look quite tired; there are black rings under your eyes; but first, just tell me about Mrs. Willis and the dear old school."

"Mrs. Willis is well," said Nan, with a yawn, "and the school is in *statu quo*. I am in the middle school now, and perhaps I shall get a drawing-room to myself before long. I'm not sure though, for I never can be tidy."

"I wish you could be; it's a pity not to curb one's faults."

"Oh, bother faults. I don't want you to lecture me, Hetty."

"No, darling, I don't wish to; but I thought you were so fond of Mrs. Willis. I thought you would do anything to please her."

"Yes, of course. I think I do please her. She gave me two prizes at the break up--one for French and one for music. She kissed me, too, quite half-a-dozen times. Look here, Hetty, I don't want you to ask Annie Forest a lot of questions about me.

I can't help having a romping time now and then at school; and there are two new girls--Polly and Milly Jenkins; they are so killingly funny; nearly as good as Boris and Kitty Lorrimer. I always had a little bit of the wild element in me, and I suppose it must come out somehow. Annie was wild enough when she was my age, wasn't she, Hester?"

"Annie will be gay and light-hearted to the end of the chapter!" exclaimed Hester.

"But she was naughty when she was my age, wasn't she?"

"She is not naughty now."

"Well, no more will I be when I am sixteen. Now, good-night, Het. Am I to sleep in your room?"

"Yes."

"How scrumptious. Look out for a fine waking early in the morning."

Nan hugged Hester in her usual rough-and-ready manner, and danced upstairs, singing as she went--

"Old Daddy-long-legs wouldn't say his prayers,   Catch him by his left leg and throw him downstairs."

This was one of Nan's rhymes which Sir John detested. Her voice was loud and somewhat piercing. He heard it in the drawing-room, and went deliberately and shut the door.

"Miss Forest," he said to his young guest, "there are moments when I feel extremely uneasy with regard to the fate of my youngest daughter."

"About Nan's fate?" exclaimed Annie, raising her arched eyebrows; "why, she is quite the dearest little thing in the world. I wish you could see her at school; she is the pet of all the girls at Lavender House."

"That may be," said Sir John, with a slightly sarcastic movement of his thin lips; "but it does not follow that school pets are home pets. If my good friend, Mrs. Willis, finds Nan's society so agreeable, I wish she would arrange to keep her for the holidays."

Annie's young face, so round, so fresh, so charming, was fixed in grave surprise on her elderly host.

"Don't you love Nan at all?" she asked, wonder in her tone.

Sir John had been giving Miss Forest credit for great tact. Up to this moment, he had considered her a very pretty, agreeable little girl, who would be an accuisition in the house. Now he winced; she had trodden very severely on one of his corns.

"I naturally have a regard for my child," he said, after a pause, "and I presume that I show it best by having her properly educated and disciplined in her youth."

"Oh, no, I don't think you do," said Annie. "You must forgive me for saying frankly what I really think. I used to be like Nan when I was a little girl, and I'd never have changed--never--never, I'd never have become thoughtful for others. I'd always have been an unmitigated horror to all my friends if my father had treated me like that. He's not a bit like you, Sir John. I don't mean to compare him to you for a moment. He is quite a rough sort of man, and he has led a rough life; but, oh dear me, from the time he came back from Australia, and I knew that I had a living father, I cannot tell you what a difference there has been in my life. I have generally spent my holidays with him, and he has loved me so much that I have loved him back again, and have learnt to know exactly what will please him and make him happy. Nothing tamed me so much as the knowledge that I was necessary to my father's happiness. I am sure," added Annie in a low voice, and with a suspicion of tears in her eyes, "that it would be just the same with dear little Nan."

She broke down suddenly, half afraid of her own temerity. There was silence for nearly half a minute then Sir John rose from his chair, and, going over to a lamp which was slightly smoking, turned it down.

"If your father has been in Australia," he said, turning again and looking fixedly at his young visitor, "you will be interested in books on that country. I have got all Henry Kingsley's novels. You will find them in the library. Ask Hester to show you the book-case."

He strode deliberately out of the room, and Annie had to own to herself that she felt crushed.

CHAPTER III.
TWO PROVERBS.

Hester Thornton and Annie Forest had been educated at the same school--the well-known Lavender House. The fame of this school, the noble character of its mistress, the excellent training which each girl who went there received, formed a recommendation for each young student in after life. Hester and Annie had gone through severe storms in these early days. Their friendship had been cemented under the influence of great trouble. It was exactly a year now since Hester had been suddenly sent for from her busy and happy school life to take care of her father through a dangerous illness. He found her company so sweet, her skill and tact in managing his house so great, that he resolved not to allow her to go back to school again. Annie Forest was now, therefore, the head girl at Lavender House. She was Mrs. Willis's right hand; her help and support in every way. Annie was as great a favourite as of old, and as love and kindness had developed all the best side of her character, she was no longer the tomboy of the school, nor the one who was invariably the ringleader when mischief was afloat. She was still impulsive, however--eager, impatient--for such a nature as hers must fight on to the end of the chapter. She did not possess Hester Thornton's steady principles, and would always be influenced, whether for good or evil, by her companions. She was only to spend one more term at school; the future, after that, was practically unknown to her.

"I wish you'd tell me about Nan," said Hester, on the first evening of Annie's visit to the Grange. "I don't know why, but I feel a little anxious about her."

"You need not be," replied Annie. "She is a dear, jolly little pet, and as open as the day."

"She seems to get wilder and wilder," replied Hester. "You must have noticed,

Annie, how she irritates my father."

"Of course I did," replied Annie. "Do you know, Het, that I had the unbounded cheek to give him a piece of my mind this evening?"

Annie was seated on the side of Hester's bed. She was in a blue dressing-gown, and her dark hair, in a mass of rebellious curls, was falling about her shoulders.

"I forgot that Nan was in the room," she said, putting her finger to her lips and glancing in the direction of Nan's small bed. "The little monkey may be awake, and I don't want her to hear my nonsense."

"She is sound asleep," replied Hester. "If she were awake, she would soon acquaint us with the fact."

"Shall I tell you what I really said to your father?" continued Annie.

"I don't know that I want to hear. I hope you did not shock him, for he is prepared to like you very much."

"I am prepared to like him. I think he is a delightful host; but, oh, *how* I should hate him for a father."

"Annie!"

Hester's delicate face flushed crimson, her eyes flashed an angry light.

Annie jumped off the bed and ran to her friend's side.

"Now you are angry with me," she said; "but if I told him the truth, I may surely tell you. I know you are as good as an angel, but I am quite certain that he ruffles you up the wrong way."

"Don't, Annie," said Hester, in a voice of pain.

She walked to the window as she spoke, drew up the blind, and looked out. The night was dark, but innumerable stars could be seen in the deep, unfathomable vault of the sky. Hester clenched one of her hands tightly together. Annie stood and watched her.

"I would not hurt you for the world," she said. "I am sorry, very sorry; the fact is, I love you with all my heart, but I don't understand you."

"Yes you do, too well," replied Hester; "but there are some things I cannot and will not talk about even to you. Now let me take you to your room, the hour is very late."

Annie's pretty room was just on the other side of the passage. Hester took her to it, saw that she had every comfort, and wished her good-night. She then stood for a moment, with a look of irresolution on her face, in the corridor.

"I don't believe nurse is in bed; I will go and speak to her," she said to herself. "I thought the day when I welcomed Nan back from school, and when Annie came to visit me, would be quite the happiest day of my life, but it would never do to make my father's home uncomfortable for him." She reached the baize door, opened it, and soon found herself in the old nursery. She was right, nurse was not yet in bed.

"Well, now, my deary!" exclaimed the old woman, "and why are you losing your beauty sleep in this fashion? When I was young things used to be very different. Girls had to be in bed by ten o'clock sharp to keep away the wrinkles, but now they're all agog to burn the candle at both ends. It don't pay, Miss Hetty, my pet, it don't pay."

"I'm all right, nursey," replied Hester. "I'm the quietest and most jog-trot girl in the world as a rule. Of course I'm excited to-night, because Nan has come back."

"Bless her dear heart!" ejaculated nurse; "but I'm not to say satisfied about her hair, Miss Hetty. I don't believe it's pointed often enough. I found a lot of split ends when I was combing it out to-night."

"Oh, I think Nan is all right in every way," replied Hester. "No one could be kinder to her than Mrs. Willis, and she is very happy at school. Nurse, I've just come here for a moment to ask you to be very careful what you say to Nan about my father. You see, the object of my life is to make him happy, and to be a good daughter to him, and, in short, to try to take my mother's place."

"Eh, dear, we all know that," replied nurse, "and a sweeter young mistress there couldn't be. Why, there isn't a servant in the house who wouldn't do anything in the world for you, Miss Hetty; and everything in apple-pie order, and the meals served regular and beautiful, and inside and out perfect order, and all because there's an old head on young shoulders. There, perhaps it isn't a compliment I'm paying you, my dearie, but in one sense it is."

"Do you really think I manage well?" asked the girl, an anxious tone in her voice.

"Manage well? You manage beautiful. Your own mother, if she were alive, couldn't do better."

"I can never forget my mother," replied Hester, tears rising to her eyes. "Well, nurse, you will be very careful what you say to Nan. The object of my life is to make my father happy. If I can do that, I am content."

"You do, you do," replied the old woman. "No mortal can do more than their best, and you do that. Now, good-night, Miss Hester."

Hester took up her candle and went away. Nurse stood and watched the pretty young figure as it disappeared down the corridor.

"There," she said to herself as she began to prepare for her own bed. "There's another victim. Don't I know what my mistress was, and don't I know that Sir John's coldness and sharpness and no-heartedness just hurried her into her grave? Never a bit of real hearty love could he give to anyone. Just as just could be--righteous as righteous could be, but hard as a flint. My mistress drooped and faded and died, and Miss Hester will follow in her footsteps if I don't look after her. Sometimes I wish the master *would* marry again, and that he'd get a tartar of a wife. He might think of another wife if things were a bit uncomfortable here, but that they never will be while Miss Hetty is at the helm. She's a born manager, bless her, with her gentle ways and her firm words and her pretty little dignity. Miss Nan's business in life, it seems to me, is to set places all in a muddle, and Miss Hetty's to smooth them out again. Of course it's due to Miss Hetty to be mistress of the Grange, but sometimes I fear the life is too much for her, and she'll fret and fade like her mother before her; if I really thought that, I'd set my wits to work, old as I am, to get a real *selfish wife* for the master, who'd teach him a thing or two, for that's what he wants."

At this stage in her meditations, nurse laid her head on her pillow and was soon fast asleep.

The next morning promised a perfect day, and Hester, Annie, and Nan met in high spirits in the breakfast-room. The post had not yet arrived, but a letter was lying on Hester's plate.

"That's in dad's writing," said Nan, going up and examining it critically; "now what's up?"

Hester took the letter and opened it. It contained a few brief words. She read them with a sinking of heart which she could not account for--

"MY DEAR HETTY,--Your young companions will make the house quite gay for you. I shall, therefore, take the opportunity of going from home for a few days. I will send you a line to let you know when you may expect me back.--Your affectionate father, JOHN THORNTON.

"P.S.--I shall have left before you are down in the morning. Give my love to Nan, and wish Miss Forest good-bye for me. By the way, she is interested in Australia, so will you show her where Henry Kingsley's novels are to be found in the library?"

Nan, who had been peeping over Hester's shoulder while she was reading, now suddenly clapped her hands, shouted "hurrah" at the top of her voice, and, running up to Annie, began to waltz round and round the breakfast-table with her.

"Oh, oh!" she exclaimed, "then little girls *may* be heard as well as seen. Annie, there are two proverbs which are the bane of my life. I wonder dad has not had them both illuminated and framed and hung up in my nursery. One of them is: 'Little girls should be seen and not heard.' What a detestable old prig the person must have been who invented that proverb! I ask you, Annie, what would life be without little girls and their chatter? The other proverb is nearly as objectionable. This is it: 'Make a page of your own age.' According to dad, that only applies to little girls, and it means that they must always be fagging round, hunting for slippers and spectacles and newspapers and books for the older people who are past the age for paging, and that no one is ever to wait on *them*, however tired or however disinclined to stir they may happen to be. Now there'll be no one to make me page, and no one to keep me silent. Oh, hurrah, hurrah, hurrah! what a dear old dad to absent himself in this obliging manner."

"For my part, I am very sorry," said Annie, for Hester had passed her on the letter to read.

Hester said nothing, and breakfast began, Nan wasting as usual a prodigal amount of energy and spirits even over the operation of eating, Hester looking a little pale and a little thoughtful, Annie in a state of suppressed high spirits, which a slight awe which she still felt at times for Hester Thornton kept rather in check.

CHAPTER IV.
THE COLTS--ROBIN AND JOE.

The Towers was situated exactly two miles away from the Grange. It was a large, old house, with a castellated roof and a high tower at one end. It was a very old family place, and the Lorrimers had lived there from father to son for several hundreds of years. Like many ancient families, their wealth had diminished rather than increased with the times. The luxurious living, which has been in vogue more or less during the whole of the present century, had obliged them to part with some of their fair acres. The present owner had married for love, not for money. More lands had to be sold to meet the wants of a large and vigorous family, and, at the time when this story opens, the Lorrimers were, for their position, decidedly poor, not rich.

Squire Lorrimer had one dread ever before his eyes. This was the fear of having to part with the dear old Towers itself. If this blow fell, he was certain that it would kill him. He trusted to be able to avert this calamity by putting down expenses in all possible ways. There were too few servants, therefore, for the size of the house, too few gardeners for the size of the gardens, too few horses for the size of the stables.

Nevertheless, there was not in the whole length and breadth of the county of Warwickshire, a jollier, happier, more rollicking household than the Lorrimers. There were ten children, varying in age, from Molly, who would be sixteen on her next birthday, to little Phil, who had not yet attained the dignity of two years. There were six girls in the family and four boys. The two elder boys went to a good grammar school in the neighbourhood; the girls and Boris had a governess who taught them at home. Neither boys nor girls were educated quite up to the requirements of the times, but the father and mother were not going to worry themselves over this fact. Mr. Lorrimer had very strong views with regard to modern education. He had a hearty preference for big bodies instead of big brains. He was intensely old-fashioned as regards all modern views for the advancement of women, and said frankly that he would rather his sons emigrated than spent their lives as city clerks. He had a good deal of faith in things righting themselves naturally, and as his wife believed him to be the cleverest and wisest man in the universe, he was not tormented by any contrary opinions from her lips.

"The children will do very well," he used to say. "If I can only keep the land together, and the old house for Guy to inherit after me, I shall die a happy man. The girls are all pretty, unless we except poor little Elinor, and she, in some ways, has the sweetest face of the bunch; they are sure to find husbands by-and-by, and the younger lads can fend for themselves in the colonies if necessary. You needn't fret about the children, mother," he would add.

"I never fret about them," replied the soft-voiced, placid-looking mother, raising her dove-like blue eyes to her husband's face. "I think we are the happiest family in the world, and the children are the dearest creatures. With all their high spirits they are never really naughty. I have only one care," she added, looking at her husband affectionately and slipping her hand through his arm, "and that is when you talk of the possibility of selling the Towers."

"Well, Lucy, that hasn't come yet," he answered.

"What about that mortgage and the suretyship?"

"Oh, pooh! They are right enough yet. I make it a rule never to think of evil days before they really come. We'll pull through--we'll pull through, no fear. By the way, my dear, I had a splendid offer yesterday for the colts Joe and Robin. I closed with it in double quick time, and the dealer who has bought them will send over to fetch them this morning."

"Very well," said Mrs. Lorrimer. She went to the window of the room where the two were talking and stood there looking out.

She gazed on a lovely scene, composed of woodland, river, and gently sloping meadows and lawns. Exactly opposite her eyes was a paddock, and in the paddock the two colts which had just been sold were contentedly grazing. As Mrs. Lorrimer stood and looked out, a girl was seen to enter the paddock and go swiftly up to the colts, calling their names as she did so. They both came to her immediately. She threw an arm round the neck of one, while she fed them in turn with carrots and apples which she had in her apron. She was a slightly-made girl, with dark hair and a sallow face. Her hair hung heavily about her shoulders. She might have been ten years old, but looked younger.

"There's Nell," said the mother. "I am sorry the colts are going, she has always made such pets of them. I never saw her take to any creatures before as she has done to those two, and they'll follow her anywhere like lambs. I'm sorry you've got to sell them, Guy."

"Sorry!" retorted the Squire, with a sort of snort. "Didn't I tell you, Lucy, that Simmons has given me a cheque for three hundred and fifty pounds for the two. Of course, the creatures are thoroughbred, and may turn out worth a great deal more; still, in these days no one gives a fair price for anything, and three-fifty is not to be sneezed at when your rents are always behindhand and your balance at the bank is overdrawn."

The Squire left the room as he spoke, and Mrs. Lorrimer, with the faintest of little sighs, presently followed his example. Meanwhile, the girl in the paddock was having a thoroughly happy time. As soon as she had finished feeding her favourites, and they had done rubbing their noses against her face and shoulder, she looked eagerly round her, and saw with satisfaction that there was no one watching her from any of the many windows which blinked like eyes all over the old house. She now approached one of the colts cautiously, laid her hand on his neck, and with an adroit, quick movement sprang on his back. He was an untamed, unbroken-in creature. He would have submitted to no burden at all heavier or at all less dear than that of the slim child who had now mounted him.

"Hey, Robin, dear," she said, bending forward, catching hold of a wisp of his mane and almost whispering into his ear, "you'll take me round the paddock three times, won't you, as swift as the wind, and then it will be Joe's turn? As swift as you can fly you shall go, my bonny, bonny Robin. And afterwards you shall have your russet apple; it's in my pocket."

From the colt's attitude, he seemed perfectly to understand every word that was addressed to him. He pricked his ear; his eye glanced backward with loving intelligence. He pawed the ground impatiently--he would not be off until Nell gave the signal, but when it came there was no doubt that he would fly swiftly over the ground. Joe, the other colt, stood near expectantly. His turn was to come, he knew.

For him, too, there would be the light weight of a loved little presence, followed by that delicious russet apple when the ride was over. Meanwhile, he would canter after Nelly and Robin, taking care not to go too near nor in any way to intrude himself mischievously.

"Now," said Nell, sitting bolt upright, "now, Robin--one, two, three, away!"

Away they went truly, mane and hair alike flying in the breeze--Nell's short skirts puffed out by the wind, Nell's cheeks with red flames on them, and Nell's dark grey eyes blazing like subdued fires.

Once round the paddock they flew--twice they went--three times. The third round was the fastest and the most delirious of all. Nell was so sure of her seat, so confident in Robin's powers, that she no longer even clasped his arched neck. Up flew her hands in the air. The delirious excitement rendered her giddy.

"Hurrah! hurrah!" she shouted.

The gay words were interrupted by eager words from approaching spectators. The gate of the paddock was pushed open, and Kitty, aged nine, followed by Boris, who was only seven, rushed on the scene. The children were followed by a couple of grooms and a strange, horsey-looking man.

"Oh, Nell, Nell!" exclaimed Kitty.

"They're sold, Nell," said Boris, in a gloomy voice. "You'd better get down. That fellow there has come"--waving his hand with immense dignity in the direction of the horsey man--"that fellow has come to take them away; they're sold."

"I don't believe it," said Nell.

Robin, who obeyed her slightest word, stood stock still when she told him. She dropped off his back with the lightness of a bird.

"Who says they're sold?" she asked. "I don't believe it."

She pressed her hand to her heart as she spoke, a pang of keen pain had shot through it; she turned pale, and her eyes still blazed.

"I don't believe it a bit," she said. "I'll go and find father and ask him if its true; I know it isn't true."

"There's father coming into the field," said Boris. "Yes, it's true enough, but you can ask him."

"Well, my man," said the Squire, who came upon the scene at this moment, "your master has sent you for the colts, I suppose? Here they are, as----Why, what's the matter, Nell? How white you are, child, and--not so tight, Nell, not so tight, you're half strangling me! What is it, my love--what is it?"

"You haven't sold Robin and Joe, father?"

"Oh, now, my little girl"--the Squire began to pat Nell's trembling hands soothingly. He looked hard into her quivering face, then, bending down whispered something in her ear.

No one else heard the words.

Nell's frantic grasp relaxed; she let her hands fall to her sides and looked piteously round.

Robin and Joe had both followed her across the paddock. Robin expected his russet apple--Joe looked for his canter with Nell on his back.

"There's a brave little girl," said her father. "'Pon my word, I wouldn't do it if I could help it."

"No, father dear; of course not."

"You're a plucky young 'un," said her father admiringly. Boris and Kitty came close; the grooms and the horse-dealer also approached. There was a sort of ring round Nell and the colts.

"Please, father, may I give Robin his apple?" she asked. "He has earned it. May he have it?"

The Squire nodded.

"Of course he may," he said; then he turned to the horse dealer.

"My little girl is fond of these creatures," he said. "I hope you will have patience for a moment or two."

The man touched his hat respectfully.

"Certainly, sir," he answered, "as long as the young lady likes; there's no manner of hurry, and perhaps little miss would like to have another canter. I never see'd no one sit so bird-like on a horse--never, in the whole of my born days."

"Do you hear that, Nell?" said her father. "Would you like another canter? I didn't know you could ride bare-backed."

She smiled up at him, a perfectly brave smile; there were no tears in her eyes, although there were black shadows under them, and her face was as white as a little snowflake.

Robin munched his apple, and Joe came close to Nell and rubbed his head against her shoulder.

She fed him also, to his own great surprise, for he did not think that he had earned a morsel, and then, without a word, turned and walked out of the paddock.

Boris ran after her.

"I say, Nell!" he exclaimed, panting. "Would you like a white rat? I have four, and I--I'll give you one if you'll promise not to forget to feed it."

Nell stood still when Boris made this offer, and looked down into his ruddy, brown, sunburnt face. Boris had bright eyes, as round as two moons. The giving up of one of his white rats meant a great deal to him. Nell carefully weighed the value of the offer.

"No," she said at last in a deliberate tone. "I might forget to feed the rat, and I don't think I ever could love it; but thank you all the same, Boris."

"Don't mention it," said Boris, in his most polite tone; he was immensely relieved by Nell's declining his offer.

She walked slowly towards the house, and Boris turned to Kitty, who had followed him.

"I offered her a rat," he said; "but she wouldn't have it. Do you think she will be very bad for a bit?"

"Yes, I do," said Kitty. "She'll creep up into one of the lofts and burrow in the hay all by herself, and if she can have a right good cry perhaps she'll be better, but if she hasn't a cry, she'll fret awfully, and perhaps she'll turn sulky; but never mind about her now. I'm ever so glad she didn't take the rat. Let's run and feed them before we go to lessons."

"I wish there were no lessons," said Boris. "I hate them. I can't think what use they are. What can it matter in a big world like this, crowded up with boys and girls and men and women, whether I can spell right or not? *I* don't mind, and I don't see why anyone else should bother."

"I like spelling," said Kitty, who had a very intelligent face. "If I were a man or an embryo man, which you are, Boris, I'd have ambition, and I'd try to get on. I'd like to walk over the heads of the other boys, if I were you, and to take their prizes from them, and to have father and mother looking on, and a lot of grand ladies and gentlemen all dressed in their best praising and cheering and bowing and smiling. But boys are no good in these days. It's girls who do everything. Now, do be quick and let's feed the rats."

"You talk such nonsense," said Boris. "You don't suppose that ladies and gentlemen care whether boys and girls spell words right or not, and what rubbish you do say about best clothes and smiling and bowing."

"I don't," said Kitty, crossly; "it's you who talk rubbish. You have never been to school, so you can't possibly tell. You ask Nan Thornton, and she'll soon tell you what's done at school. Oh dear, oh dear, I wish I were at Lavender House instead of doing my lessons with stupid Jane Macalister!"

"You talk very dis'pectful," said Boris.

"Do I? I don't care. Oh, I *am* glad you didn't part with the white rat!"

CHAPTER V.
NOT MISSED.

Jane Macalister was the governess. She was old--at least the Lorrimers considered her old--she wore spectacles, and her hair was slightly tinged with grey. She had a queer mixture of qualities. She was affectionate and narrow; she was devoted to her pupils, and thought she could best show her devotion by an unceasing round of discipline. Fortunately, both for her and the little Lorrimers, this discipline never extended beyond the hours devoted to lessons. It never showed its stern visage in play hours, nor at meals, nor at night, nor on half holidays, nor on Sundays. During all these times, Jane was the intelligent and much belaboured companion. She was at everyone's beck and call. She was to be found here, there, and everywhere--darning the rent in Molly's frock, or helping Nora with her drawing, or trying to find a story-book for Nell which she had not already read at least six times, or healing the small squabbles with which Boris and Kitty helped to beguile the weary hours. Mrs. Lorrimer consulted her with regard to the cook and the servants generally. The Squire would shout to her to spare him a quarter of an hour in the study to see if he had totted up his accounts right. In short, Jane Macalister was as much part and parcel of the Lorrimer household as if she were really one of themselves. She was by no means educated up to the standard of the latter half of the nineteenth century, but what she did know, she knew thoroughly. She was methodical and helpful. The kind of person whom Mrs. Lorrimer was fond of quoting as invaluable. The children, one and all, loved her as a matter of course, but, in school hours, their love was certainly mingled with awe. In school hours, Jane allowed no relaxing of the iron rod.

Kitty and Boris, having just heard the dismal sound of the schoolroom bell, started from their fascinating occupation of feeding the white rats and ran as fast as their small feet could carry them in the direction of the house. They went in by a side entrance, and with panting breath and hot little steps began to mount the spiral staircase which led to the schoolroom in the tower. They were late already, and they knew that they could not possibly escape bad marks for unpunctuality. They pushed open the green baize door which admitted them to the sanctum of learning and came in. All the other children whom Miss Macalister taught were already in the room. Kitty and Boris were the sole delinquents--the only ones in disgrace, even Elinor was present. Their faces fell when they saw her. They had built great hopes on having at least Elinor's company in their disgrace. The swift thought had darted through both their minds that she would be safe to be extra naughty that morning, and in consequence would divert some of the storm of Jane Macalister's wrath from their devoted heads; but no, there she sat in her accustomed place, her hymn book open on her knee, marks of tears on her cheeks, it is true, but in all other respects she looked a provokingly model Elinor.

It was too bad; Kitty made a face at her across the schoolroom, and even Boris gave her a reproachful glance.

Jane Macalister fixed two awful spectacled eyes upon the culprits, and, scarlet blushes tingling in their cheeks, they took possession of their vacant chairs.

The children all sang their usual hymn, although Elinor's voice was a little husky and Boris held his book upside down.

"All things bright and beautiful,
All creatures great and small,
All things wise and wonderful,
The Lord God made them all."

"I wonder if He really made that dreadful horsey man," thought Nell, as she looked out of the window.

Boris smothered a sigh as he reflected again over the problem which had often before puzzled his small head--Why God, when he made everything so beautiful, had forgotten to give Jane Macalister a beautiful temper in school hours?

The singing was followed by the Bible reading, and then lessons began. Molly and Nora acquitted themselves admirably, as was their wont--Nell's dark grey eyes grew full of interest as she read the fascinating story of the "Field of the Cloth of Gold" in her history book--Kitty worked at her sums with fierce persistence and tried to fancy herself at boarding-school, going up rapidly to the top of her class, while Boris made more mistakes than ever over his dictation, and inked his fingers unmercifully.

"What was the use of fussing over such a stupid, useless thing as spelling?" This was his thought of thoughts.

The day was a warm one. Jane Macalister was icily cold, however, as unapproachable as an iceberg. Boris watched her with anxiety. He knew well that there was no chance for him and Kitty; they would both be punished for being late for prayers.

Oh, dear, oh, dear; *why* was Jane so unbeautiful, so unapproachable in school hours?

"I know she'll keep Kitty and me in during the whole of the play hour," he muttered to himself. "I'm certain of it, because the tip of her nose is getting red; that's a sign that she's worried, and when she's worried she's twice as bad as she is at any other time."

"What noise is that? Oh!--I say--Miss Macalister----"

Jane Macalister was always spoken to in this correct fashion during school hours.

"I say, there's a visitor!" burst from the eager lips of the little boy.

He started to his feet as he spoke, upsetting the ink-pot over his own copybook and also over Kitty's white-frilled pinafore.

"Boris, you are incorrigible!" exclaimed Jane. "You lose all your conduct marks for the week, and must stay indoors for an hour and learn a piece of poetry after lessons."

Boris got very red and tried to smile. The blow had fallen, so he wasn't going to whimper over it. He would stand up to his punishment like a man. He meant to be a soldier some day, and felt exactly now as if he were facing the guns. He met Elinor's full, troubled grey eyes, and seated himself slowly once more in his chair.

The steps had come nearer, the schoolroom door was burst open, and Nan Thornton rushed in.

"Here I am," she said. "I have come to torment you, Miss Macalister, and to beg off lessons at once. How do you do, children? How are you, Kitty? How are you, Boris? How do you do, Nell? Molly and Nora, I'll kiss you when I can get breath. Oh, what a climb those stairs are! Why do you have lessons in the tower? All the same, it's lovely when you *are* here. What a view! What a darling, darling, heavenly, scrumptious, *ripping* view. Oh, dear! oh, dear! I am out of breath. Jane, aren't you glad to see me? Aren't you glad to know that all the children are to have a holiday immediately? Shut up your books, young 'uns, and let's be off. You don't mind, do you, Jane?"

Certainly Jane Macalister did mind. The icy expression grew more marked on her face. Boris gave her a glance, felt that he was very close to the guns, and lowered his eyes. Nan began dancing about the room. Nan was in white--white hat, white frock. Her fluffy golden hair surrounded her like a cloud. Boris felt that she was something like a very naughty and very beautiful angel. Why was she tempting them all when Jane Macalister was like ice?

"I think, Nan," said Miss Macalister--"(how do you do, my dear? Of course I'm glad to see you)--I think I must ask you to leave the schoolroom for the present. Recess will be at half-past eleven, and then you can talk to all the children except Boris, who I grieve to say will have to undergo punishment. As to holidays, the summer holidays will begin in a fortnight, until then I cannot permit any such indulgence. Go away, Nan, for the present. Molly, I can attend to your German now. Bring your exercise book with the grammar and history."

Nan was not accustomed to being vanquished, but she was very near defeat then. The next moment she would have found herself ignominiously outside the baize door if other steps had not approached, and Hester, looking cool and sweet, Annie, all radiant and laughing, and Mrs. Lorrimer, with her usual gentle motherly expression, had not appeared on the scene.

"Jane," said the mother, smiling round with her blue eyes at each of the children, "Hester wants us to get up a hasty picnic to Friar's Wood. The day is perfect, and this is the first of Nan's holidays, so I hope you will not object, particularly if the children promise to work extra well to-morrow."

Jane began to close up all the books hastily. Nan's petition was not to be listened to for a moment. Mrs. Lorrimer's was law, and must be cheerfully obeyed.

"Certainly," she said, in a pleasant tone, dropping her frozen manner as if by magic. "It is a **perfect** day for a picnic. Leave the schoolroom tidy, my loves, and then go and get ready. You'd like me to see the cook, wouldn't you, Mrs. Lorrimer? I can help her to cut sandwiches and to pack plates and dishes."

"Jane, you're an angel," said Mrs. Lorrimer.

Jane Macalister kissed Hester, was introduced to Annie, and then rushed down the spiral stairs, intent on housekeeping cares.

The Lorrimer boys and girls surrounded Hester and Annie. Nan flitted in and out of the group, and was here, there, and everywhere. All was excitement and laughter. Presently the children left the schoolroom in a body.

No, there was one exception. Boris stayed behind. He looked wistfully after the others as they streamed away. Miss Macalister had not said a word about remitting his punishment, and he must be true to his colours. He found it very difficult to keep back his tears, but he would indeed think badly of himself if even one bright drop fell from his round blue eyes.

It would have comforted him if Kitty had noticed him. Kitty might have stayed if only to bestow a kiss of sympathy on him, but she was whirled on with the others. No one gave him a thought. He was only Boris, one of the younger children. He was alone in the schoolroom.

He looked at the clock; it pointed to half past eleven; he would not be free until half past twelve. Picnics at the Towers were hastily improvised affairs. Long before his hour of punishment was over the others would all be off and away. It was scarcely likely that any of them would even miss him. Kitty would be in such a frantic state of excitement at having Nan Thornton to talk to, that she would not have room in her heart to bestow a thought on him. He could not walk all the way to Friar's Wood, the day was too hot. How delicious it would be there in the shade. How interesting to watch the squirrels in the trees, and the rabbits as they darted in and out of their holes. Well, well, there was no use fretting. His heart felt sore, of course, but he wouldn't be half a boy in his own opinion if he didn't take his punishment without a murmur.

He drew his chair up to the table, pushed his ink-stained fingers through his curly brown locks, and looked around him.

Miss Macalister had forgotten to set him any task, but he supposed he could set himself something.

He was just wondering what would be the least irksome form of punishment he could devise, when a small head was pushed in at the door, and a voice, in accents of extreme surprise, shouted his name.

"Why, Boris, what are you doing? They'll be off if you don't look sharp."

"I'm not going, Nell," said Boris; "but please don't fuss over it, it's nothing."

"***Nothing!***" said Nell, coming into the room and seating herself by the side of her little brother. "Don't you love picnics?"

"I *adore* them," said Boris.

He shut up his lips as he spoke and winked his eyes.

"Don't make a fuss," he said again after a pause. "Do you think I might learn a bit of the 'Ancient Mariner' for my punishment task? I like that old chap, he's so grisly."

"It's a splendid poem," said Nell with enthusiasm, "particularly that part about--
    'Water, water everywhere,   And not a drop to drink.'

Can't you picture it all, Boris? The sea like a great pond, and the thirsty old mariner looking at it, and longing, and longing, and longing to drink it, and the dead people lying round. Sometimes at night I think of it, and then afterwards I have a good, big, startling dream. A dream that's not ***too*** frightful is almost as good as a story-book. Don't you think so?"

"No, I don't," said Boris. "I hate dreams. Perhaps I'd better learn the first six verses of the 'Ancient Mariner,' and perhaps I'd better begin at once. Jane Macalister is very stern, isn't she, Nell?"

"Awful in lesson times," said Nell.

"Well, the only way I can bear it," said Boris, "is this--I think of her as the general of an army. I don't mind obeying her when I think of her in that way. Soldiers have to promise obedience before anything else, and I'm going to be a soldier some day. I'd better not talk now, Nell, for I must get the first six verses of the 'Ancient' into me in an hour, and I can't if you keep chattering. The general was rather sharp with me this morning, I must say, for all my conduct marks are gone, too, and I won't get sixpence on Saturday, and I'll have nothing to subscribe to mother's birthday present; still, of course, 'tis 'diculous to fuss. You'd best go, Nell. Why aren't you ready for the picnic?"

"I'm not going," said Nell. "I have a headache, and a drive in the sun would make it worse. Besides, Nan Thornton does chatter so awfully."

"Chatter," repeated Boris; "you don't mean to say you mind her chattering?"

"Yes, I do, when I have a headache."

"Well, I think she's sweet," said Boris.

"You had better learn your 'Mariner,' Boris, and I'll sit in the window and look out."

The schoolroom was so high up in the tower that people who sat in one of its windows had really only a bird's-eye view of what went on below.

Boris, in his rather tumbled sailor suit, sat with his back to Nell. He kicked the rungs of the chair very often with his sturdy legs. His inky fingers took fond clutches of his curls, his lips murmured the rhyme of the "Ancient Mariner" in a monotonous sing-song. Nell pushed open the lattice window and looked out. There was a waggonette drawn by a rather bony old horse standing by the side entrance; behind the waggonette was a pony-cart, a good deal the worse for wear. The pony, whose name was Shag, stood very still and flicked his long tail backwards and forwards to keep the flies away. Nell saw Miss Macalister and two of the servants come out with those flat delicious picnic baskets which she knew so well, and which had so often made her lips water in fond anticipation; they were placed with solemnity in the waggonette. Then Molly and Nora, in their white sun-bonnets, took their places, and Hester and Annie sat opposite to them, and Mrs. Lorrimer took the seat of honour, and two or three of the smaller children were packed in heterogeneously, while Nan and Kitty and Miss Macalister bundled themselves into the pony-cart.

Nell's heart beat high as she watched. Was no one going to think of her and Boris? Was no one going to miss them?

Apparently no one was.

The gay cavalcade got under weigh and disappeared from view down the long and lovely beech avenue.

Nell did not wish to go to the picnic, not to-day with her heart so sore, but it made that heart feel all the sorer not to be missed.

CHAPTER VI.
FRIAR'S WOOD.

A s a matter of fact, the picnic party imagined that Boris and Nell intended to follow on later in the donkey-cart. The Lorrimer picnics were well known in the neighbourhood. They always passed through the village in the following order--first the waggonette, drawn by the bony horse and packed to overflowing with baskets and young people, who waved their arms and shouted in high glee as they went by; then the pony-trap, driven sometimes by Jane Macalister, sometimes, when Jane was in a very good humour, by Kitty or even Boris; and last, at an interval of about half an hour, the donkey-cart. The donkey-cart as a rule contained kettles and pots, for the Lorrimers would consider a picnic only half a picnic if they did not boil their own potatoes out of doors and make their own tea in the woods. Consequently, the coarser utensils which were required for the feast were usually reserved for the donkey-cart. The donkey, as a rule, was driven, or rather led, by Guy, the tall schoolboy, aged thirteen, who would be owner of the Towers, if it were not sold over his head, some day. Harry, the brother next in age, would also accompany the donkey-cart, and sometimes one or two of the younger children would prefer this rough mode of travelling to the more refined waggonette or the fleeter pony-carriage. The donkey-cart had of course to be late, as Guy and Harry would not be home from school until quite an hour after the rest of the party had started.

"Where is Boris?" asked Hester, addressing herself to Molly when they had driven about half of the distance.

Molly had tranquil blue eyes, like her mother.

"Isn't he in the pony-carriage?" she asked.

"Who is Boris?" interrupted Annie Forest. "Is he the pretty little round-faced boy in the sailor suit?"

"Yes," said Nora, joining in the conversation.

"Then he's not in the pony-trap," replied Annie. "I don't think he left the schoolroom."

"Cute little beggar," laughed Nora. "He wants to come in the donkey-cart."

Annie raised her brows in inquiry; the mystery of the donkey-cart was explained to her, and no further questions were asked with regard to Boris.

Elinor had not yet been missed.

Friar's Wood was a perfect place for a picnic, and in due course of time the happy cavalcade arrived there. The younger children and Miss Macalister began to make preparations for the first meal. The Lorrimers always had two hearty ones whenever they went on a picnic. Kitty, Nora, and Annie Forest went off to explore the Fairies' Glen, a lovely spot about a quarter of a mile away. Mrs. Lorrimer took out her knitting and sat with her back against a great beech tree, and Molly and Hester found themselves thrown together.

"That's right," exclaimed Molly. "I wanted to have a talk with you, Hetty. Will you come to the top of the knoll with me? We can sit there and cool ourselves. There is not the faintest chance of dinner being ready for quite an hour."

The girls set off at once. Molly was not yet sixteen, Hester was past seventeen, nevertheless they had been intimate friends for a long time.

"Why have you got that little frown between your brows, Molly?" asked Hester. It smoothed out the moment Hester spoke.

"I surely ought not to have a frown to-day," retorted Molly. "The weather is glorious, we are all in perfect health, we are out for a picnic, you are here, you have brought your friend, Annie, about whom we have always heard so much, and Nan is home from school. Yes, I certainly ought not to frown; but let me retort on you, Hester. Why have you those grave lines round your lips?"

"Because I'm a goose," answered Hester. "Sit down here, Molly. You have not got me up to the top of this knoll just to make me recount my grievances. Out with yours; you know you have one at least."

"Well, yes, I have one," said Molly. "A horrid little cankering jade--a sort of black imp. I thought I had tucked him up snug in bed until the evening, and there, you have loosened the sheets, and he has sprung up again to confront me."

Molly's honest face was undoubtedly troubled now, and there was a suspicion of tears in the blue eyes, which were nearly as frank and round as Boris's.

"I suppose I must confess," she said: "it's only that the colts, Joe and Robin, have been sold."

"I don't think I know them," said Hester.

"Well, you must imagine them. They are not broken-in yet. They were born at the Towers, and we used to feed them when they were foals. Then one day Robin got rather wild, and kicked Boris severely, and father said we were to leave them alone; but Nell somehow managed to evade the order; she never could be got to fear any four-footed creature. She spent almost all her leisure time with the colts, and I believe she used to ride them bare-backed. Well, they were sold this morning, and Nell will fret awfully. Fretting is very bad for her, for she is not at all strong, you know. That is one thing that troubles me," continued Molly, after a brief pause. "I am sorry the colts are sold, on account of Nell, for I know, although she won't pretend to fret a bit, how she will secretly grieve and grieve; and the other reason is, that I know father would not have sold them if he had not been hard up for money again. Oh, I wish, I wish," continued Molly, her face turning crimson, "that there was no such thing as money in the world."

Hester looked at her with a mingling of sympathy and surprise.

"I think you must be wrong," she said slowly. "I mean, of course, that I know you're not rich as my father is rich, for you are such a large family, and father has only Nan and me; but still, it cannot be true that your father wants money to the extent of having to sell the colts to get it, Molly."

"I'm afraid it is true," said Molly, in a sad voice. "I wish it were only my imagination. You would never take me for a fanciful girl, would you, Hester? I am always called matter-of-fact, and I think I am. I really don't care a bit for poetry, and not much for music, and even story-books don't amuse me unless they're the downright sort, like 'Little Women,' or unless they tell all about housekeeping and that sort of thing. I love cooking, and I rather like accounts, and I delight in overhauling the linen cupboard, and I am not a bad hand at darning the linen. I'm just a commonplace, matter-of-fact sort of girl; it isn't in me to imagine things."

"Well?" said Hester, for she saw that Molly was intensely in earnest.

"I know I'm right about the money," said Molly. "You cannot think how troubled father looks sometimes; and mother told me only yesterday that we were not to go to the seaside this year, and she thinks our shabby old hats will do quite well for church. You don't suppose I care about shabby hats, or even about the seaside, but I do care when I see father looking troubled. Once a stranger came to see him, and they were shut up together in the library for a long time, and when he went away I noticed that father looked quite old. Oh, I know there are money troubles, and I am sure things will get worse. I know what father dreads, and dreads and dreads. Oh, Hester, if it happens it will kill him!"

"Molly, dear, how white you are. If what happens?"

"Don't whisper it, Hester; but I dread it. If he has to sell the Towers it will kill him."

"To sell the Towers!" echoed Hester. "I should think so, indeed; but----"

"What are you two doing up there?" shouted the voice of Nora from below. "Come down at once and make yourselves useful. The donkey-cart has come, and so have Guy and Harry, and we are washing the potatoes and want you to rub them, Molly. Come along down and help, you lazy good-for-nothings."

The girls hastened to obey. As if by magic all trace of a cloud left Molly's face. It became radiant, smiling, and dimpled. She was once more matter-of-fact, charming, capable Molly, who could work with a will and never once think of herself. Molly was so generally self-forgetful, that her happiness was not put on. Good-nature shone from her eyes. She was not a particularly brilliant or witty girl, but she was a strong rock to rely upon, as all the other Lorrimers knew well.

Nora, who was very pretty and very gay, gave herself up to heedless enjoyment as soon as Molly appeared upon the scene. The potatoes would certainly be done to a turn now. The table-cloth would be laid in that part of the wood where the midges were least troublesome. Jane Macalister would not have to complain of no one helping her. Guy, who was very like Molly, and nearly as good-natured, would also do his best to make the picnic lively, and Nora, one year Molly's junior, could give herself up to the fascinations of Annie Forest's society.

Nora had never before found herself in the company of such a completely grown-up and such a very pretty girl. Nora could give herself little airs when occasion required. She could put on rather a killing grown-up sort of would-be society manner. She never dared adopt it when Guy and Harry were near, but she contrived to get Annie away by herself, and then indulged in what the other children called her "high-falutin" talk.

It was nipped in the bud, however, by Annie herself. Annie Forest was nothing if she was not frank and fearlessly matter-of-fact. She quickly discovered how hollow and insufficient poor Nora's attempts to maintain a worldly conversation really were. She crushed her by telling her that she had never been in society herself in the whole course of her life, that she knew nothing whatever of it or its ways, that she had just left school, and that in all probability she would have to earn her bread in the future.

"But, look here, Nora!" she exclaimed, suddenly, "why should we two stand here chattering? I'm sure we ought to help the others."

"Oh, no; there's nothing really to be done," replied Nora, in a languid voice. "I like picnics, but I hate the fuss of preparing the meals, and as all the others adore it, I generally leave it for them to do. Won't you sit here? There is a charming little peep between those two oak trees. You can just see the Towers from there, and I think the Grange also. Don't you think the Grange a very beautiful place?"

"Yes; but not half as beautiful as the Towers."

"Don't you, really? Well, I am surprised! Of course, the Towers is very old. We are quite one of the very oldest of the county families round here, but my father likes us to live quietly just at present. Molly and I will have to be presented by-and-by. It is a pity father and mother don't think more about society, but they'll have to when we are grown up, and Molly is sixteen now. Hester will be very rich, and so will Nan. I'm surprised that you prefer the Towers to the Grange."

"I beg your pardon," said Annie, "but did not the donkey-cart arrive about half an hour ago?"

"Yes, of course."

"And two of your brothers with it?"

"Yes," replied Nora, suppressing a yawn, "Guy and Harry. How hot it is to-day--the heat makes one dreadfully languid, does it not?"

"I must go and tell Hester that Boris has not come," exclaimed Annie.

She put wings to her feet as she spoke, and left the astonished and indignant Nora to her own reflections.

Annie ran quickly through the wood. The sound of many voices floated on the summer breeze to greet her. She had almost reached the party when she suddenly came upon Kitty, who was standing alone. Kitty had just had a furious quarrel with Nan, and was in consequence feeling considerably out in the cold. Kitty knew that Boris was not of the party. She had known this from the beginning, but in the excitement and fun of having Nan Thornton to herself had been too selfish to mention the fact. Kitty guessed why Boris had remained behind. She remembered the severe punishment which Jane Macalister had inflicted upon him--a punishment which Jane had doubtless forgotten, but which Boris himself remembered.

Kitty thought of Boris now as she stood by a blackberry-bush, and pricked her finger on purpose against one of the thorns. Nan had been very snubbing and very disagreeable, and Kitty cordially hated her for the time being, and wished with all her heart that Boris was there. She could snub Boris, who would never retort, but now there was no one for her to play with.

"What is your name?" asked Annie, stopping and looking at her kindly; "you are one of the Lorrimers, of course, but I have not caught your name yet. Do you mind telling it to me?"

"I'm Kitty," answered the little girl; she raised her brown eyes and looked full at Annie. She had never seen anyone so lovely as Annie before. She had never even imagined that the world could contain anyone so sparkling and so gay.

"You're Kitty; that is capital," replied Annie. "Then, Kitty, I am sure you will do just as well as Hester. Can you tell me why your dear little brother Boris has not come to the picnic?"

"I was thinking of him," said Kitty. Tears slowly welled up into her eyes; her heart began to ache; she tried to prick her finger again to relieve the pain inside.

"Boris has not come," she replied. "I'll tell you why. He spilt some ink, and Jane Macalister said he must be punished by staying indoors for a whole hour after lessons were over. I expect she forgot all about Boris when we got a holiday so suddenly, but Boris didn't forget, and he stayed behind."

"Dear little Boris!" exclaimed Annie; "dear, good, plucky little Boris! The moment I looked at him I knew I should adore him. But see here, Kitty, the hour is up now, isn't it?"

"Oh, yes, of course; some time ago."

"Then he'll follow us, won't he?"

"How can he? He can't come alone; it's nearly an hour's drive to Friar's Wood."

"Of course he cannot walk," said Annie, impatiently; "but haven't you got a trap or carriage, or horse, or something?"

"No, I'm afraid we haven't," said Kitty, looking very sorrowful. "There's only old Rover, who draws the waggonette, and Dobbin the pony, and Jacko the donkey. Of course, there's father's mare, she's quite a beauty; but we are none of us allowed to have anything to do with her."

"Then we are not to have dear little Boris at the picnic?" said Annie; "I declare I shan't enjoy it a bit. I want him to be my own special knight."

"What do you want a knight for?" asked Kitty, looking up with interest.

"What do I want a knight for? You silly child, all fair ladies want their own true knights."

"You are a very fair lady," said Kitty. "At least, I mean you're a very lovely lady--very, very lovely; but can't you do with Guy or Harry for a knight?"

"No; I have fallen in love with Boris, and I won't have anyone else. Kitty, can't we manage to get him to the picnic?"

"I don't know, I'm sure. He could ride Harry's bicycle, but I don't think it would once enter into his head."

"It would if I went back and told him to."

"How can you go back? You can't walk."

"Yes, I am a splendid walker. Besides, I am sure the road is longer than by the fields, and you could take me part of the way and show me the short cuts."

"It would take a long, long time," said Kitty, "and when you came back dinner would be over, and you'd have lost quite half the fun."

"No, you dear little thing, I wouldn't. I mean to go and fetch Boris; virtue shall be rewarded, and the knight shall be rescued by the lady. Now, come with me part of the way and show me the short cuts. Why, I'm as strong as a lion. You don't suppose a walk of a few miles tires me? Come along, Kit, we are wasting time."

In reality, Kitty was charmed beyond words with any move which was to bring Boris on the scene. The moment Boris seemed at all unattainable, he became wonderfully precious in Kitty's eyes. She would, of course, snub him in five minutes after he did arrive, but that really did not matter. The fascination of Annie's secret mission also delighted her much, and she skipped along now by the side of this beautiful lady in a state of high good-humour.

"I'll show you a lovely short cut," she said. "It will take two miles off the distance. There's a bog, and a sunken ditch, and a wire fence; but you won't mind them, will you?"

"Not a bit," said Annie, laughter in her eyes.

"And there's farmer Granger's bull-dog, and perhaps the bull himself may be in the four acre field; but you won't mind," continued Kitty.

"Not a bit, not a bit."

"Well, let's run down into this little dell. I'll start you from the wicket gate at the end of the dell."

"It sounds quite Pilgrim's Progressy," said Annie.

"Annie," said Kitty, in an ecstatic whisper, "is it to be a secret?"

"Of course; if you dare to reveal it my knight shall execute vengeance on you."

"Oh, Annie!" said Kitty, "I do love you; its so perfectly delicious to have a secret."

"Well, see you keep this one faithfully. Now we have come to the wicket gate. How shall I go? Can I see the bull from here?"

"No."

"Can I hear the bull-dog bark?"

"No."

"Kitty, you little wretch, you've been trying to frighten me with imaginary dangers. Yes, I see my road. I follow the winding path wherever it leads. Keep a bit of dinner for me, Kitty. I'll be back in a couple of hours."

Kitty promised, and Annie started with great vigour on her long walk.

Kitty stood at the stile and watched her. Suddenly she raised a cry.

"Annie."

Annie turned.

"You'll find Nell at home, too, Annie."

"Is Nell another Lorrimer?"

"Yes; the ugly one of the family; the duckling, we call her most times."

"Well, the duckling shall come, too," shouted heedless Annie; and Kitty, with the full weight and delirious importance of her secret radiating all over her stout little person, slowly returned to the other members of the picnic party.

CHAPTER VII.
THE STORY BOOK LADY.

Annie found the road hot and the way long. As she said, she was a very good walker, and was never daunted by difficulties or dangers either real or imaginary. She was impressed by Boris's bright little face, and Kitty's story of his fidelity to the path of duty touched her quick and affectionate nature. Annie Forest, the grown-up girl, was very like Annie Forest, the child. She was still intensely impulsive, wayward, and eager. Her faults were in a great manner subdued, but they were not eradicated. She was intensely affectionate, brave, and true as steel; but she was apt to be both heedless and thoughtless. When rushing away to rescue Boris, it never once entered into her head that the secret of her absence might prove very troublesome to poor Kitty, and that the rest of the party might suffer uneasiness on her account. Without any adventure from bull or bull-dog, without endangering her life in the bog, which turned out to be almost non-existent at this time of year, she reached the Towers at the most sultry time of the day, and appeared upon the scene between one and two o'clock, a tired, flushed, and very thirsty Annie. All during her walk she pictured Boris's state of despair. She saw in her mind's eye a vision of his little, flushed, tear-stained face. She thought of Nell, too, and imagined the rapture with which the ugly duckling would greet her, the deliverer of the oppressed.

Annie entered the Towers by a side entrance, and, skirting a pretty, shady lawn, approached the house by the nearest way. As she did so, she was attracted by voices which seemed to proceed from out of a clump of trees. She stepped close to the spot from where the sound proceeded, and, craning her neck, looked over the thick laurustinus bushes, which enclosed a very tiny lawn or plot of grass.

Seated here, in the utmost peace and apparent contentment, were the poor victims for whom she had exerted herself so terribly. Nell was lying full length on her back on the grass. Boris was seated tailorwise on the ground a little way off. Nell had a white rat curled up in her hair and another nestling in her neck. Boris was feeding some white hares and some pet rabbits. The children were eagerly talking to their animals, and Annie had to own to herself that there was nothing in the least unhappy or even morbid in the sound of either of the voices.

For a moment the children's perfect happiness almost vexed her. It seemed provoking to have taken that long, exhausting walk for nothing, and oh! how hungry and thirsty, how very hungry and thirsty she felt.

The next instant, however, her good-nature asserted itself. She said "Hullo!" pushed her way through the laurustinus hedge, and stood in the midst of the group.

Nell started into a sitting position, tumbling the white rats on to her lap. She looked up at Annie. What a tumbled, dishevelled, hot, but oh, what a pretty strange lady was this! Nell worshipped beauty with the passion of a very hot and fervent little soul. She had scarcely noticed Annie in the schoolroom, but now her heart went out to her with a great throb.

"Who are you?" she said. "Where do you come from? What is your name?"

"Oh, I'm not a fairy, my good child!" said Annie. "I'm a poor, exhausted girl, who thought she was performing a very heroic feat and finds herself mistaken."

"Pray come in and take a seat," said Boris, who was always the soul of gentlemanly politeness. He stood up as he spoke, tumbling his rabbits and hares helter skelter in all directions, and tried to push back the laurustinus hedge for Annie. She squeezed through, tearing her cotton dress as she did so.

"Oh, dear, dear, your sweet dress is spoiled!" said Nell, in a tender voice.

"Never mind," answered Annie; "one must lose something to attain to this perfection."

"Won't you seat yourself?" said Boris.

He pointed to the grass, and Annie sat upon it with a sense of delight.

"How hot you are," said Nell. "What can we do for you? Would it soothe you to stroke one of the rats? This darling, for instance. His name is Crinklety."

Annie took the rat on her lap and looked at it reflectively.

"It's a darling," she said, "and so are the rabbits, and so are the hares; but oh, I'm so hot and so thirsty! and oh, children, don't you know what I've come about, and don't you know who I am?"

"No, I'm sure we don't," answered Boris. Nell stared solemnly; she did not speak.

"Well," said Annie, "I see I must introduce myself. I am Annie Forest. I'm Hester Thornton's friend, and I came here this morning with Hetty and Nan, and we all started on a picnic, and when we came to Friar's Wood, I found that you, Boris--you see I know your name--and you, Nell, were left behind, and I could not stand it somehow; it seemed too cruel and unfair, so I--I came back for you."

"How did you come?" asked Boris. "Did you drive back with Dobbin or Jacko?"

"No; they will have plenty to do this evening, and why should I give them double work, poor dears? No; I came back with these," she pushed out her dainty, but very dusty, feet as she spoke.

"You mean that you **walked**?" said Nell. "You walked all that long way just because of us two children that you knew nothing about. I didn't believe it was true. I never believed anything so perfectly splendid could be true out of a story book. Boris, do you hear? She walked from Friar's Wood all by herself."

"Are you awfully dead beat?" asked Boris, standing in his sturdy attitude in front of Annie and looking at her with immense attention.

"Yes; I never was hotter in my life, and I don't think I ever felt more tired. It is such a blazing day."

"Then you don't want to walk back again?"

"Well, I suppose I must, only I think I'll rest a little bit first, and perhaps one of you can bring me a glass of water. I consulted Kitty about it, and Kitty said you could ride your brother's bicycle, Boris. She only told me about Nell just when I was starting, but perhaps Nell can get on the bicycle sometimes, too. I'm not quite sure how it can be managed."

"You need not trouble about me," said Nell, "for I'm not going to the picnic. I don't wish to."

"And I don't wish to either," said Boris; "there's nothing to go for now, for dinner will be over. I always think the fun of a picnic is washing the potatoes and lighting the bonfire, and they'll be all over long ago."

"Well, then," said Annie, "I see that I have made myself a martyr in an unnecessary cause. You bad children, you are not a bit unhappy at staying at home, and I pictured you both such miserable little victims."

"Would you rather have seen us miserable?" asked Boris.

"Of course I'd much rather have seen you miserable, you little wretch. How dare you look at me with those smiling, bright blue eyes? If I had seen you and Nell pale and wretched, and a little bit withered up, I'd have felt that my walk had been taken for a good purpose; but now----"

"Perhaps you think," said Nell, looking at Annie with great earnestness, "that you did nothing when you took that walk and when you made the story books come true. You did a great deal for me. We are Lorrimers, Boris and I, and it isn't the fashion for a Lorrimer ever to fret when things can't be helped. Boris would have liked to go to the picnic, and I'd have liked it, too, if it had happened on another day, but as we couldn't go, we meant to have a picnic at home. Will you stay with us and help us to make up a jolly picnic at home?"

"Of course I will, only too gladly."

"Then, Boris," said Nell, "we had best fetch the food while the story book lady is resting."

The children disappeared, and Annie lay back on the grass and laughed to herself. She was absorbed as usual with the fascination of the moment, and forgot all about Kitty, who would be carefully guarding her secret far away in Friar's Wood.

The picnic, which was partaken of by Annie, Nell, and Boris on the tiny lawn, surrounded by the laurustinus hedge, was a truly gay affair. The white hares, the rabbits, the rats, joined the company of diners, and Annie became her gayest and wildest self. When dinner was over, Boris reluctantly took his pets back to the out-house where they were kept, and then returned once more to the fascination of strawberries, cream, and Annie Forest's society.

Meanwhile, in Friar's Wood, Kitty was keeping an eager look-out. It was almost time for Annie to come back, and all the other members of the party who did not know where she had gone were becoming anxious about her. They would have been much more so but for Hester and Nan. But Hester and Nan were both well accustomed to Annie's many vagaries.

"If it were anyone else, I should fret about her," said Hester, answering Nora's eager inquiry for about the twentieth time. "She has wandered away in the wood by herself and will come back when she pleases, or perhaps she may have gone straight back to the Towers or to the Grange. Annie is grown up now, and she can take care of herself. There is no manner of use in fretting about her."

"If you only knew Annie at school!" exclaimed Nan. "Why there is quite a proverb about Annie at school. Let me see, this is it: 'The only thing to be expected of Annie Forest is the unexpected.' Now don't let's talk of her any more. She is a dear old Annie; but why should she spoil this lovely, perfect day, the first of my holidays? Guy, I wish you'd come and sit next me. Let us get up a jolly game of hide and seek."

"No," said Guy, "It's too hot at present. We will presently, when the sun gets a bit lower."

"Then tell me a story, there's a darling Guy."

Guy complied rather lazily. Nan moved a little apart with him, and the two began an eager, whispered conversation. Molly and Hester once more joined forces and resumed the interrupted talk of the morning. The others wandered away in different directions, and Nora and Kitty found themselves together. Nora felt rather discontented. She missed Annie Forest, not because she particularly liked her just now, but because Annie's conduct during their morning walk had rather piqued her. Nora was quite sharp enough to read Kitty's secret in her troubled, demure, watchful and impatient eyes. She thought it would be rather good fun to bully Kitty a little.

"What are you staring through that long line of trees for?" she said. "Come here, and out with it at once. You know you're bursting with a secret. If you don't tell soon you'll explode, and there'll be nothing left of you. Come here, I say, and out with it."

Nora thought it quite unnecessary to put on her society manners for Kitty's benefit.

"Come here, Kit, at once, when I call you," she said, in a cross voice.

"I needn't come if I don't like," answered Kitty. "I'm not obliged to obey you, so don't you think it."

"Highty tighty. Do you suppose I'm going to take impertinence from a little chit like you? You know perfectly well where Annie Forest has gone, and it is your duty to tell."

"I won't tell. There!"

"Ah!" laughed Nora, now thoroughly exasperated. "I guessed you had a secret. I knew it when I saw you shutting up your lips so straightly, and putting on that little demure expression whenever Annie's name was mentioned. Now you have confessed it."

"I have confessed nothing," said Kitty in alarm.

"Yes, you have; you said you wouldn't tell. How could you say you wouldn't tell if you had nothing to tell? I know mother is uneasy about Annie, and I know Jane Macalister is uneasy, and you know where she is and you dare to keep them in suspense. Come along to mother at once. She'll soon get this secret out of you."

"I won't go, Nora--I won't. I'll climb up into this tree, where you can't catch me. Here," continued Kitty, suiting the action to the word, "you can't catch me up here; you can't. I won't go to mother--no, I won't."

"You will if I make you," said Nora. "You think I can't climb."

"You wouldn't dare to climb!" exclaimed Kitty, shouting down from the foliage of the tree into which she had hastily swung herself. "You'll get your frock all torn, and Molly and Jane will be just mad. You daren't climb, Nora--you daren't. You can't catch me Nora--you can't."

Nora had a quick temper, and Kitty's manner was most exasperating. Under ordinary circumstances the ladylike Nora would have hated climbing trees, but now all was forgotten in her fierce desire to lay hold of the daring, exasperating little Kitty and to force her secret out of her. How dared Annie Forest snub Nora and then confide in a baby like Kitty?

"Unless you come down this minute, I'll follow you into the tree and drag you down," said Nora. "Now you know what I mean to do, so come down this instant."

"Not I, not I," laughed Kitty. She had been rather frightened while Nora was taunting her on the ground, but now she felt so secure that she could afford to laugh, and even in her turn to use taunting words.

"I knew you were too much of a coward, fine, ladylike Miss Nora, to climb up here," she said; "and I'm going to stay here just as long as I please."

"Oh, are you?" said Nora. "There'll be two people to decide that point." She was in a blind fury now, and, before Kitty could say another word, began to swarm up the tree. She managed to catch the branch where Kitty had planted herself, and in another instant would have caught hold of the little girl's dress; but Kitty and

Boris could both climb like monkeys, and it did not take the little girl an instant to swing herself on to a higher branch. Nora's mettle was now up. She was resolved that Kitty should not conquer her. The spirit of defiance in Kitty made her resolve to die rather than be taken.

"You shan't catch me--you shan't," screamed the child. "I'm lighter than you. I'm going to creep on to the end of this bough; it will bear my weight, but it won't bear yours, Nora. Don't attempt to get on it, Nora; if you do the bough will break."

Kitty, as good as her word, crept on to a dead branch of the forest beech tree; it was high above the ground and nearly bare of leaves. It looked what it was, thoroughly rotten; but it bore Kitty's light weight without strain. She reached almost the end, and turned her flushed, laughing, defiant face towards Nora. Nora had reached the bough, but hesitated a moment before trusting herself on it.

"Who said I was going to be caught?" exclaimed Kitty. "Hurrah! hurrah! I'm safe enough."

"I will catch you!" exclaimed Nora. "You horrid, sneaking little cheat. This bough looks firm enough. It will hold me as well as you; anyhow, I'm going to try."

"Don't, don't!" screamed Kitty. She was really frightened now, for she saw the danger from the position where she was sitting far more plainly than Nora did. "Don't do it, Nora," she shrieked. "I'd rather come back to you. I would really, really. You'll be killed--we'll both be killed if you get upon this rotten bough. Oh, dear! oh, dear! Nora, are you mad? Are you mad?"

Blind passion had made Nora almost mad. She did not believe Kitty's words. The bare bough looked safe enough from her position. She stretched out one cautious hand, then another, and propelled herself slowly along. Her whole weight was now upon the bough. It was thoroughly rotten and very brittle. Kitty gave a shriek of terror, and, with a wild leap, managed to throw her arms over the bough just above. She was not a minute too soon. The rotten branch cracked and broke with a loud report, and poor Nora was hurled with great violence to the ground.

CHAPTER VIII.
ALONE IN THE WOOD.

There was a dizzy moment for Kitty when she seemed to hang between heaven and earth, and everything swam in circles before her dazed eyes. Then, with a supreme effort, she managed to clutch the bough, to which she clung with a firmer grasp, and slowly but surely to drag herself up into safety on its broad, firm stem.

"I'm coming, Nora. I'll be down in a minute," she shouted.

She crept along the bough, and soon, much scratched and covered with moss and leaves, her dress torn, her face hotly flushed, she reached the ground and rushed to Nora's side.

Poor Nora had fallen from a height of nearly twenty feet. Her fall had been slightly broken by the rotten bough which had come to the ground with her; but, notwithstanding this fact, she lay now on her back, faint and sick and moaning, as if she were in great pain.

Poor Kitty's repentance was intense.

"Oh, Nora, Nora!" she sobbed, bending over her, "are you hurt badly? Can't you get up? Oh, dear! oh, dear! you do look ill, and it's my fault of course. Why did I have a secret? and why did I tease you? Oh, Nora!" she added, terror in her tone as she noticed the increasing whiteness of Nora's pretty face, "are you in dreadful, shocking pain?"

"I feel sick," said Nora, "and--and faint. Can't you fetch some water. Oh, everything seems miles away. What shall I do?"

"I'll go for mother," said Kitty. "Lie very still, Nonie, darling; you have got an awful shake from that fall, but you'll be all right soon--I'm sure you will; and, oh, here's some water in one of the picnic bottles."

Kitty sprang towards this welcome sight, wetted a handkerchief with part of the contents and put it on Nora's forehead, and then gave her a little to drink.

The cold refreshing water revived the poor girl; but when she attempted to sit up, she fell back groaning and very faint once more.

"You *must* let me fetch mother," said Kitty. "I won't be a minute. I'll go as if I were a bird. I'll be back in no time, really."

"No; I can't be left alone," said Nora. "It--it's awful. The pain in my back gets worse and worse. Kitty, don't leave me. Kitty, I'm frightened. I'm sorry I was so cross to you."

"And I'm sorry I aggravated you," said Kitty; "but, oh, dear! what's the use of being sorry? That won't mend your poor back. I wish you'd let me get mother."

"No, no; you mustn't leave me."

Nora tried to stretch out one of her hands, but the pain of the least movement was extreme, and she was forced to lie absolutely still, while Kitty wetted her lips at intervals with a few drops of the precious water left in the bottle.

Nora was in too great pain to care anything about the loneliness of their position. She was in too great suffering even to be keenly sorry for her own wrongdoing. The one only desire she had was to keep Kitty by her side. But poor Kitty's little heart was full of absolute terror. She had never seen anyone look so ill as Nora. Her face was white; her lips were blue; she was evidently in severe pain; but, with the pain, there was a strange faintness, which Kitty had never encountered before in the whole course of her ten sturdy years.

Many and many a fall had both Kitty and Boris had in the wild expeditions and daring feats which they performed in each other's company. Kitty knew of the fall which stings; of the fall which shakes you all over, which raises a great bump and causes great soreness of the injured part; she knew of the fall which scratches and even renders you giddy; but she had never before seen the effects of such a serious fall as poor Nora's.

Friar's Wood was a very lonely place, and when, in utter exhaustion and pain, Nora closed her eyes, poor Kitty felt almost as if she were sitting alone in this great solitude with a person who was dead.

Oh, suppose pretty Nora was dead. Pretty Nora, who had been so mocking and full of life only ten minutes ago. If this were the case, to her dying day Kitty would feel that she had killed her by tempting her on to a rotten bough. It was terrible, terrible to be here alone with Nora, who might be going to die. Why could not she slip away and fetch someone to her aid?

Nora had clutched a very tight hold of Kitty's hand when first the little girl had proposed to fetch her mother, but now, in the kind of torpor of pain into which she had sunk, she relaxed the firm grip, and Kitty found that by a very gentle movement she could release her hand altogether.

She did so, and rose slowly to her feet.

Nora felt the movement and spoke.

"Kitty."

"Yes."

"You're not going away?"

"I'm only looking to see if there's anyone coming."

"Well, don't go away."

Nora's voice had sunk to a hoarse whisper, and Kitty's terrors and her certain fears that Nora was about to die became greater than ever.

She looked all around her, to right and left, before and behind.

No one was in sight. Not even the voice of a living creature broke the stillness. The birds were silent, the creatures of the wood seemed to be all asleep, the other members of the picnic had evidently wandered far afield; but, hark, what sound was that? Oh, joy! Who was this coming swiftly through the trees? Kitty's heart gave a bound of rapture, and then, forgetting all Nora's injunctions to keep by her side, she flew with lightning speed towards the figure of a horseman who was riding through the wood.

The man on horseback was Squire Lorrimer himself.

He had promised to join the children in time for dinner, but had not turned up. It was not his custom, however, on any occasion to disappoint his young people, and although late in the day he was now hastening to the scene of revelry.

Kitty's frantic speed in his direction by no means surprised him.

"Well, little woman," he said, pulling up the mare as he spoke. "Shall I give you a mount on Black Bessy's back? and where are all the others? I expected quite a swarm of you to rush forth. Where is Molly, and where is Nora, and where is the beautiful Annie Forest, whom everybody seems to rave about, and mother and Jane

Macalister? Are they all hiding and ready to rush out upon me with wild whoops?"

Kitty panted visibly before she replied.

"No, father, it isn't that," she said. "I and Nora are alone, I--get down please, father, won't you?"

"Why, what's the matter with you child?" The Squire hastily dismounted. "Are you hurt, Kit? What a red, excited face."

"No, 'tisn't me, it's Nora. She fell; I think she'll die. It was my fault. The beech tree had a rotten bough, and I crept out on it, as I didn't wish to be caught; and Nora followed me, and the bough broke, and she's lying on her back now and she can't move, and I think she'll die, and they're all away--I don't know where--somewhere else in the wood, and I think she's going to die, and it's my fault."

"There, Kitty, keep your pecker up," said the Squire. "I'm glad I came round this way; it was a lucky chance. Wait a minute until I tie Black Bess to this tree. Where is Nora?"

"Over there, lying on that knoll of grass. I think she'll die."

"Tut, tut, monkey, what do you know about people dying? Give me your hand, and bring me to her."

Oh, the comfort to Kitty of that firm, cool, strong hand of father's--oh, the support of looking into his face. A burden as of black night was lifted from her. She ran in eager accompaniment to his great strides. He was bending over Nora in a minute.

"Now, my poor little maid, what is this?" he asked, dropping on one knee and trying to put his hand under her head as he spoke.

Nora opened her pretty, dark eyes.

"Oh, father, is it you? I'm glad," she said in a faint voice. "I've been naughty, father; I--I'm sorry."

"Well, you can't be more than sorry, can you, Nonie? Don't bother about anything now, but just tell me where you are hurt."

"Oh, it's my back. Oh, don't touch me; it's dreadful!"

Squire Lorrimer's face looked very grave.

"Where did she fall from, Kitty?" he asked.

Kitty pointed to the gash made in the beech-tree by the broken bough.

"Over twenty feet," murmured the Squire to himself. "God help my poor little girl!"

"Look here, Kitty," he said aloud, "Nora is in a good deal of pain; but I hope we'll soon have her easier. We must try and get her home somehow, and it would be a good thing if your mother were here; you had better fetch her. Don't frighten her, Kit, for Nora may not be badly hurt after all; but bring her here as quickly as you can, and Guy, too, and Molly; they are both strong, and have their wits about them. We must contrive a litter of some sort. Now, be quick and find the folks."

"Yes," replied Kitty, who was almost happy again under the influence of her father's encouraging words.

She was soon out of sight, and in less than half an hour Mrs. Lorrimer, Jane Macalister, and every other member of the picnic party, were gathered round the prostrate figure of little Nora.

She was more conscious now, and looked eagerly for one face, the solace of all sick children.

"Let Mummie hold my hand," she said.

Mrs. Lorrimer took it, bent down, and kissed her; Nora smiled as if a load had been lifted from her heart.

A rough litter was presently constructed, and with great difficulty the poor child was lifted into it. The pain of even this slight move, however, caused her to faint completely away.

It was at this juncture that Hester Thornton came forward with a suggestion.

"The Grange is nearly three miles nearer than the Towers," she said; "had not we better bring her there? And had not Guy better ride off at once to Nortonbury for the doctor?"

"That is a good idea," said Mr. Lorrimer. "Guy, mount on Black Bess's back and off with you. Bring Dr. Jervis back with you to the Grange if you can."

The merry little picnic party looked dismal enough as they slowly, and almost in funereal fashion, left the scene of festivity. The strongest of the party had to take turns to carry poor Nora's litter, for she could not endure any less easy movement.

Nan came up to Hester and took her hand.

"I don't know what the meaning of all this is," she said; "but, somehow or other, I think Annie must be at the bottom of it."

"Where is Annie?" queried Hester. "How completely she seems to have lost herself. Oh, how miserable poor little Kitty looks. Come here, Kitty, dear, and tell me all about the accident."

"I cannot," said Kitty. "Don't ask me; it's part of the secret."

"I knew Annie Forest was at the bottom of it," murmured Nan. "Oh, what a horrid, horrid, dreadful ending to the first of my holidays!"

CHAPTER IX.
"I BROKE MY WORD," SAID ANNIE.

In utter ignorance of the tragic events which were happening in Friar's Wood, Annie Forest and her two little companions were having a gay time at the Towers. Annie's old passion for children had not deserted her. She was often heard to say that she was happier with a frank, original child than she was with most grown people. Boris was certainly frank; Nell was certainly original. Annie's beauty and brightness had won Boris's heart from the moment of her arrival; Nell's affections went out to her also, but for a different reason. Nell lived in a world of romance, and Annie's conduct in giving up her own pleasure had seemed to Nell to fit in with her fairy tales and other story-books. The three were, therefore, supremely happy during that long afternoon. The picnic behind the laurustinus hedge being quite a thing of the past, they proceeded to explore the tower, the old ruined chapel, where services used to be held morning and night more than three hundred years ago, the dungeon under the chapel, and all the other places of historic interest. Then the children's gardens were visited; and, finally, Annie was persuaded to seat herself in the swing and be sent up into space as high as Boris's and Nell's united efforts could accomplish. In their turn they were swung by Annie; and then followed tea in the play-room, where Nell presided, sitting solemnly in front of the dolls' tea-service and helping Annie and Boris and herself to unlimited weak tea, with heaps of cream.

The heat of the day was over at last, a perfect summer's evening had set in.

"When are they all likely to be back?" asked Annie.

"Not until night, dark night," said Boris with a little sigh.

"What are you sighing for?" asked Annie. "You look quite sad, and I don't like you sad; I like you with your eyes smiling and your face puckered up with laughter.

Nell looks pale and sad, too. What is it Nell? what is it Boris?"

"I'd like to be at the picnic now," said Boris, "I didn't mind it in the daytime when it was so hot; but now they're lighting another bonfire and they're going to have tea, and after tea Guy will tell stories."

"All about bogies," struck up Nell; "yes, I wish I were there."

Annie looked at them both reflectively. She never cared to be with children unless she could succeed in making them almost boisterously happy.

"But it doesn't matter a bit," said Nell, seeing the shadow cross her face; "I shouldn't be very happy in any case to-night."

"Why?" said Annie.

"I'd rather not say, please. You have been good to us; you have helped us to have a beautiful day; we are grateful to you, aren't we, Boris?"

"We love her," said Boris.

"You are two darlings," said Annie. "Well, now, suppose we have a bit of fun on our own account. How far is it from here to the Grange?"

"By the road, three miles," said Boris; "but across the fields, only a mile and a half."

"We'll go to the Grange across the fields," said Annie. "I heard Hester say this morning that she was going to try and induce you all to come back to the Grange to supper, so we three will join the rest of the party at supper, and if we start at once well be ready to welcome them when they arrive."

"What a spiffin' plan," said Boris; "do let's start at once."

Nell clapped her hands.

"Now I've made you happy again, that's all right," said Annie. She took a hand of each child, and they started on their pleasant walk. Boris was very messy and untidy, his face was stained with fruit and his hands were dirty. Nell's blue cotton frock was also considerably out at the gathers round the waist, but the children did not give a thought to their clothes or personal appearance in the sudden rapture with which they hailed Annie's suggestion.

The walk across the fields in the sweet freshness of the summer's evening was all that was delightful, and in an incredibly short space of time, the three found themselves at the other side of the turnstile which led into the grounds of the Grange.

"We'll be there long before the others," said Boris. "Suppose we light a great bonfire on the lawn to welcome them." But even wild Annie did not see the propriety of this suggestion.

"No, we won't do that," she said. "If the Grange were our own place we would. We'll just go and sit on the terrace and watch for them."

"Won't Kitty jump when she sees us?" said Boris, a look of satisfaction radiating all over his face. "She'll see that we have had our lark as well as the rest of them; oh, I call it real spiffin' fine."

They were walking rapidly through the shrubbery now, and as Boris finished his speech they came out on the broad sweep in front of the house.

Just before the entrance a brougham was standing, and instead of solitude they found themselves surrounded by familiar figures.

Kitty was the first to observe them. She gave a stifled sort of scream, and pushing aside Boris, who was prepared to rush into her arms, came up to Annie, took one of her hands, and looked into her face.

"I kept the secret true as true," she said; "but it almost killed me, and it has nearly quite killed Nora." Her poor little voice broke with these last words, and she burst into the frantic sobs which she had bravely kept back until now.

"What in the world is the matter?" said Annie, kneeling down and putting her arm round the excited child.

"Why, that's Dr. Jervis's carriage," shouted Boris. "What can be up?"

"Why are you back so early from the picnic?" asked Nell.

But Kitty sobbed on unable to reply.

She felt the comfort of Annie's arms round her, and presently she laid her hot, flushed, little face on Annie's neck and wetted her frill with her plentiful tears, but no information could be got at present from poor Kitty's lips.

"There's Molly, and there's Hester," exclaimed Boris, "they'll tell us; oh, and there's Nan, too. Hullo Nan, come here and tell us what the rumpus is about."

Nan rushed up excitedly.

"Nora is nearly killed," she said; "she fell from a tree over twenty feet from the ground, and her back is hurt awfully, and Hester said she'd better come here, and she's lying in the library and Dr. Jervis is there. I haven't the faintest idea how it happened," continued Nan; "only it seems to be your fault, Annie; it seems to have something to do with you and a secret, only Kitty won't tell."

Kitty ceased to cry; she raised her face and looked at Annie. Annie struggled to her feet.

She was about to reply to Nan when Hester came up and spoke to her.

"Oh, Annie," she said, "where have you been all day? We have been dreadfully anxious about you; and poor Nora has been hurt, and Kitty seems in trouble of some sort, and says that she won't tell her secret. What can it all mean?"

"Well, really!" said Annie. She paused a minute; the rich colour mantled her cheeks; her bright eyes seemed to flash fire.

"I'm awfully sorry about Nora," she said; "but I fail to see how I am to blame. From your manner, Nan, and yours, Hester, I seem to be accused of something. What is it, pray?"

"Oh, it's nothing, indeed," said Molly, who had come up now and joined Hester. "What does it matter, Hetty, when we are all so awfully wretched? Poor Annie did not mean anything. Do let her alone!"

"I did not mean anything?" echoed Annie. "I'm afraid I can't allow myself to be let alone. I must find out what I'm accused of. Kitty, you say you kept my secret safely. Speak now and tell everybody."

"I can't stay to listen," said Molly, turning away; "it's too--too trivial!"

Hester and Nan, however, still stood facing Annie, and the boys, Guy and Harry, also came and joined the group.

"Speak, Kitty," said Annie.

"You were kind," said Kitty; "it's wicked to say you weren't kind. You found out that Boris hadn't come to the picnic, and you said you'd go back for him; you'd walk back all in the heat, and you didn't mind the bull, nor the bull-dog, nor--nor--anything; and you said I wasn't to tell, and 'twould be a surprise when you came back with Boris and, perhaps, Nell, too--and I promised. Then we had dinner, and you weren't there, and everybody asked for you and everybody wondered where you could be; but Hester said you were a sort of 'centric girl, and that you was grown up and we needn't fret; and Nan said you was nothing if you wasn't unexpected; so nobody fretted, and I kept my secret locked up tight. But Nora wanted you more than the others, and she saw my lips shut tight and my eyes watching for you through the trees, and she guessed I had a secret; and I said I had, but I wouldn't tell; and she said she'd take me to mother, and that mother would make me tell, and so I climbed up into the beech-tree to get away from her; and I was naughty and cross, and she was naughty and cross, too, and she followed me up into the beech-tree, and I got out upon a rotten bough, where I thought she'd be sure not to come; but she did come, cause I was real naughty and I taunted her; and the bough broke and she fell, but I didn't fall 'cause I caught on to a bough higher up. It's been dreadful ever since," continued Kitty, pressing her hands tightly together. "Worse than when I forgot to give water to Harry's canary and it died, and worse than when I pulled up all Guy's canariensis in mistake for weeds; its been awful, but I did keep the secret."

"Is that all?" said Annie.

"Yes, that's all," replied Kitty. "I did keep the secret."

"I understand," said Annie. "I should have come back, of course. I did not remember that I might get you into trouble, Kitty; it did not occur to me that you were the plucky sort of child you are."

"Plucky?" echoed Guy with some scorn. "I don't call it plucky to be just decently ***honourable***. We don't tell lies. Kitty would have told a lie if she had broken her word."

"And I promised to come back, and I broke my word," said Annie. "Yes, I fully understand; it's just like me."

She turned away as she spoke, and, plunging into the shrubbery, was lost to view.

"Leave her alone, children," said Hester to the astonished children, who were preparing to follow her. "I knew it would cut her to the heart, but it can't be helped. She'll be all right by-and-by, but she can't stand any of you now; you must leave her alone."

Boris came up to Kitty, put his arms round her neck, and kissed her. His kiss was of the deepest consolation to her; she walked away with him slowly, and Nell took Hester's hand. Nell's face was like a little white sheet; she was trembling in her agitation.

"Oh, what is the matter?" she gasped. "Is Nonie awfully hurt? Is it dangerous? Oh, Hetty, it's worse than the colts! Oh, I felt bad this morning, but it was nothing to this--nothing! May I stay with you for the present, Hetty?"

"Yes, darling," said Hester in her kindest voice. "Come into the house with me. We are all very anxious until we get the doctor's opinion. Your father and mother are both with Nora; and Dr. Jervis is there and Jane. Everything is being done that can be done, and we know nothing at present. Come, Nell, we must be brave--and here is Molly; she is just as anxious as you."

Nell looked at Molly, who was standing in the porch; she flew to her eldest sister's side, clasped her arms round her neck, and shed a few of those silent, rare tears which only came to her now and then, for Nell was no ordinary child, and rarely showed her deepest feelings.

"I don't know how I'm to live through this suspense," said poor Molly.

But even as she spoke it came to an end.

Mr. Lorrimer came out of the study, closing the door softly behind him. He strode quickly through the hall, and entered the porch where the three girls were standing. Molly stepped forward quickly and seized his arm.

"Well?" she asked.

He gave her a quick look; his face was very pale, and a sudden contraction of pain flitted across his brow.

"Well, my loves," he said, "we must all try to be as cheerful as we can and not break down; there isn't a bit of use in breaking down."

"But how is she, father?" asked Molly. "What does Dr. Jervis say?"

"He says, Molly, that poor Nora is very seriously hurt; but it is impossible to form a reliable opinion on her case so soon. He wishes us to get Dr. Bentinck from London to see her, and I am going to drive to Nortonbury to telegraph to him to come at once. Now, don't keep me, my dears. By the way, Molly, mother says you had better take the children home as soon as ever you can."

"Oh, may I not stay?" asked Molly.

"No, my dear, I think not; there must be some head at home. Jane Macalister will stay and help your mother to-night until we can get the services of a proper nurse. Take the children back as soon as you can, Molly. God bless you, my love."

The Squire stepped into the doctor's brougham and was driven rapidly away. Molly raised her hand to her forehead.

"I feel stunned," she said. "Nora was the gayest and the brightest and the prettiest of us all. Nothing ever seemed to happen to Nora, and now she is so ill that I may not even see her."

"She will be better to-morrow, I am sure," said Hester.

"Oh, Hetty, if I could only stay here," cried poor Molly.

"I wish you could, Molly, with all my heart."

"We'll know nothing of how she's getting on at the Towers," continued Molly. "I think it will drive me mad not to know."

"I'll come over very early in the morning and tell you, and perhaps something may be arranged to-morrow so that you can stay here."

"I might stay instead of Jane. I know I could help mother far better than Jane can. But there, I suppose I must have patience. Come, Nell."

CHAPTER X.
AN AWFULLY FRIVOLOUS GIRL.

D r. Bentinck, the great London surgeon, arrived early on the following morning. Poor Nora was quite conscious now, and in great pain. This pain, however, was considered rather a good sign than otherwise, for had the spine been much injured the little girl would have been numbed and stupid. Dr. Bentinck examined his little patient with great tenderness and care. His opinion, when it was given, was a great deal more favourable than anyone dared to hope. He thought that Nora would eventually be as well as ever again; but although he was sure that there was no permanent injury to the spine. there was a great deal of present distress and discomfort to be got through. The little girl must lie perfectly still on her back for many weeks, and it would be many a long day before the dancing, romping Nora of old would return to the Towers.

After the night of suspense and terror, however, which poor Mrs. Lorrimer, by Nora's bedside, and Molly in her lonely little bedroom at the Towers, had undergone, the great London doctor's news seemed all that was delightful. Hester hurried to the Towers to put Molly's anxious heart at rest, and Mrs. Lorrimer returned to the room where Nora was lying very white and still.

Nora had received a shock the day before which must influence her during all the remainder of her days. It seemed to shake all her little artificial affected nature off and to reveal the real Nora, who was frightened and weak and silly, and yet who had somewhere beneath her frivolous exterior a real little heart of gold. If there was one person whom Nora really adored, and in whose presence she was ever her truest and best, it was her mother. She looked at her mother now as she re-entered the room.

"Stoop down and tell me," she said in a whisper.

Mrs. Lorrimer bent over her.

"Yes, my love," she said. "What do you want to know?"

"Am I going to die, mother?"

"Die? not a bit of it, my darling. Dr. Bentinck has given us quite a cheerful opinion of you. He says there is no very serious injury, and that you will be your usual self by-and-by."

Nora's eyes brightened.

"I am very glad," she said. "I didn't want to die. I don't think I'm quite fit."

"My little daughter will have learnt a severe lesson by this accident," said Mrs. Lorrimer; "but now you must lie still, love, and think of nothing but how quickly you can get well again."

Nora closed her eyes, and Mrs. Lorrimer sat down in an easy chair by the bedside.

The next day the little girl was considerably better, and Mrs. Lorrimer proposed that she and Jane should return to the Towers and send Molly to look after Nora. A good surgical nurse had arrived from town the evening before; Molly's services, therefore, would only be of the lightest.

Mrs. Lorrimer went into the morning room, where Hester and Annie were sitting together.

The moment she did so Annie jumped up and came to her.

"How is Nora?" she asked.

"She is much better, my dear; in fact, almost quite like her old self to-day. She cannot, of course, move without the greatest pain, but when she lies perfectly still she is tolerably easy."

"Then I may go to see her, may I not?" asked Annie.

"If you will promise to be very quiet. It would not do to excite her in any way."

"There never was such a good nurse as Annie," exclaimed Hester. "She has a soothing influence over sick people which is quite marvellous. Did I ever tell you how she saved Nan's life years ago at Lavender House?"

"Oh, that's an old story," said Annie, laughing and reddening. "Well, granted that I possess a sort of mesmerism, may I use it for Nora's benefit?"

"Certainly, my love," said Mrs. Lorrimer, smiling affectionately at Annie's bright face.

She ran off, singing as she went.

Nora was lying perfectly flat on the little bed which had been hastily improvised for her in the study. The room was now turned into a comfortable bedroom, but was also in part a sitting-room. A large screen effectually shut away the bedroom part of the furniture and partly screened Nora also.

Annie had not gone straight to the sick room. She had rushed first into the conservatory and made frantic mad havoc amongst the roses there. The choicest blooms, any quantity of unopened buds, were cut by her reckless fingers. She gathered a whole quantity of maidenhair to mix with the roses, and then, a tender colour on her own cheeks, her dark eyes bright as well as soft, she appeared like a radiant vision before the tired, sad eyes of the sick child.

Nora was just well enough to feel the monotony of her present position, to think longingly of the life of active movement which was hers at the Towers. Even lessons in the old schoolroom, even that hateful darning and mending to which she had to devote a portion of her time each day, seemed delightful in contrast to her present inertia. She was thinking of Friar's Wood and of Annie's bright face just when Annie herself, looking like a bit of the summer morning, appeared in view.

"Now, don't get excited," said Annie smiling at her. "You'll see such a lot of me during the next few weeks that you need not get into a state just because I've come into the room. I feel that in a certain fashion I am to blame for your accident, so I am going to take your amusements upon my shoulders; and if you just allow me to manage matters, I'll promise that you shan't have a dull time while you are getting well. Have you a headache?"

"No, not a bit."

"That's all right; then you won't mind my talking. Are you fond of pretty things?"

"Yes, very fond."

"Well, I'll sit here, just where you can comfortably see the flowers and me. I expect we'll make a very pretty picture, but you need not say so. I wonder where there's a looking-glass. Oh, yes, in that corner, decently covered with an antimacassar. Well, then, glass, you have got to uncover for my benefit. I wish to see whether I look pretty or not."

Annie danced up to the glass; Nora could watch her each movement.

Her steps were as light as a sylph's, nothing rattled in the sick-room as she moved about it. She took up a comb and re-arranged her dark, curling hair. She placed a rose in her belt, nodded to her own bright image, and then, seating herself before a small table, began to arrange the flowers. "Nora, you can't think what a mass of roses there are in the green-house this morning. Of course the garden is full, too, but I did not wait to go to the garden to get these for you. You can watch me just as long as you fancy and then shut your eyes. These half-open buds are to be placed on a table close to you, where you can smell them. The other flowers we'll put here and there about the room. It's a good thing you were brought into this pretty study, for from where you lie you can fancy you are in a sitting-room, and that you are just having a stretch on the sofa to rest yourself. Fancy goes a long way, doesn't it?"

"I don't know," replied Nora. "I'm afraid I can't fancy that."

Tears filled her eyes as she spoke.

"How cool you look," she said presently, "and--and active and happy."

"It wouldn't do for me to look unhappy when I am with you, would it?" asked Annie. "Now tell me, do you like this dress?"

"Yes, it's very pretty. What stuff is it?"

"Only pink cambric, trimmed with pink embroidery. Would you like me to make you one?"

"What do you mean?"

Nora's eyes brightened perceptibly.

"What I say," replied Annie. "I made this dress for myself. I make all my dresses, for I am not at all well off; in short, I am poor, and Mrs. Willis is so sweet and dear that she gives me a couple of hours every day to devote to needlework. In consequence I have got some pretty things, although they cost next to nothing. Now, I think you and I are something alike. We are both dark, and we have both got bright colour. Oh, I don't mean that you have a bright colour just now, you poor little darling; but when you are well, you are sweet, like a wild rose. Suppose I make you a pink cambric frock, and a white one and a blue one? I have got a white and a blue. When you're well again you'll look quite lovely in them, Nora. What do you say?"

"I'd like it awfully," said Nora. "You are very good, very good; but I haven't got any money. I--I am even poorer than you."

"Are you? How delightful. I adore ***poor lady*** girls, because they are always contriving, and that's so interesting. We'll make the dresses out of odds and ends, and they shan't cost you a penny."

"It's very good of you," said Nora. She was too weak to argue and protest, and the vision of her pretty little self in alternate dresses of pink and white and blue cambric was decidedly refreshing.

She lay and looked at Annie and acknowledged to herself that she made a pretty, a beautiful, picture, and the discontented lines round her mouth vanished, and the time did not seem long.

That evening Molly, excited and in high spirits, arrived on the scene.

Molly was absolutely trembling as she came into the room where Nora was lying; but although her love was ten times deeper, she had not Annie's marvellous tact, and soon contrived to tire poor Nora dreadfully. The nurse seeing this sent her away, and Molly came back to Hester with a very crestfallen expression of face.

"I can't make out how it is," she said; "but Nora does not seem a bit glad to see me."

"Oh, nonsense," said Hester; "what do you mean?"

Annie was sitting in a corner of the room busily engaged over Henry Kingsley's novel, "Geoffrey Hamlyn." She did not raise her eyes, but bent her curly head still lower over the fascinating pages. Nan had gone to spend a few days at the Towers, and the great house at the Grange seemed very quiet and still.

Molly sank down into a chair near Hester.

"I have been so excited about this meeting," she said. "Nora is almost my twin-sister, and I have suffered so terribly about her. I cannot tell you the relief and joy of being allowed to come here to look after her, but now I fear I shall be next to no good."

"Well, you'll be no end of good to me," said Hester; "and, of course, Nora will like to have you by-and-by, but she is still very weak and cannot bear the least excitement."

"But nurse tells me that you, Annie, spent some hours in her room to-day."

At these words Annie sprang to her feet, and "Geoffrey Hamlyn" fell with a bang to the floor.

"I did spend hours in her room," she said, "and I don't think I tired her; but, then, perhaps you kissed her a lot, Molly?"

"Kissed her?" exclaimed Molly; "I should think so, at least a hundred times."

"Oh, good gracious, how dreadfully fatiguing for a sick person. Well, you see, I didn't kiss her once, nor even touch her."

"But you aren't her sister," said Molly.

"No, no; and that is the reason that I am a very good person to be with her, because I amuse her without exciting her. All I did to-day was to sit in the room where she could see me, and arrange some flowers and have a little talk about dress-making."

Molly opened her eyes in astonishment. Nora had been at the brink of death. Had not Molly spent a whole night in fervent and passionate prayers for her recovery? Did not Nora love Molly, and did not Molly love Nora as only loving sisters can love? and yet Molly exhausted poor Nora, while Annie Forest, who was a stranger, soothed her.

Molly looked at Annie now without in the least comprehending her, and for the first time in all her gentle life a distinct sensation of jealousy was aroused within her.

Annie left the room a moment later, and Hester turned to Molly.

"I see you don't understand Annie," she said.

"Yes, I'm sure I do; what an awfully frivolous girl she must be. Fancy her talking of dress to Nora, and she so ill."

"But it did Nora heaps of good; nurse said she was quite jolly this afternoon, and that Annie was the companion of all others for her."

"Don't say that again, Hester," said Molly; "it makes me feel quite wicked."

"I know well," replied Hester, "that Annie is thoughtless."

"Thoughtless? I should think so; but for her Nora would never have been hurt."

"But she has the warmest heart in the world," continued Hester. "I did not understand her for a long time. Indeed, Molly, I don't mind telling you that once I hated her; but, oh, if you could only see Annie at her best. She can be--yes, she can be noble."

Molly stared in non-comprehension.

CHAPTER XI.
THE DIAMOND RING.

Those of my readers who have read "A World of Girls" will know all about the early story of Annie Forest; but, to those who have not, I may as well explain that she was a motherless girl, that she had been in her day a sad tomboy, that she had a father living, but that it was absolutely necessary for her before long to earn her own living. She was still at school, however, although she now occupied the post there of pupil-teacher. Mrs. Willis, the headmistress of Lavender House, the school where Annie was educated, was her warm and devoted friend. Mrs. Willis loved all her pupils and had an extraordinary influence over them, but Annie was almost like her adopted child.

She stood now in the wide, cool hall at the Grange, and reflected for a moment as to what she should do. She then ran lightly up to her pretty bedroom, and, opening her trunk, began to rummage eagerly among its contents. Annie would not be Annie if she were not the most impulsive creature in the world. She meant to devote herself to Nora; she had a great gift for reading character, and a quick glance showed her how best she might amuse this little girl. Nora was pretty, but Nora was not richly endowed with pretty frocks. Annie felt sure that she would arouse the keenest sympathy in the sick girl if she used her skilful fingers to cover the defects in Nora's wardrobe. She had made her own cambric frocks, and imagined that she had plenty of stuff in her trunk to make similar ones for Nora; she saw, to her dismay, however, that she had left the cambric behind her at school and, as Mrs. Willis was away, and Lavender House was shut up during the summer vacation, it would be impossible for her to send for it. She had only a few shillings in her purse; she was well aware that Nora was possessed of no money. How, then, could she redeem her promise? Annie could not bring herself to ask Hester to help her, and yet, at the same time, it would never, never do to disappoint Nora! Annie had brought herself to consider Nora her own special patient. She had spent an hour with her in the morning and nearly two hours in the afternoon, and during the afternoon visit the girls had talked a good deal about the frocks. It was arranged between them that they were to be surprise frocks, and that Mr. and Mrs. Lorrimer were to know nothing about them until they saw Nora well once more and arrayed in the prettiest of the three. Annie had hunted up some fashion-books, and had consulted Nora about the shape and the cut of the sleeves, and the way the skirt was to be hung and the embroidery sewn on. Both girls had been animated over the discussion, and Nora had been too interested to feel fatigue.

Well, that happened a few hours ago; now Annie, on her knees, bent over her empty trunk with an expression of keen dismay.

What was she to do? How could she possibly raise the money necessary to the purchase of the cambric? She calculated that the cambric and embroidery necessary for the making of three simple dresses would cost from twenty-five to thirty shillings This was not a large sum, but everything is by proportion, and for poor Annie, with five shillings in her purse and very little chance of any more money coming to her until the end of her visit to the Grange, thirty shillings seemed absolutely unattainable.

"But I must get it somehow!" she murmured, flinging herself on the floor by her open trunk as she spoke. "I'm not going to be beaten by a little paltry sum like that! I promised Nora the frocks, and she shall have them! I didn't care a bit for Nora yesterday--she didn't suit me, and I thought her affected; but if I hadn't been so desperately thoughtless, she'd have been well now; and, as I have been in part the cause of her accident, I'm simply bound to look after her. Have those frocks she must! Poor little bit of frivolity, nothing in the world will soothe her nerves so much as seeing me making them for her. But that money--that thirty shillings! Oh, *dash* that thirty shillings! Why should a mean little sum like that worry a girl almost into fits? Get it, I *will*; and ask Hester to help me, I *won't*! The frocks are to be a secret between Nora and me; the secret will be half the fun. Now, how am I to get the money? Have I anything to sell?"

Annie rose from the floor, where she had seated herself, and, going to a drawer, opened it. She took out a little leather box, and looked anxiously at its contents.

There were a few treasures there, dear from association, but not of a valuable sort. There was a silver brooch, shaped like a horn, with a little bell attached; a schoolfellow had brought it to her from Switzerland; it probably cost a franc, and, although Annie admired it immensely on her neck, she did not believe any jeweller would give her sixpence for it. Then there was a basket beautifully carved out of an apricot-stone, and a narrow silver chain broken in many parts; and there was a bog-oak brooch and an old jet bracelet. Annie also possessed a gold locket and chain which she had won as a prize on a certain memorable occasion, but this treasure she had also stupidly left behind her. How provoking! She had really nothing she could sell for thirty shillings. But stay, she had forgotten. She coloured high as a memory came to her. She had one article of solid value--a ring. In one sense it was not hers; in another it was. It was a gold ring, with a single diamond; this ring had belonged to Annie Forest's mother. On her dying bed she had given the ring to Mrs. Willis One day Mrs. Willis had shown it to Annie, had yielded to Annie's entreaties that she might borrow it for this visit to the Grange, and had told her that, although she could not part with her mother's last gift during her lifetime, she would leave the ring to Annie in her will.

With her dark eyes full of excitement, Annie now took the ring out of its little morocco case and looked at it.

She had meant to wear it proudly on her finger during her stay at the Grange; but, in the excitement of passing events, had forgotten to do so up to the present time. The ring was of value; no one had seen it on her finger, therefore no one would miss it. It occurred to Annie that she might ask a jeweller to lend her thirty shillings on the ring. With this thirty shillings she could buy the stuff for Nora's frocks; and as her father always sent her a pound on her birthday, and that birthday was only a little over a month away, she thought that she might manage to scrape together thirty shillings to redeem the ring before she returned to school.

Annie's mind was quickly made up. She would pawn the ring to someone, and trust to her lucky star to get it back before she returned to Lavender House. She knew well that Mrs. Willis would ask her for it as soon as ever she went back to school. Mrs. Willis was a person who never forgot: big things and small things alike found a place in her memory; but long before then Annie would, of course, have the ring in her possession.

Having made up her mind to sell it, she wondered how she could accomplish this feat. She would have not only to sell the ring, but also to buy the cambric and embroidery without anyone knowing anything about it. The secret would lose half its fascination if anybody guessed. Annie thought anxiously for a moment, then an idea came to her. Nan had talked a good deal about her old nurse. Annie was a prime favourite with nurse, who always considered that she owed Annie a good deal for having rescued her darling from the gipsies some years ago. Perhaps nurse would help Annie now; she resolved to go and sound the old woman.

Putting the ring in its morocco case, she opened the baize door which led to the nursery part of the house, and soon found herself in Mrs. Martin's apartments. Mrs. Martin was known by three different appellations: to Hester she was nurse, or nursey, to Sir John Thornton she was Patty, but to the servants and to strangers she was always spoken of as Mrs. Martin. She was extremely punctilious as to the manner in which she was addressed; and now, as Annie entered her room she wondered which of her three titles would best propitiate her.

"Well, my dear, what do you want?" said the old lady, looking up with a pleased smile from her knitting as Annie's pretty head was pushed roguishly round the door. "Oh, come now, Miss Forest; I know your collogueing ways. But you ought to be in bed, my dear, for it's past ten o'clock."

"And so ought you to be in bed, you dear, naughty, old thing," said Annie; "but you know people don't always do what they ought. If going to bed is what I ought to do at the present moment, you ought to do the same, nursey. May I call you nursey?"

"Well, Miss Annie, you're almost like one of the family; but still I'm properly only nurse to my own two bairns--Miss Hetty and Miss Nan."

"And this is a motherless bairn who would like you to be nursey to her," said Annie, seating herself on a low hassock at the old woman's feet and looking into her face.

"Well, and nursey it shall be," said Mrs. Martin. "Eh, but God has given you a very bonny face, my love."

Annie took up one of the horny hands, and rubbed it affectionately against her soft cheek.

"Nurse," she said, "I am quite in trouble. I wonder if I might tell you a secret?"

"Well, dear, if you like to trust me, safe it shall be. Inviolate it shall be kept, Miss Annie, and you know that violet's the colour of truth."

"Of course I do, you dear old thing. What a wonderful comfort it is to talk to you. I knew you'd let me confide in you, and it will be such a load off my mind."

"My dear, I hope you haven't been at any mad pranks. The young ladies of the present day are wonderful for audaciousness."

Annie sighed.

"I wish I wasn't audacious," she said; "and I wish I wasn't thoughtless and reckless. I'm always meaning to be kind to people, and somehow or other I'm always kind in the wrong way; it's very, very trying."

Annie's pretty eyes filled with real tears of contrition.

"You're but young, my bairn," said Mrs. Martin, "and the heart's in the right place; anyone can see that who looks at you, Miss Annie."

"Nurse, you are a comfort to me. Now I will tell you my trouble. At the picnic the other day I got into a state of mind because little Boris Lorrimer had not come, and I confided in Kitty Lorrimer and went off to fetch him, and Kitty promised she would not tell where I had gone until I had brought him back; but when I got to the Towers I was very hot--very, very hot with my long walk, and I found that Boris did not wish to come back with me, and I forgot all about my promise to Kitty, and stayed at the Towers for the rest of the day; but poor Kitty kept her word and did not tell, and Nora got cross with her, and climbed up the beech tree after her, and crept out on to the rotten bough, and so got the dreadful fall which has made her so ill. Nora would not have met with this terrible accident but for me; so I have taken upon myself to amuse her, and I promised to make her three dresses."

"Sakes alive! Three?" interrupted Mrs. Martin; "and why three, Miss Annie? Wouldn't one be enough to content her?"

"No, nursey, no; three cambric dresses or nothing. I promised to make them, and I thought I had the cambric and embroidery in my trunk, but when I looked I found I had left it all behind me at school. You can't think how upset I am about it, for I must keep my promise to Nora, and Nora has got no money, and I have only five shillings, which I must keep for stamps and odds and ends; and I would not ask Hester or Nan to lend me sixpence for the world."

"But why not, my dear? I am sure Miss Hetty would be proud to oblige."

"No, nurse, it must not be," said Annie; "Hester is to know nothing about the frocks, and Nan is to know nothing and Molly is to know nothing. The fun of the thing is its being a great, great secret. Why, the making of those frocks in the room with Nora and only Nora knowing; why, the mystery of the thing will almost cure her, it will, really. Oh, nursey, nursey," patting Mrs. Martin excitedly as she spoke, "you must, you shall help me."

"And you want me to lend you the money, my pet?"

"No; how can you imagine such a thing. But I'll tell you what I want you to do. I want you to get up early to-morrow morning, quite early, and to make one of the grooms drive you into Nortonbury."

"Sakes alive! What for? I'm not used to the air without my breakfast."

"I'll get up and get you your breakfast. I'll boil the kettle here, and make your tea and toast your bread. You must go to Nortonbury, and you must be back between ten and eleven o'clock."

"And when I go what am I to do there, my dear? Oh, dear, dear, the ways of the young of the present day are masterful beyond belief. You make me all of a quiver, Miss Annie."

"I knew you'd rise to it," said Annie. "I felt if there were a soul in this world who would pull me out of the horrid scrape I have got myself into, it would be you, nursey."

"Well, my love, you have got a blarneying tongue, and no mistake; but now, when I do get to Nortonbury, what am I to do?"

Annie pulled the morocco case out of her pocket. She opened it, and slipped the ring on Mrs. Martin's little finger.

"You are to sell that," she said; "or, rather--no, you are not to sell it for the world--but you are to borrow thirty shillings on it."

"My word! Is it to the pawn-shop you expect me to go, Miss Forest?"

"How nasty of you to say Miss Forest. I'm Annie Forest, in great trouble, and looking to you as my last comfort. You are to borrow thirty shillings on that beautiful diamond ring. I don't mind where you get it; and then you are to buy me seven yards of pink cambric, and seven yards of white cambric, and seven yards of blue cambric. These shades, do you see? And I want embroidery to match. I have put the number of yards on this slip of paper, and a list of buttons and hooks and waistbands and linings. Oh, and, of course, cottons to match. Now, will you or won't you? Will you be an angel or won't you? That's the plain question I have got to ask."

"It's the pawn-shop that gets over me, Miss Annie."

"Oh, *please* don't let it get over you. What can the pawnbroker do to you? Most people call him uncle, so I expect he's awfully good-natured."

"Uncle, indeed," exclaimed Mrs. Martin, tossing her head; "it's a word you shouldn't know, Miss Annie Forest."

"But why shouldn't I? I never heard that uncles were wicked, except the one who killed the babes in the wood. Now you will go; you will be an angel! I know this special uncle who is to lend money on my ring will be delightful!"

CHAPTER XII.
THE LAND OF PERHAPS.

There are some people who always get their way in life. They are by no means the best people, nor the most amiable, nor the most thoughtful. Sometimes, and not a very rare sometimes either, the poor, thoughtful people go to the wall, when the thoughtless and impulsive and careless come triumphantly out of their difficulties.

There never was a girl who got into a greater number of scrapes than Annie Forest; but neither was there ever a girl who managed to right herself more quickly. She knew the art of twisting other people round her little finger. Having performed this feat to perfection on Mrs. Martin, alias Patty, alias nursey, she went happily to bed, knowing that all would be right for the present, and never giving a thought to the evil but still distant hour when she must return her mother's ring to Mrs. Willis.

Annie rose in good time in the morning, and took upon herself the preparing of Mrs. Martin's breakfast. She lit a fire in the old lady's sitting-room, and toasted her bread with her own fair hands, and made the tea for her to drink.

Mrs. Martin started on her journey to Nortonbury with many fervent blessings from Annie, who then returned in a high state of content to her own room.

The parcel of cambric arrived in due time, and Annie cut out the first of the three frocks that morning.

In order to keep their secret quite to themselves, Nora and Annie decided to keep the door of the library locked while they were at work. This arrangement was delightful to Nora, but it irritated Molly not a little. When she came to see her sister, to be greeted by a locked door--and to hear Annie's clear voice singing out from within, "Oh, we're so busy, you darling of a Molly asthore. Don't disturb us for the present, there's a love," and when this remark was followed by silvery laughter from Nora--poor Molly felt herself decidedly out in the cold.

Jealousy was for the first time fiercely stirred in her gentle breast and she shed some tears in secret over the change in Nora, who had hitherto clung to her and loved her better than anyone else in the world.

But what will not a rather frivolous little heart do for the sake of a pretty dress?

Nora in her own way was as thoughtless as Annie, and it never occurred to either of them as even possible that Molly should be pained by the fact of the locked door.

A fortnight passed away. The pink dress and the white were both finished and the blue was rapidly approaching completion, when one day the whole party at the Grange were considerably electrified and their attention turned into a completely new quarter by a letter which arrived for Hester from Sir John Thornton.

After writing on various subjects, he concluded his lengthy epistle as follows:--

"I shall not be home for another week. For some reasons I am sorry for this delay; but when I explain matters to you, my dear Hester, on the occasion of my return, you will, I am sure, agree with me that my absence from home is, under the circumstances, allowable. In the meantime, I have not forgotten that Nan's birthday is on the 15th of August, and that that date is only a week distant. If in any way possible, I shall return either on the fifteenth or the evening of the day before; but, meanwhile, I give you carte blanche to celebrate the auspicious event in any manner you like. You need spare no expense to make the day as truly festive to yourself and your young friends as you possibly can. I enclose in this letter a blank cheque to which I have affixed my signature. You may fill it in for any sum within reason, and then if you take it to the bank at Nortonbury it will be cashed for you. Buy Nan a handsome present from me, and please choose presents for Annie Forest and all the Lorrimer children. I am sorry to hear bad rumours with regard to the Squire, and that there is a possibility of the Towers being soon in the market; but I trust these rumours are either grossly exaggerated or without any foundation. I am sorry, also, to hear that Nora Lorrimer has met with an accident, but am glad that you are taking care of her, as I know by experience that no one could have a kinder nurse than my good little Hetty. Get every possible thing you can want, my love, for Nan's birthday. Make it a festival to be long remembered by you all. Set your wits to work to make the day a really brilliant one, and expect your loving father, if not to share in the whole of the festivity, at least to be present at a portion of it.

"Now good-bye, my dear Hester; give my love to Nan, and remember me kindly to your young friend, Miss Forest.--Believe me, your affectionate father,

"JOHN THORNTON."

Hester received this letter at breakfast time. She read it through gravely--not once, but twice. Annie's gay voice, her peals of merry laughter, and her gay and irresistibly funny speeches were diverting the attention of Molly, and to a certain extent of Nan; but Nan knew the handwriting on the envelope. She was also well aware of the fact that the birthday, when she would have the glorious privilege of counting nine years as her own, was close at hand. When Hester, therefore, folded up the letter, she called to her from the other end of the table.

"Toss it over, Hetty," she said. "I know it's from the Dad; let us hear what he says."

"Yes, it is from father," replied Hester in a grave voice.

"May not I read what he says?"

"The beginning part is business."

"Well, I'll skip the business; you can point out where the fun begins. What are you looking so mysterious and solemn about? Why may not I read the letter?"

Nan looked almost cross; Hester was disturbed. She showed this by slipping the letter into her pocket. This fact aroused Annie's curiosity, who looked at her with sparkling eyes full of mischief.

"You are a cross-patch," exclaimed Nan in her most spoilt tone. "I never knew such a thing. Is not a father's letter meant for one child as well as for another?"

"No, Nan, dear, not on this occasion," said Hester in a firm tone. "Now, try not to be silly; finish your breakfast, and I will speak to you afterwards."

Nan pouted.

"When is Sir John coming back, Hester?" inquired Molly.

"In about a week," replied Hester.

"A week," shouted Nan suddenly recovering her good humour. "Hurrah! my birthday will be in a week. My dear, good girls all of you, I am getting elderly as fast as possible. I'll be nine in a week; isn't that scrumptious? Did Dad say anything about my birthday in that mysterious letter, Hetty?"

"He is coming home for your birthday," replied Hester.

"Good, kind, considerate old gentleman," responded Nan in her most flippant voice. "Did he say anything more about that great and auspicious event Hetty?"

"He said a great deal more about it; in fact, the largest part of his letter was about it; but I'm not going to talk it over now. I propose that we all go to Nora's room after breakfast and discuss the letter. There is a good deal to discuss, and it is very exciting," continued Hester, a flush of brilliant colour coming into her cheeks.

The news that there was a good deal to discuss of an exciting character restored even Nan's good humour. Breakfast was hurried over, and Annie Forest and Nan rushed off to Nora's room to prepare her for the fact that she was soon expected to hold a *levee*, and that the subject under discussion was likely to be of a very rousing character.

Molly lingered behind in the breakfast-room; she looked anxiously at Hester, who avoided her eyes. Hester did not wish to say anything to make Molly unhappy, and she knew that her father's allusion to the possible sale of the Towers would fill the poor little girl's heart with the most acute misery.

Making a great effort, therefore, to fight down a nameless apprehension on her own account, for what important business could be keeping Sir John so long away from home, she said in a cheerful voice--

"Now, Molly, we're not going to croak, nor spend the day imagining all kinds of unpleasant things. Father has written me a long letter, and there are some things in it which I don't quite like; but I am not going to talk them over at present. All the end of the letter is taken up with Nan's birthday, and that is the matter we have to discuss just now. Come along now to the library, and let's get it over."

Nora was still lying flat on her back; but all pain had long left her, and she was practically quite well.

The subject of the letter was therefore discussed with intense animation by the five eager girls.

Unlimited money, any amount of presents, and *carte blanche* how to spend the birthday in the most agreeable way was surely enough to turn the brains of most people.

Many and wild were the plans which Nan proposed.

They would start for a picnic at six in the morning. They would order ices from Nortonbury to arrive by special messenger at some impossible place at an un-earthly hour. They would have bonfires on the top of every hill within a reasonable distance. Although it was not Christmas time, they would end up with the largest Christmas tree ever seen, and it should stand in the centre of the lawn, and every poor child for miles round should be invited to see it and to share the wonderful presents which should hang from every branch and twig.

Nan's cheeks were flushed and her eyes bright while she made these suggestions; but, after all, it was Annie's proposal in the end which carried the day.

"Let's have the picnic by all means," she said; "and let all who will go to it. If Nan wishes to be charitable, and to think of others rather than herself, let her do so; and let all the school children be taken in waggons and waggonettes to Friar's Wood or any other beautiful place in the neighbourhood, and let Nan herself give them presents before they go home. All that, of course, will be very delightful; although, of course, neither Nora nor I can be present."

"What do you mean by *your* not being present?" asked Molly, her brown eyes growing dark with anger. "I suppose if anyone is to stay with Nora, it ought to be me."

"No, it oughtn't," said Nora. "I wish for Annie; she's more fun."

"And I can't do without you, Molly, darling," interrupted Hester. "You always are my right hand when anything important is going on; and then you know all the school children by name, which, frankly, I do not."

"Well, now, *do* hear me out," said Annie; "I have not half done. What I say is this, that as Sir John Thornton is so generous, and as he wishes everyone in the house to be happy on the day of Nan's birthday, I think something should be done to make it up to Nora and me. Now, why shouldn't we have a real glorious time in the evening? You have a billiard-room in this house, haven't you?"

"Yes."

"Can't we have a ball there?"

"What are we to do with the table?" said Hester.

"Oh," exclaimed Nora, her eyes sparkling, "we have such a heavenly ball-room at the Towers; a great enormous room, never used and full of rubbish which can easily be turned out."

"Is there a gallery to that room?" interrupted Annie.

"Yes, at one end."

"Then the whole thing is complete," continued Annie. "We'll have a children's fancy ball in the evening, and Nora shall look on from the gallery. Nora shall be, in a sort of way, princess of the ceremonies. We'll make her up the sweetest dress, and everyone shall come up and talk to her; and if presents are to be given away at the end, she shall give them. What do you say, girls? Could anything be more perfectly lovely than a children's fancy ball in the old ball-room at the Towers? Oh, I hope it will be a moonlight night, and the whole place will look like fairyland!"

This suggestion was so daring and brilliant that it carried Nora away on a storm of enthusiasm immediately. Nan clapped her hands and screamed with glee; and even the more sober Hester and Molly could find no objections to raise. The ball-room was certainly at the Towers; it contained a gallery where the musicians could be, and where, if necessary, Nora might rest; it contained what seemed to the children like unlimited space, and if to unlimited space unlimited money could be added, what brilliant results must be produced!

"If I consent to this," said Hester--"and I think my consent is essential--it must be on condition that not a single Lorrimer is put to even a shilling's worth of expense. The ball must be Nan's ball; the Lorrimers will most kindly give her a room to hold it in, all the rest will be our affair. Do you clearly understand, Molly? Do you, Nora?"

"Oh, I understand fast enough," said Nora quickly.

"Yes, I understand," replied Molly in a graver tone.

"Do you agree?"

"Yes," answered Molly.

"Well, your consent being obtained," continued Hester, "I will go with you to the Towers this morning, Molly, and look at the ball-room, and see Mrs. Lorrimer on the subject."

"The worst of it is," continued Annie, "that we have such a very short time to prepare--only one week to make all our fancy dresses and to see to all the other arrangements!"

"Fancy dresses!" exclaimed Nora from her sofa. "What am I to wear?"

"You are to be dressed as Queen of the Fairies. You shall lie on a bed of rose-leaves, and have gossamer, cloudy sort of drapery all around you. Never fear, Nora, you will look lovely--leave it to me."

Nora's eyes sparkled.

"Annie, you're a darling!" she exclaimed, with enthusiasm.

"And what character am I to be, Annie?" cried Nan, pouting her full lips. "I'm not jealous, and I don't mind Nora being Queen of the Fairies; but please remember that it's my party, and I am really the queen of the day."

"So you are, you sweet!" exclaimed Annie. "Don't think for a moment that I'll forget you; but you must really give me a little time to think the characters over. Suppose I consider everything carefully and jot down a few ideas, and suppose we discuss them to-night; and then to-morrow we can go to Nortonbury to buy the materials for the dresses."

"But we can't possibly make our own dresses," exclaimed Hester.

"Oh, yes, we can; they'll be twice as original. If you can get in a couple of good workwomen to help us, the dresses can easily be made at home," exclaimed Annie, her eyes sparkling.

"Hester!" cried Molly, suddenly springing to her feet, "if we are to go to the Towers this morning, don't you think we had better start?"

Hester stood up.

"The day is such a delightful one," she said, "that I think we will just walk across the fields. I'll run up to my room and fetch my hat and gloves, and bring yours down at the same time, Molly."

Five minutes later the two girls had set off. It was now holiday time at the Towers, and almost immediately on their arrival they were greeted by a whole bevy of children, who rushed up the avenue in a state of breathless excitement.

"What do you think, Molly?" exclaimed Kitty, stammering almost in her eagerness. "Oh, you'll never guess, for it is so uncommon and unexpected—father and mother both went to London this morning?"

"Both--to London?" exclaimed Molly, stepping back a pace or two, while a look of surprise, and even consternation, spread itself over her round, fair face.

"Dear me, yes!" exclaimed Nell.

"And they were awfully jolly about it," exclaimed Boris; "and mother has promised to bring me a rabbit."

"And me a dove," screamed Kitty.

"And perhaps I'm to have a shaggy pony all to myself," exclaimed Nell; "but it's only perhaps. It's perhaps, too, with you, Boris, and you, Kitty; you oughtn't to forget that."

"Oh, bother perhapses!" exclaimed Kitty. "I know I'm to have my rabbit; he's to have lop-ears and long fur, and he's to be snow-white, if possible. I described him fully to mother last night when she came to tuck me up. I kept pulling my eyes open to stay awake for the purpose."

"And I told mother that I wished for a ring-dove," said Boris. "I want a ring-dove awfully, for there's an empty cage in the attic that will just fit it. Oh, I do hope. I do hope, that it will come!"

He looked almost sad as he spoke and glanced at Nell, who was not looking at him.

"Nell, come here," exclaimed Molly suddenly. "Hester, you can explain to Boris and Kitty what you have come about, and they can take you round and show you the ball-room. Come along, Nell, I want to talk to you."

Molly put her arm round Nell and drew her down a side walk.

"Now, Nell," she said, "you must explain all this to me. Why has mother gone to London? I am not so much surprised about father; father does go sometimes, but mother. Why has she gone? Answer me, Nell; tell me what you know."

"I don't know anything," said Nell. "Father was out all day yesterday, and mother looked very sad. She didn't cry or anything of that sort, of course; but she looked sad, and then father came home about tea-time quite jolly and in high spirits, and he said something to mother and they went into the study together; and then father shouted to Jane Macalister to come to them, and Jane went; and presently we were told that father and mother were to go to London this morning, and that they'd be away perhaps a week, perhaps ten days. Jane told us that, and then mother came into the room and she said the same thing, and she looked kind of ***pretence***-merry you know, and said that ***perhaps*** she'd bring us back things. It was then Kitty asked for the rabbit, and Boris for the dove, and Guy wanted Star-Land and Harry some new carpenter's tools, and mother promised everything with a perhaps tacked on; but I don't think anyone noticed the perhaps except me, and all the time she kept smiling with her lips, but her eyes were so sad."

"And you asked for a pony, Nell?"

Nell coloured crimson.

"No, I didn't," she replied; "but mother turned to me and put her arm round me and said, 'If the others get their things you shall have the wish of your heart, a shaggy pony.'"

"And what did you say to that, Nell?"

"I whispered back to her that I didn't want her to spend her money; and then she kissed me very hard."

"And did father promise things?"

"He said that the house should be refurnished, and that we should go to the sea, and he would buy new horses and a lovely carriage for mother. Father was lively; I never saw him so gay."

"And they went off this morning?"

"Yes, very early; I wasn't even dressed, but I jumped out of bed and ran to the window and saw them driving away."

"And that's all you know, Nell?" exclaimed Molly.

"Yes, that's all I know."

"Now, tell me what you think."

"What I think?" replied Nell. "I--" she hesitated. "No, I'd rather not."

"You must, Nell, you must. Remember I'm your own cosy old Moll; remember I understand you, and I'm the eldest girl and mother's right hand. There's something that you think very, very hard, Nell, and you have wise thoughts, though you are so young. Tell me what they are; tell me at once."

Molly knelt on the grass as she spoke and put her arms round Nell, who leant up against her and laid her head on her shoulder.

"Now, Nell, speak."

Nell rubbed her cheek against Molly's, as if she found great comfort in the contact.

"I think that mother is unhappy," she said, "and that, that we won't get the presents."

"Come along and let's find Jane Macalister," exclaimed Molly suddenly. She caught Nell's hand and rushed with her towards the house.

When Jane was not teaching, she was, generally, cooking, or mending clothes, or putting the store-room in order. Jane never wasted a moment of her time, and she was extremely fond of taking up all the loose threads of work which other people had dropped. When the girls, therefore, now found themselves in the great central hall, and Nell's clear, high voice shouted for Jane, the single word, "store-room," seemed to echo back to them from somewhere in the clouds.

The store-room, where the largest supply of preserves and dried goods was kept, was high up in the old tower--higher up even than the schoolroom.

"You stay downstairs, Nell," exclaimed Molly; "I wish to see Jane alone." She reached the spiral stairs, which she began to mount quickly. By-and-by with panting breath she arrived at the store-room. The door was open, but there was no Jane.

"Where are you, Jane Macalister?" called Molly.

"Linen press," called Jane from still higher up.

Molly mounted once more. Jane, with an old pillow-case pinned round her head and a huge apron on, was on her knees sorting feathers.

"What are you doing?" exclaimed Molly.

"Don't speak to me for a moment, Molly; I'm in a perfect rage," exclaimed Jane. "There stand out of the draught, child, or you'll get all this fluff into your hair. I have just discovered that the feathers put into these last pillows were not properly cured, so I've been obliged to take them all out, and I'm sprinkling them with lime. Faugh, what a mess the place is in. This is what comes of taking in an incompetent kitchen-maid like Susan Hicks. She did not half do the work of sorting and curing these feathers. Now, what is it you want, Molly? You can see for yourself that I'm up to my eyes in work."

"I can," said Molly. "Well, I'll wait for a moment."

"You'll wait for a moment!" screamed Jane. "I tell you I shan't have done for hours. There are at least a dozen pillows to be unpicked and their contents well sorted, and sprinkled with lime. I brought up a sandwich in my pocket, and don't mean to come downstairs until the job is done, and well done, too. Nothing frets me like half-finished work, and these pillows would get on my brain at night if I didn't see to them."

Molly slowly crossed the linen-press room, and stood by the window.

"There, child," exclaimed Jane, "you're exactly in my light. If you have anything to say, say it and have done with it. By the way, how is Nora? I hope they're not spoiling her at the Grange."

"Nora is getting on nicely, thank you."

"It was a lucky chance for her," continued Jane, "that she happened to be near the Grange when she got hurt. Hester Thornton is sure to give her every comfort. Molly, you're exactly in my light."

Molly moved to one side of the window.

Jane Macalister went on vigorously with her work, the fluff from the feathers rose in the air, the smell of the lime was pungent.

"Faugh," continued Jane; "here's a lump for you. Susan Hicks, you'd better keep out of my way for the present. 'Pon my word! look at this quill, why I could make a pen with it; disgraceful, perfectly disgraceful. Molly, I wish you wouldn't fidget. What in the world do you want to say to me?"

"I want to ask you this," said Molly. "Why has mother gone to London?"

Jane bent low over her work, some fluff got into her nose and made her sneeze.

"Look here, Molly," she exclaimed; "your mother went to London with your father because she wished to, I suppose."

"Yes, but why did she wish it?"

"That I am not prepared to tell you, my dear."

Molly stamped her foot.

"I wish you'd look at me, Jane," she said, "and leave off fiddling with those horrid, detestable feathers. When--when one is quite wretched, what do feathers matter? I have come home to find father and mother gone."

"And me over the feathers," interrupted Jane. "Well, I suppose people want pillows, whether they're happy or miserable. I never knew before, at least, that they didn't."

"Jane," said Molly, "you're hiding something from me."

Jane Macalister suddenly rose to her feet. She came up to Molly and took her hand. "I didn't know you'd come over this morning, my love," she said. "I have been told certain things, and what I'm told in confidence cart-ropes won't drag from me. Your father and mother have gone to London because there is a hope, just a hope, that terrible trouble may be averted. It's all uncertainty, and it's all suspense at present, Molly; and those who are cowards will bear it badly, and those who are brave will bear it well. That's all I can tell you, my love; and now let me get back to the feathers, or I won't have them done by night."

CHAPTER XIII.
THE FANCY BALL.

The best cure for anxiety, short of removing it altogether, is plenty of work. Molly came down from her interview with Jane Macalister with a sickening sense of coming disaster filling her heart. Hers was not a particularly hopeful nature. By nature she was inclined to look at the dark side rather than at the bright. She had plenty of courage and was unselfish to a fault; but when she arrived in the hall now and found all the rest of the children gathered round Hester and was greeted by peals of excited laughter and shouts of excited joy, she would have given a great deal to have been able to run away and hide herself.

This was impossible, however; she was dragged into the eager group of children, and was obliged not only to listen to their remarks, but to make suggestions of her own. In the absence of Mr. and Mrs. Lorrimer, Molly had to decide whether the ball-room could be used or not. She would have given the world to say no, but scarcely dared to do this with all those eager delighted faces gazing at her.

"I am sure mother will consent," she said after a pause. "I will write to her to-day and ask her; but I think we may act as if her consent were already given. Now, shall we come to the ball-room and see what is necessary to be done?"

"Oh, what a darling Molly you are," exclaimed all the other Lorrimers in a breath. She found herself whirled in their midst to the old ball-room, and the rest of the morning was spent in eager and animated discussion.

This magnificent old room was apart from the rest of the house. It was entered by a covered way from one of the drawing-rooms; but this entrance had long been closed, and the room itself--since the family purse had become so low--was only made use of as a play-room for the children in wet weather, and as a place for all kinds of lumber and rubbish. Hester and Molly were neither of them artistic in their tastes or ideas, but they were intensely practical in all they said and did. Molly proposed that the room should be first cleared out and thoroughly cleaned, and that early on the following morning Annie Forest should come and see it. The room was lit by seven tall Gothic windows, and had a high arched roof of oak. Round the windows the thick ivy which only years can produce hung in heavy masses. Some of this must be cleared away, and some light draperies must relieve the dark tone of the walls. The gallery was pronounced sufficiently sound for the band to stand there, and Annie's original idea of placing Nora in the gallery as a sort of queen of the ceremonies was superseded by a better one. She was to have a special throne made for her at the other end of the ball-room. There she would not only see perfectly, but would also be seen. It seemed simple enough to have a ball in such a lovely room, and Hester arranged to send some men over that very afternoon to begin the work of clearing out the rubbish.

"We don't wish to take possession of the Towers," she said. "We only want the loan of the ball-room, and of this delightful lawn just beyond, where we can put up a marquee or tent."

"No, no," exclaimed Molly, "it must be all or nothing. You know how big our entrance hall is, Hester, and those great half-empty drawing rooms. The whole ground floor is to be at your disposal. If we do it at all, let it be a real merry-making. It will be nice to have a merry-making once again at the Towers."

Molly sighed as she spoke. Hester glanced at her, and the remark in her father's letter flashed through her brain.

While the others were planning and talking at least twenty words to the dozen, Nell was looking solemnly up at the tall windows with an expression of ecstacy on her small face. Boris came up presently and pulled her hand.

"What are you in a brown study for?" he asked.

"Oh, Boris," she exclaimed, flashing round on him; "it is more a white dream than a brown study. Fancy this room all lit with Chinese lanterns and the moon outside, and us sitting up until twelve o'clock, and music, Boris, and everybody dancing. The story books will have come true--oh, it will be too lovely."

"I'm thinking of the supper," said Boris. "I expect I'll get awful peckish sitting up so late. I hope there'll be jellies--I love jellies; don't you, Nell?"

"Yes; I heard Hester say there was to be a real band. I wonder if they'll play any of the airs out of ***Faust***. I do so love the Soldier's Chorus, don't you?"

"Yes; I'll march to it when I'm big. Nell, do you think I'll be allowed to have as many cakes as I wish, and ***pate de foie gras***? I tasted it once and 'twas ripping."

"I like it, too, rather," said Nell in a contemplative voice. "I mean to be a fairy in the dance, though, and I'll have wings. Wings! how I wish they'd bear me upward."

"Oh, do come out," exclaimed Boris. "I want to show you my dove's cage; it was ever so musty, but I've cleaned it out, and it's as sweet as a nut now."

The children left the room, and a few moments later Hester and Molly returned to the Grange.

That evening Annie Forest had a very comprehensive scheme drawn out with regard to the proposed characters which the different members of the party were to adopt. Molly would make an ideal shepherdess. Hester was to be in white, and was to represent St Agnes. Nora was to be Queen of the Fairies, and Nan little Bo-Peep. Annie had not yet decided on her own character, but was strongly inclined to act the part of a gipsy. Annie further suggested that it would save a great deal of trouble and have a decidedly pretty effect if all the girls under twelve years of age were dressed as white fairies, with wings, and all the boys of the same age as brownies. She considered that so many fairies and brownies would have a very picturesque effect, and would help to throw up the gay ***bizarre*** colours of the older girls and boys.

Her suggestion was immediately adopted, and Hester and Molly sat down then and there to write invitations.

Besides the Lorrimers, about a hundred and forty other children were invited, and the girls expected that quite sixty or seventy of these would take the parts of fairies and brownies.

"You don't know how relieved the mothers will be," exclaimed Annie. "When people have no imagination it is the most difficult thing in the world to think of a dress for a fancy ball which has not been adopted dozens and dozens of times before. Please keep the notes open for a moment, Hester, for I mean to slip into each of them some very simple directions with regard to the dress, which will insure our having a certain amount of uniformity."

Annie was in her element now, and even Molly was constrained to admire the absolute genius which she showed in all matters which required tact and brisk, quick work. Annie could write fluently, and her little slips of paper, with their simple and plain directions, were soon ready, and Molly and Hester set to work making copies of them as fast as they could. The letters of invitation were all posted before they went to bed that night. Nora shut her eyes to dream of herself as queen of the fairies, and Molly and Hester sat down to write letters which required a little more thought than the invitations which had just been got through. Hester wrote--

"DEAR FATHER,

"I am sorry you are still away; I like to feel that I am of use to you. Whenever you come back you will have a hearty welcome from me. We are all well here and the weather is splendid; even Nora is quite well, although the doctor says she must lie on her back for some weeks longer. Annie is still with us, and Molly has been staying here to help look after Nora; not that she is wanted much for that post, for Annie is the most indefatigable nurse, and Nora simply adores her. But Molly is great company for me and I am delighted to have her, she is such a dear girl. I hope what you say about Squire Lorrimer is not true. I can see that Molly is very anxious, and the Squire and Mrs. Lorrimer have just gone to London, which is quite unusual. There is evidently something the matter, but none of the children have been told what it is. How I wish you could help the Squire, father. I know you are very very rich, and oh, it will break Molly's heart if they have to leave the dear old Towers. Now, I must talk to you about Nan's birthday. We are going to have a children's ball in the old ball-room at the Towers. It is going to be quite lovely. Annie is designing our dresses. She makes us all quite enthusiastic, she has such exquisite taste. I hope you will come home in time to see us in our pretty dresses. I am to be St. Agnes, and Annie says that I shall look like a dream! Did you ever think that your sensible Hetty would talk such folly?--Your affectionate daughter,
"HESTER THORNTON."

Hester finished her letter, folded it up, and addressed it. She then glanced towards Molly, whose fair head was bent low over the sheet of paper which she was filling. She wrote--

"DARLING MOTHER,

"I went to the Towers this morning with Hester and found that you had gone. Is anything the matter? Oh, if I had been at home you might have told me. I can't bear either you or father to have a burden that I don't share. I feel anxious and unhappy, but I will try very hard to be brave. Nonie is getting on so nicely, and Annie Forest is very kind to her. Mother, darling, there is going to be a great big party on the fifteenth, Nan's birthday, and Hester and Nora and Annie and I are very anxious that it should be a children's ball--a fancy ball, you know, mother, and that it should be held in our beautiful old ball-room. It is the Thorntons' party, and they will go to all the expense, but they haven't a big room like ours, so I thought we might lend them the big hall and the drawing-rooms and the ball-room, and they are beginning preparations already. If by any chance you or father object, will you send me a telegram to-morrow? I wish I could kiss you good-night.--Your most loving

"MOLLY."

Molly's letter was also directed and stamped, and when these important epistles had been taken to the post, the whole household went to bed.

That is, with one exception.

Annie Forest, notwithstanding her gaiety and the high spirits she had been in all day, had a care upon her mind.

It was three weeks now since the day when Mrs. Martin had pawned Mrs. Willis's beautiful ring for the small sum of thirty shillings. That thirty shillings had purchased cambric and embroidery and lace, and even a few knots of coloured ribbon, to make three charming frocks for Nora Lorrimer, but alack and alas, though the frocks lay neatly folded up in their drawer waiting to be worn on the first festive occasion, poor Annie had not the faintest idea how to get back the ring. That morning's post had certainly been an important one. It had not only brought a letter for Hester which had nearly turned the heads of two households, but had brought Annie two epistles of a profoundly and painfully interesting character. One was from her father, telling her that he must postpone sending her her usual birthday present for a time, and the other was from Mrs. Willis herself. Mrs. Willis wrote from Paris. She was staying there for a short time on her way home, and asked Annie to send her the diamond ring without delay by registered post. The ring was of a very antique pattern and she wished to have it copied for a wedding present for one of her pupils.

"Try and post it to me at once, dear," she said, "for I shall not
be in Paris after Saturday. I return to London that day and shall
very likely accept Hester Thornton's invitation to come to the
Grange for a few days. You shall then have the ring back to make
your finger look smart for the remainder of your visit. I am
writing in great haste in order to catch this post, so do not fail
me, my love. The ring will be perfectly safe if you register it.
My dear love to Hester and Nan, and much to yourself.--Your
affectionate

"M. WILLIS."

Annie had glanced her eyes quickly over the contents of this disquieting letter at breakfast time, but it was only now, in the solitude of her own room, that she ventured to take it out and study it. What was she to do? How could she possibly get the ring out of pawn without any money to redeem it? She dared not confide this trouble to Mrs. Martin. She thought and thought until her head ached and her bright eyes looked dull.

What kind of man was the pawnbroker? Why were pawnbrokers called uncles? Was it because they were really good-natured and helpful? She wondered if it might be possible for her to induce the pawnbroker to let her have the ring out on condition that she paid for it by instalments? If he really was quite a good-natured order of uncle, he might consent to such an arrangement. Annie felt, however, that it would be useless to get Mrs. Martin to make such terms with him.

"She was very proud about him," thought Annie. "She did not wish to go to him at all. I'm afraid he's disagreeable. I'm afraid he's not the sort of man who would help a girl out of a difficulty. What *shall* I do? The ring *must* go to-morrow if Mrs. Willis is to do anything with it before she leaves Paris. It ought to have gone to-day, but to-morrow is the very last, the very last chance. We are all going to Nortonbury to-morrow to buy the materials for the dresses. Oh, suppose I go and see the pawnbroker and tell him of my difficulty, and assure him that I will honestly pay him back that money if he will only let me have the ring again. I have four shillings still in my purse, and father's sovereign will be certain to come sooner or later. I could show uncle father's letter, he would then see that I was not humbugging. I expect he would like me to call him uncle, as it seems to be *the* name. Yes, I really think I will go, but I must on no account whatever let Mrs. Martin or Molly or Hester know anything about this. I should rather like to confide in Nora, for she would think it no end of a lark; but if I did, the poor darling would know that I had got into all this trouble on account of her dresses, and that would simply never do. Yes, there seems nothing for it but to visit my uncle, the pawnbroker."

Annie presently laid her head on her pillow and went to sleep.

When she awoke in the morning she still thought an appeal to the pawnbroker the only available solution of her difficulty. The girls were much excited about their gay shopping, and the landau was ordered to be round at an early hour to convey Hester, Nan, Molly, and Annie to Nortonbury. Nora had to resign herself to the company of her nurse, but her thoughts were so full of pleasurable anticipations that under the circumstances she did not mind the loss of her favourite Annie.

Before starting, Annie ran quickly round to Mrs. Martin's rooms.

"Here I am," she exclaimed in her bright way. "I have just rushed up to say good morning to you before we start. You have heard of all the fun that we are going to have, haven't you, nursey?"

"Folly, I call it," said nurse. "Throwing away good money on fallals and wings and clouds. Miss Nan was up here last night so late that I thought I'd never get her to bed, bamboozling me with stories of all the children round the country being turned into fairies, which you know, Miss Annie, is sheer nonsense and impossible to do, and Miss Nora, who has narrowly escaped her death, is to lie on rose leaves with clouds under her. The folly of it is beyond belief, even if it can be done, which I sincerely hope it can't. In old days people took their pleasures properly. Children were kept in the nursery and were sent early to bed, and young ladies were presented to her Gracious Majesty the Queen, and then went to balls in good stiff silks and no wings nor clouds about 'em. They met the gentlemen they were to marry at the balls, and then there was a proper wedding breakfast and all the rest, as it should be. I don't hold with the scarum days of the present."

"Look here, nursey," exclaimed Annie, "the fairies will look lovely, and I'll show you myself how innocent and simple the clouds are, and as to the wings, I'll make a pair for you if you like."

"No, thank you, Miss Annie, I hope I know what's due to myself."

"Well, I must run away," continued Annie. "You know we're just off to Nortonbury."

"So I hear, miss."

"It was to Nortonbury you went when you sold my ring; you were a dear to do it."

"I wouldn't do it for no one else, miss, and I don't know even now how I came to demean myself by such a job."

"Was," said Annie in an almost trembling voice, "was the uncle very disagreeable, then?"

"Miss Forest, such a word oughtn't to pass your lips."

"Why so, nurse? I cannot imagine why you dislike such helpful people."

"We won't argue the point," said nurse; "the subject is not suited to the young."

Annie fidgeted. Nan's voice was heard down stairs shouting for her.

"Nurse," she said in sudden desperation, "I want to get the ring back; tell me the name of the uncle."

A look of relief came over Mrs. Martin's face.

"I'd be glad if you had that valuable ring again," she said. "Have you got the money for it? It would be thirty-two shillings; thirty shillings for the loan and two shillings interest."

"Annie, we're all waiting," shouted Nan.

"Oh, do tell me the address," said Annie.

"You had better let me get the ring out of pawn for you, miss."

"No, no, I must get it to-day."

"Have you got the money, Miss Forest?"

"What would be the use of going if I hadn't?" prevaricated Annie.

"Well, but you're not going to take my young ladies to a pawnbroker's?"

"No, I promise not to take any of them; I'll go alone, quite alone. You may trust me, really. Oh, nursey, nursey, I'm in such trouble."

Again the bright lovely eyes and sweet voice did their work.

Mrs. Martin fumbled for her keys, and taking a small piece of blue paper out of her work-box, put it into Annie's hand.

"There," she said. "I'm sorry I ever made or meddled with this thing. Mind you don't take one of my young ladies with you."

"I promise," said Annie. She thrust the paper into her pocket and rushed from the room.

CHAPTER XIV.
POOR MRS. MYRTLE.

The girls spent a busy morning in Nortonbury, and if Annie had any care on her mind she certainly did not show it. She was a splendid girl to go shopping with. She could make up her mind quickly with regard to the exact material she required. Her choice was practically made before she entered a shop, her taste in colour and texture was excellent, and with her to guide them, Hester and Molly got through their business with great celerity. Many parcels were piled up on the front seat of the landau, but work as they would, the girls could not get through their necessary shopping in the morning. Hester therefore determined to lunch at a restaurant which she knew well, and to finish buying the rest of the materials for the fancy dresses before they returned to the Grange. It was while they were at lunch that Annie seized the opportunity to secure a few moments to herself. She had not yet had time even to glance at the address which nurse had given her on the little slip of blue paper. But it was now or never, if she were to seek the pawnbroker without the others discovering where she was going.

Hester had ordered a very tempting lunch, and Nan was attacking her nicely roasted chicken and bread sauce with appetite, when Annie, snatching up a sandwich, sprang suddenly to her feet.

"I'm not hungry," she exclaimed, "and as there is so much to be done, I won't waste time eating. Mrs. Willis wrote to me yesterday and asked me to send her a small parcel. It contains a ring which she lent me, and as it ought to be registered, I will go to the post-office now and get it done while you are at lunch."

"But you really must eat something first," exclaimed Hester. "You will be ill if you don't; the carriage is to call for us in a few minutes, and you may just as well drive to the post-office in it; you would do it in half the time."

"But I would rather walk," replied Annie. "I am perfectly sick of driving. I see by Nan's face that lunch will be quite an affair of half an hour, and I'll be back long before then."

She left the shop before Hester had time to remonstrate, and the next moment found herself in the street.

"Now for it," she exclaimed, a little catch of excitement in her breath. She took out her purse, opened it, and removing the slip of blue paper, looked at the words written on it. The address rather surprised her. It was a fancy goods shop, and was kept by a woman of the name of Myrtle.

"MRS. MYRTLE,
"Haberdashery and Fancy Goods Warehouse,
"30, Eden Street,"
was the address on the sheet of paper.

Annie had never in the course of her life come in contact with a live pawnbroker, but she had a vague idea that pawnbrokers were of the male species, and that they invariably had three gilt balls over their establishments.

She was relieved rather than otherwise to find that this pawnbroker was of the female sex, and fancied that it would be easier to deal with her on this account. A policeman directed her to Eden Street, which was a thoroughly respectable broad thoroughfare off the High Street.

Annie walked quickly until she came to number thirty. Then, raising her eyes and seeing Mrs. Myrtle's name over the door, she boldly entered. The shop was the sort that ladies delight in. One side of it was entirely devoted to the best class of haberdashery, the other was extremely attractive with coloured wools and silks, and all sorts of materials for crewel and other fancy works. A thin, pale girl, of about sixteen, was attending to the haberdashery department, and a little old lady, with pink cheeks, bright dark eyes and white hair, was busily serving several customers at the fancy goods side.

Annie had to wait until these customers had completed their business. The girl who had charge of the haberdashery asked if she could serve her.

"I wish to speak to Mrs. Myrtle," replied Annie in a decided tone. The little woman raised her head at hearing her own name pronounced, and said in a respect-ful voice--

"I'll be at leisure to serve you in a moment, miss."

"She seems very nice," said Annie to herself; "she has a decidedly kind face. What can there be objectionable in pawnbrokers, if she is one? Perhaps I'd better call her aunt; she'll be sure to like it."

In a couple of moments Mrs. Myrtle was at leisure, and Annie went up to the counter. Now that the critical instant had come, she felt her heart beating quickly, and knew that her cheeks were pale. Annie could look wonderfully pathetic when any emotion stirred her. She had a voice full of vibrations, and her eyes could as-sume the dumb pleading expression of a dog's.

"I want to speak to you about a very private matter," she said, looking full at Mrs. Myrtle.

The little woman could not help giving her a glance of great surprise. What could such a pretty, nicely-dressed young lady want with her; then suddenly it flashed through her mind that Annie must want to buy a present; perhaps the pres-ent was for her sweetheart; if so, the state of affairs was perfectly natural.

"Yes, miss," she said, in a cordial voice of sympathy, "but Netty, my niece, is a bit deaf and won't hear a word you're saying. I have got some really nice things, miss, and quite suitable; tobacco pouches made of different coloured plushes, and flowers traced very beautifully on them; you could work the pouch yourself, miss, and it would look most suitable; then I've got braces, too; they're quite the newest thing, and can be embroidered with any colour, and cases for gentlemen's evening ties, they really are very new; shall I show you some, miss?"

"Oh, no, thank you," said Annie in a choking voice. "I'm in an awful hurry and I don't want to buy any present for a gentleman; I don't know any gentleman except my father well enough to think of giving presents to. No, no, I don't want to buy anything, but I want--I want you to give me something, aunt."

Mrs. Myrtle looked at Annie as if she were now quite sure that the poor pretty young lady was not quite right in her head. She did not speak at all, but waited for Annie to continue.

"You're a female pawnbroker, are you not?" said Annie.

"A female what, my dear?" said Mrs. Myrtle, her face growing crimson. This was really the last straw. "I don't understand you, miss," she said in a stiff tone. "I have nothing whatever to do with the trade you indicate."

Just then some ladies, very good customers, entered the shop.

"You'll excuse me for a moment, miss," said Mrs. Myrtle; "but if you don't want to buy, I shall be obliged to leave you to attend to my customers. Good morning, Lady Dalgetty; what can I show your ladyship?"

Poor Annie found herself pushed into a corner. Lady Dalgetty and her suite occupied all Mrs. Myrtle's attention. Even the humble-looking Netty was busy serving out spools of cotton, needles, and pins to a prim-looking lady. Neither of the women in the shop had a moment to attend to Annie's sore need.

She began to think that Mrs. Myrtle was not so kind as she looked, and to understand a little of nurse's repugnance to the pawnbroker class.

"They must be low people," she murmured to herself; "for this woman won't even own to the fact that she is a pawnbroker."

The shop became empty once more; and Mrs. Myrtle, who was really quite as kind hearted as she looked, raised her eyes, and encountered a very forlorn glance from Annie.

"Poor, pretty young lady," she said to herself. "She's gone in the head without any manner of doubt, calling me aunt, and asking me if I'm a female pawnbroker; but I'd best humour her a bit, and try to find out who she belongs to."

Accordingly Mrs. Myrtle called Annie back to the counter in a kind voice.

"I can attend to you now, miss," she said; "but if you have anything to say, perhaps you'll say it quickly, for this is market day, and heaps of farmer's wives come in for no end of small matters."

"Do they pawn rings, and then take them out by degrees in instalments?" asked poor Annie in an eager voice.

"Poor, poor young lady, she's very, very bad," murmured Mrs. Myrtle to herself.

"I couldn't say for positive, miss," she replied, "that a farmer's wife has never pawned a ring; but if they are reduced to such straits, I know nothing about it."

"Then you are not a pawnbroker yourself?"

"I am **not**, miss. Wouldn't you like to come into my parlour and rest a bit if you're tired, and maybe you'll tell me your name?"

"She's getting quite kind again," thought Annie. "Of course she is a pawnbroker, but she doesn't like to own it; it evidently is a very disgraceful calling."

"My name is Annie Forest," she said; "and I'm not at all tired, thank you, aunt. You don't mind me calling you aunt, do you? for we always call the men in your trade uncles."

"I hope heaven will preserve my patience," muttered poor Mrs. Myrtle. "I must get this young lady to her friends whatever happens. Netty!"

"Oh, don't call Netty here," exclaimed Annie. "Now, look here, do you see this piece of blue paper?"

"Yes, miss. It's my address, sure and certain."

"Do you know the handwriting?"

"Well, I can't say that I do; it seems a sort of an ordinary hand, don't it, miss?"

"Is Mrs. Martin, who lives at the Grange, a friend of yours?" asked Annie suddenly.

Mrs. Myrtle's face glowed all over with pleased relief.

"Mrs. Martin of the Grange," she exclaimed, "old nurse to Miss Hester and Miss Nan Thornton? I should rather think she is a friend of mine. I have known her ever since we went to school together, and that's many a year ago."

"Oh, how glad I am," exclaimed Annie; "then I am sure, quite sure, you will be kind to me. You will do what I ask for the sake of your friend Mrs. Martin. You won't mind just confiding to me that you are a pawnbroker? I promise most faithfully not to call you aunt if you really dislike it."

"I'm afraid I don't understand you, Miss Forest. I am *not* a pawnbroker; not one of my belongings would own to such a trade; and if Patty Martin gave you to understand that I am, I'll quarrel with her, late as it is in the day."

"But she pawned a ring to you," said Annie; "an old-fashioned gold ring with one big diamond in the middle. You lent her thirty shillings on it, and the interest is two shillings. That ring is mine. She did pawn a ring to you, did she not?"

A light at last broke over Mrs. Myrtle's face.

"Well, well," she exclaimed: "I begin to see what you're driving at. Won't I have a crow to pick with Patty Martin for this. No, no, miss, she pawned no ring to me; but she gave me a diamond ring to keep for her early one morning about three weeks ago. 'And keep it safe until I ask for it, Martha Myrtle,' said she and safe I will keep it until then, Miss Annie Forest."

"But it's my ring," said Annie in great distress. "You'll give it back to me now when I ask for it?"

"I'll give it back to Patty Martin, miss, and to no one else."

"Oh, but really, really, don't you understand? It's *my* ring."

"I've only your word for that, miss. It was given to me by Mrs. Martin."

"But I know Patty Martin would let you give it back to me. Why, she gave me your address and told me to go to you; and I thought, of course, you were a pawn-broker."

"Won't I have a crow to pluck with her for this?" exclaimed Mrs. Myrtle. "Pawnbroker, indeed! Why my poor mother who's dead would rise up from her grave if she thought I was called by such a name. No, miss, I'm sorry not to oblige, but Mrs. Martin gave me the ring to keep for her, and she must come herself to fetch it away, for to no one else will I give it."

Some farmers' wives, looking flourishing and handsome and full of purpose, now entered the shop. Mrs. Myrtle devoted all her energies to serving them, and poor Annie with sinking heart had to go away.

CHAPTER XV.
"THE WAY OF TRANSGRESSORS."

The week that followed passed all too quickly. There was no hitch whatever in the girls' plans. Mrs. Lorrimer wrote to Molly to express her complete satisfaction with the arrangement proposed by Hester. The workwomen who had now taken up their abode at the Grange were both efficient and clever. With Annie's help the different dresses began to assume form and completion with marvellous rapidity. Annie was the life and soul of the dressmaking. She sketched pictures of the proposed toilettes; she coloured these sketches; then she tried on and cut out, and basted, and tacked. She helped to hang draperies and to arrange the wings of the fairies. The women became interested themselves in such an artistic assistant, and did everything in their power to help her. At the Towers the ball-room began to show its noble proportions to the best advantage. Hester and Annie and Nan and Molly went backwards and forwards at all hours of the day. By Monday evening, the ball-room was in complete order. Every possible direction was given with regard to the different refreshments, and the last stitch in the pretty fancy dresses had been done. The news of Nan's fancy ball had spread far and wide. Almost every invitation met with an acceptance, and the Thornton and Lorrimer households were borne forward just at present on a full tide of victorious excitement. Even Molly felt herself obliged to enter into the full spirit of the fun. Not a murmur of anxiety from her father and mother in London reached her. Mrs. Lorrimer, in writing to Molly, had assumed as cheerful a tone as possible; she had alluded to no possible care, had hinted at no canker root of possible trouble. She had said, it is true, that it was rather unlikely that she and the Squire would return in time for the ball; but if this could not be managed, she hoped the children would enjoy themselves to the full in their absence; and finally, she said how heartily she rejoiced in the thought of their having such a delightful time. Hester also forgot the small worrying thought which came to her now and again about her father, in this week of rush and pleasure. Hester was by nature a very quiet-mannered girl, but she became nearly as lively now as Annie; she laughed, and joked, and danced, and skipped until Mrs. Martin, who watched her from the nursery window, began to shake her head gravely, and to say that such mirth was not "fey" as she expressed it, and that it surely forbode a season of gloom by-and-by.

Annie's high spirits being natural to her, no one specially noticed them, and according to her custom, she put dull care aside and was as lively as she looked.

It is true that she had been obliged to ignore Mrs. Willis's letter; it is true that the ring was still being jealously guarded by that dreadful Mrs. Myrtle, for Annie had not the courage to ask Mrs. Martin for it. The whole situation was now quite plain; Mrs. Martin had never gone near the pawnbroker's, but had lent Annie the money herself. Why she had parted with the ring under these circumstances was a problem which poor Annie could not attempt to fathom. All she could do now was to abide the issue of events as patiently as possible. All her life long she had found that, somehow or other, matters did right themselves for her, and she trusted to her usual good luck on this occasion.

The preparations were almost all completed for the fancy ball by Monday night. Nan's birthday would be on Wednesday. No second letter had arrived from Sir John Thornton, and Hester wondered whether he would be present on the birthday or not. The day was to be one long scene of triumph for the young birthday queen. Annie and Hester both stole out of bed at an early hour that morning, and going out into the garden, they picked baskets full of flowers with the dew on them, with which they made wreaths to decorate the breakfast table, and to cover the piles of presents which lay not only on Nan's plate, but all round it.

As soon as Nan appeared in the breakfast-room, Annie tripped up to her, bent on one knee as if to a liege lady, told her that she was her lawful sovereign for that entire day, and then begged leave to crown the birthday queen with flowers. Nan's cheeks were flushed already, and her eyes bright with excitement. Molly came in by-and-by, and Nora, who was now much better, was wheeled into the room on her sofa. She wore the white cambric dress which Annie had made for her. Her dark hair was swept back from her pretty, low forehead, her cheeks had roses in them, and her eyes sparkled.

"Molly, Molly," she exclaimed, "look at me, look at me. Now you know the secret of the locked door. Annie made me this frock; she had some bits of cambric over from dresses of her own, and she made this and a blue one, and a pink one also; I have the other two in my drawer; I know they are all sweetly becoming, aren't they? It's nearly as good as having a *trousseau*. Oh, do kiss me and congratulate me, Molly; you know how I have always longed for pretty dresses. Was not it perfectly *darling* of Annie to make them for me?"

Before Molly could reply a loud exclamation from Hester turned all eyes in her direction.

"What do you think?" she exclaimed. "The crowning bliss of our day is come. Nan, you will never guess. Annie, dear, how charmed you will be. Here is a letter from Mrs. Willis; she expects to reach Nortonbury by the mid-day train, and asks me to send to meet her. Oh, dear, this is lovely. I have not seen my dear Mrs. Willis for over a year. What a rest and comfort it will be to talk to her again. Molly, you will delight in her; she is just the woman to captivate you completely. Nora, you will lose your heart to her, too. I don't know what wonderful thing there is about her; she is so strong, so noble, so gentle, that she wins all hearts; it is impossible for anybody to be naughty when Mrs. Willis is in the house. Nan, the arrival of Mrs. Willis on your birthday is the happiest possible omen for the whole year. Oh, how truly rejoiced I am!"

"Yes, it's awfully jolly of her to come," said Nan. "Of course I'm very fond of her, but I hope she won't remind me of my holiday task, for, frankly, I have not looked at it yet, and I don't mean to do so until the last week of the holidays. Now, do let's all begin breakfast; even though I am queen, I happen to have an appetite. Annie, what are you in a brown study about? Why, you look quite pale!"

"I expect Annie is so glad about Mrs. Willis that she can scarcely speak," said Hester, glancing at her friend in an affectionate manner. "Yes, we had better get breakfast through. I shall give Mrs. Willis the maple room, with that lovely west view. There is a little sitting-room which goes with it, where she can be quiet whenever she wants to be quiet. How glad nursey will be when she hears that dear Mrs. Willis is coming."

Hester began to perform the duties of tea-maker in a rather abstracted manner.

As she kept on filling up cups of tea, she also glanced from time to time at the letter which gave her such delight.

"It is such a surprise," she said; "perhaps that is half the pleasure."

"Please don't put any more sugar into my tea," exclaimed Annie in an almost cross voice; "you know I never touch sugar, and that is the fourth lump."

"Oh, I am sorry," exclaimed Hester; "I'll take that cup and you shall have mine."

"You put five lumps into your own cup, I watched you; oh, dear, it doesn't matter, of course."

"No, it doesn't matter," said Hester, still reading her letter. "Molly, will you pass the tea on, please. Oh, yes, I'll have some honey; you can put a piece on my plate if you like."

"The only plate you have before you at present contains eggs and bacon," exclaimed Molly. "I think I won't help the honey for a few minutes."

"This is a delightful surprise," murmured Hester; "but, dear me, it is rather strange, Mrs. Willis says she wrote to you last week, Annie, and said that she would try to give us a couple of days at the Grange on her way back to Lavender House. How was it you never mentioned it?"

There was just a pause long enough to be noticed before Annie replied.

"I did not get the letter," she said then, in a steady voice.

She hated herself the moment she had uttered the words. She felt as if she had fallen from a height, and was lying maimed and bruised, bleeding and ugly in some dismal abyss; but all the time her eyes looked bright and her face was cheerful.

Hester exclaimed, "How strange! what a pity! How could the letter have gone astray?" but other thoughts soon chased this one from her mind.

Breakfast being over the young housekeeper had much to attend to.

Nora held out her hand to Annie, who stooped down and kissed her affectionately.

"Are you really glad that she is coming?" asked Nora.

"Of course I am, Nonie; she is--" a stab went through Annie's heart--"she is my best friend."

"Is she really as good as Hester says she is?" continued Nora.

"Yes, yes, better; no one quite knows how good she is."

"I shall be afraid of her," said Nora shuddering. "I hate such perfectly good people; they make me feel small and mean."

Annie took up a basket of flowers, and began deftly to form them into wreaths for the further decoration of the ball-room.

"It's dreadful to feel mean," she said almost in a whisper.

"You can't surely know what it means," replied Nora.

"Oh, can't I though; don't let's talk of it any more. I like you in white, Nora. White, toned with lace and coloured ribbons, makes a charming dress for you. You have such a pretty face. It is so full of *esprit*--so *piquant*. Some day you will be a beautiful woman."

"As beautiful as you are?" asked Nora. "I don't desire to be more beautiful than you."

"In some ways you will be more beautiful," replied Annie. "I don't pretend that I am not pretty, I know I am; but in some ways you will be superior to me. You will have a greater air of distinction. *Noblesse oblige* will be abundantly manifested in you. Oh, yes," continued Annie, "it is all very fine for us *parvenus* to despise race. We don't really despise it; we adore it, we envy it; we can never, never, never get what race confers."

"How excitedly you talk," said Nora; "you seem angry about something."

"I am angry with myself," said Annie; "my low ways and my meanness. *Noblesse oblige* has nothing to do with me. Now, look here, Nora, forget all this rubbishy talk; be thankful that you are a beautiful girl of good family, who could not do a shabby action. I must leave you now, for Mrs. Willis is coming, and I should like to go into Nortonbury to meet her."

Annie ran off to find Hester.

"Hester," she exclaimed, "may I go in the carriage to Nortonbury to meet Mrs. Willis?"

"That is an excellent idea," said Hester; "take Molly with you, the drive will do her good. I am so busy this morning that I can scarcely be spared from home. Yes, that is an excellent idea. I was wondering who would go to meet her.'

Molly was very pleased to accompany Annie to Nortonbury, and Annie was glad of her company. Molly would be a sort of shield to her; not that it really mattered, for she had already quite made up her mind how to act.

The girls enjoyed their pleasant drive together. Mrs. Willis's train was punctual, and she was soon driving back to the Grange, Molly seated by her side and Annie on the seat facing her.

Mrs. Willis had the knack of making all girls perfectly at home with her. Molly felt sure that a certain feeling of restraint would come over her when she sat by the side of this excellent and adorable woman; but the moment she looked into Mrs. Willis's kind eyes, and Mrs. Willis returned her glance, and said in that full, rich, motherly voice of hers, "Oh, I have heard of you; you are Molly Lorrimer, you live at the Towers, and you have a great many brothers and sisters, and your schoolroom is reached by a spiral stair, and is somewhere up in the clouds. I have heard all about you many times from Nan." Then Molly laughed, and felt at home. She felt more than at home, for her heart gave a strange flutter, and then a curious sense of peace pervaded it. It was something like being near her mother, and yet it was something different. The magnetic influence of a good and great spirit was already making itself felt.

Annie sat opposite to the two with dancing eyes.

"How well you look my love," said Mrs. Willis. "I am delighted to see that the change has done you so much good."

Annie drooped her long lashes for a moment.

"I am as well as well can be," she said, "and as jolly as jolly can be, and you have just come in the nick of time to make everything perfect. Molly, do tell Mrs. Willis about our fancy ball to-night."

"I will listen to you in a moment, Molly," said Mrs. Willis; "but first of all I want to ask Annie a question. I hope you did not send the ring to Paris, Annie, for, if you did, I never received it."

"What ring?" asked Annie, looking up in pretended amazement. "Do you mean my mother's ring, Mrs. Willis, the--the one you lent me?"

"Yes, dear. I wrote to you last week about it. I was surprised at never hearing from you, for my letter was quite urgent. I wanted the ring for a special object, and was disappointed at its never coming."

"That must have been the letter you never got, Annie," exclaimed Molly.

"You never got my letter?" exclaimed Mrs. Willis. "How very, very strange! But I posted it myself, and I know I put the right address on it. I am relieved, of course, that you did not send the ring when it was too late; but it is odd about the letter."

"No, I didn't send the ring," said Annie in a light voice. "How could I?"

"Certainly not, dear, if you did not know that I wanted it."

"Hester was surprised this morning," continued Molly, taking up the thread of the narrative, and unconsciously giving Annie immense assistance. "You said, in your letter to her, that you had told Annie a week ago that you were coming. Then Annie said that she had never got your letter."

"It is very queer," said Mrs. Willis. "I must write to the post office in Paris and make inquiries. Well, I am glad the ring is safe."

"Of course, it is as safe as possible," said Annie. "It is too bad about the letter," she continued. "Did you want the ring very badly?"

"Yes, very badly; but it is not too late yet to manage matters. I want to have the ring copied as a wedding present for Margaret Cecil, but I have already spoken to a jeweller about it, and if I send him the ring to-day or to-morrow he will have it in time. Don't forget to give it to me, Annie, dear, when we get home."

"Oh, no," said Annie, "I won't forget."

A few moments later they arrived at the Grange, where Mrs. Willis was received with a kind of trembling joy by Hester, who took her into the house and showered every imaginable attention which her love could suggest upon her.

"Time, time," muttered Annie to herself as she rushed away. "Something must happen between now and to-morrow. I'll keep out of her way to-day, and in the fuss and excitement she'll forget about the ring. I have told one big lie about it, and I have insinuated a dozen more, and I vow and declare one thing--that I will not be discovered now. I'll go on to the bitter end now, come what will. Heigh-ho, is that you, Nan? What are you doing? Don't you know that Mrs. Willis has come? What is that you have in your hand?"

"It's a letter of yours," said Nan; "I found it in the garden under a rose bush; it's in Mrs. Willis's handwriting; didn't you say that you did not hear from her last week?"

"No more I did; give me that letter; it's quite an old one." Annie stretched out her hand, snatched the letter from Nan, and pushed it into her pocket.

"You didn't read it?" she asked.

"No, I'm not so mean; what is the matter with you?"

"I hate to have my letters read."

"They're not read by girls like me; you needn't be afraid."

Nan rushed off in a huff, and Annie walked slowly down the corridor. Her heart felt like lead. She fully believed that Nan had not read the letter, but Nan's eyes might have happened to glance at the postmark on it. That postmark contained a date only one week old. Nan was the last child to whom Annie felt she could confide her guilty secret.

"Oh, dear, dear," she murmured under her breath, "what a true saying it is, that 'the way of transgressors is hard.' I am a mean, low sort, not a doubt of that. Why, if the Lorrimers and Thorntons really knew me as I am, they wouldn't speak to me. Well, there's nothing for it now but to carry matters with a high hand, and to let nothing out. If Nan does happen to have noticed the date on the letter, I'll tell her she was mistaken. How could I have been so mad as to carry this letter about in my pocket? Well, to make all things sure, I'll destroy it now."

"Annie, Annie, we're just going to lunch," called out Hester; "what are you running into the garden for?"

"I'll be back in a minute," shouted Annie.

She ran quickly out of the house and down the broad grass walk which led to the arbour at the farther end. By the side of the arbour lay a basket of tools. Annie snatched up a small trowel, and going to the back of the arbour, dug a hole for her letter. She tore it then into fragments and buried it, looked round her eagerly, saw that there was not a soul in sight, and then, with a certain sense of relief, hurried back to the house.

CHAPTER XVI.
PERHAPS.

The ball was to begin at nine o'clock. The festive hour grew on apace. Mrs. Willis said nothing more about the ring, and Annie Forest heaved a deep sigh of relief.

"Reprieved until to-morrow," she murmured to herself; "and now for high frivolity."

The horses from the Thorntons' stables were in great request during that eventful day. Hester, who was most anxious to spare her friends all possible trouble, had decided that she and Nan, and all the rest of their party, should dress for the ball at the Grange, and come over in their separate characters prepared to act their different parts at once. Molly and Hester were to be the two hostesses for the occasion. Guy, who was a very gentlemanly boy, was to assist them to the best part of his ability. Annie promised to look after the refreshments, and also to establish Nora in a becoming attitude on her bed of rose leaves and clouds.

Nora made a most beautiful queen of the fairies. She was dressed in a sort of transparent white; her large, clear wings were very slightly toned with rose colour, and the whole dress was bespangled with light sprays of silver. Nora's hair was crimped, and hung in masses over her shoulders. The silvery dust also shone in her hair. Her eyes were dark and deep, and natural roses of happiness and excitement bloomed on her pretty round cheeks. To Annie's ingenuity and genius the whole of the charming dream-like effect of this fairy queen was due. Mrs. Willis, who insisted on coming to the ball in the part of the schoolmistress, "The only part which I shall ever play in life," she had said with a smile to Hester, was much delighted with the arrangement of everything. Mrs. Willis was in grey silk, with her favourite Honiton lace. She was a very striking and beautiful woman, and in her grand simplicity, made a perfect foil to the fantastic appearance of the younger members of the party.

Amongst the honoured guests on this occasion, Mrs. Martin shone conspicuous. Hester had insisted on her coming over early, and when the good woman entered the ball-room and saw Nora on her cloudy throne, she could not help muttering, in an almost angry tone of great excitement--

"Eh, eh, why this is almost witchcraft. I didn't believe in them wings and clouds till now, but sure enough there they are. Seein' is believin'. I don't hold with it, but I don't deny as it ain't clever."

"I'm glad you think it clever, Patty Martin," said a very gay voice in her ear.

She turned almost in alarm, to be confronted by the most impudent-looking, and yet the most charming gipsy lass she had ever looked at.

Mrs. Martin loathed gipsies.

"None of your sauce," she said in an angry voice. "This is no place for the like of you; get out at once or I'll let Miss Hester Thornton know."

"Oh, nursey, nursey, you'll kill me," exclaimed Annie in a voice choked with laughter. "Do you mean to say you don't know me?"

"My sakes alive, Miss Annie Forest!" exclaimed the old woman. "Who'd have thought you'd have been up to this folly? What are you doing, masquerading like them hateful gipsies? It's bad enough to have wings and clouds about; but gipsies-- 'tain't respectable; my word, no."

"This gipsy is eminently respectable," said Annie, with a sort of bitter emphasis. "Here, nursey, take my hand, and let me lead you up the ball-room. I have many strange characters to introduce you to. I see plainly that you won't recognise them without my kind assistance. Here, come along, be quick."

"My head is getting *moithered*, and that's the only word," said nurse Martin. "Dear, dear, what *are* the young coming to? And sakes alive, what in the world are those?"

The creatures thus apostrophised by the almost frightened nurse Martin, were a troop of fairies and brownies, who now rushed into the ball-room from every direction. The band struck up a merry waltz, and the fairies and brownies began to dance with vigour.

"Its past belief," said Mrs. Martin "and did you make all them wings, Miss Annie?"

"Oh, dear, no," replied Annie; "they were made by the mothers of the fairies--at least, I presume so. Now come into the supper-room and let me get you a comfortable seat."

Mrs. Martin was glad enough to comply. She said the slippery floor of the ballroom, and the uncanny creatures that were all round her, made her feel as if the top of her head would come off. She uttered a little shriek of terror as Jane Macalister, dressed as Minerva, glided fiercely by, and was glad to seat herself in a safe corner behind one of the long supper tables. Annie desired a servant to give her all the refreshment she required, and then ran off to attend to the other guests.

Fast and furious rose the fun. During the whole of the present century the old ball-room at the Towers had not reflected so gay and animated a scene. Grim ancestors of the house of Lorrimer looked down from their tarnished frames at the last Lorrimers as they danced away their precious time in this frivolous and yet enchanting manner. The grown people, who sat in the gallery and on benches near the walls, talked in whispers to one another about the lovely scene. The Lorrimers were popular in the county, and although rumours of coming trouble were rife about them, yet their friends and well-wishers augured happy results from this present gaiety.

But why was not the Squire present, and why was Mrs. Lorrimer absent?

Molly, who made the gentlest of shepherdesses, came up as these remarks passed the good people's lips. She stopped to speak to an old friend of her mother's.

"I'm so glad you were able to come," she said; "and how sweet your children look."

"It was very kind of you to ask us, my dear," responded this lady, "and the sight is a charming one--quite charming; but I am sorry to miss your mother."

"Mother is in London at present; she is away on special business. She is ever so sorry to be absent to-night."

"And the Squire, is he quite well?"

"Yes, thank you. He is in London with mother."

At this moment a brownie with a hot face and looking rather uncomfortable in his brown-velvet tights, accompanied by the most spiritual-looking fairy it was possible to see, revolved slowly round in the mazes of the waltz.

The brownie's honest face was raised to Molly's; his brown eyes were full of a question; the fairy by his side had a far-away look. They both floated away.

"Oh, what a charming little pair," said Mrs. Fortescue, Molly's friend. "Do you know who they are, Miss Lorrimer?"

"That poor, hot brownie is my brother, Boris," exclaimed Molly; "and that little girl is Nell, my sister."

The lady sat down again; and, Molly's partner coming up to claim her, she joined in the dance, and forgot the question in Boris's eyes.

There was a commotion near the entrance door. Hester was seen to move hastily forward. There was a call for Nan, who, accompanied by her partner, Little Boy Blue, rushed quickly across the room, and the next moment a tall, aristocratic-looking man was seen moving up the ball-room with Hester's hand on his arm. Sir John Thornton had kept his word. He had returned in time if not for the whole of Nan's birthday, at least to see it out.

The matrons who sat about the room remarked on his appearance, and said that they had never seen him look better, younger, or more cheerful. They said what an admirable thing it was for Sir John to have Hester at home; and, as Sir John himself was the best possible company in society, he soon made his presence agreeably felt all over the room. In the Squire's absence he naturally took the part of host; and no one could be a more polished or charming host than he.

One of the many delightful features of this great fancy ball was the presents which the fairy queen was to bestow upon her many subjects at the end of the festivities. These presents lay piled up in comical shapes all round her, and helped to form some of the billowy clouds on which she was supposed to be resting. The poor little fairy queen certainly looked most charming, and when the moment came for giving away the presents, she would enjoy herself to the full; but just now she could not help envying those fairies and brownies, who could jump about and skip and dance and have a very good time, without being in quite such a grand position as she was. On the queen fairy's head rested a spangled crown of light texture. She felt it almost heavy just now, and murmured to herself in a sentimental voice, "Uneasy lies the head that wears a crown."

Boris, with his eyes still full of that unanswered question, came near and looked at her.

"Are you having an awfully dull time, Nonie?" he asked.

"Oh, it's all right," said Nora, who would have scorned to complain.

"You're going to give us our presents by-and-by."

"Yes."

"You'll feel jolly and hop o' my thumb, won't you?"

"Oh, I'll feel nothing special," replied Nora, who did not wish to encourage this brownie in his efforts after familiarity.

"How hot you look, Boris," she said, with a slight laugh.

"Hot?" echoed Boris. "I'm boiling. It's these abominations of tights. Nonie, I'd like to tell you something; it's very important, very."

"You can't possibly tell it to me now, Boris," replied Nora; "don't attempt to come too near, disarranging my clouds. Oh, what a naughty, troublesome boy you are; you have trodden upon that piece of white tarlatan, and it has all got out of shape. Do run away; do leave me alone."

Boris scampered off; he had suddenly caught a glimpse of the round, smooth face of the shepherdess, Molly, in the distance. If he could only catch her up, she would allow him to whisper in her ear. Nora was always rather a cross patch, but Molly was kind. Molly would be interested, even though she was a shepherdess. He trod on some long trains as he skimmed by. People called him a tiresome child and an awkward little worry, but he did not heed them; he was gaining on Molly, and Molly would be sure to listen to him. Everything would be all right when Molly knew. Now, he had all but reached her, but no, how tiresome--how more than tiresome--a shepherd came up and held out his crook to Molly, who held out hers to him, and then they joined hands, and then they danced away, away, away, far, very far from Boris and his question.

He turned round and stamped his pointed shoe in his vexation.

Nell suddenly came up and touched him.

"Did you find Molly? Have you told her?" she asked.

"No, I can't get to her," replied Boris; "she's dancing over there with that horrid shepherd; he's only Hugh Pierson, and he doesn't look a bit well. Let's dance by ourselves, Nell; let's forget; 'twasn't nothing but nonsense, I'm sure."

"I can't forget," replied Nell.

"Well, aren't you a little bit hungry? There's lobster and pink champagne in the supper-room. I'm going in for some; I heard Hugh Pierson say it was ripping; come and let's have some."

"I couldn't touch any," said Nell with a little shudder of disgust.

Boris looked at her and gave vent to the faintest of sighs.

"While I'm having my lobster, you could eat a jelly, couldn't you?" he said in the most insinuating of whispers.

"No, I couldn't; I couldn't touch anything. Go and eat if you want to, and then come back to me here. I'm going to stand by that window; perhaps he'll come back and take another peep."

"It couldn't have been him, Nell; you know it couldn't; he's away in London, you know."

"I tell you it was him."

"Has he brought back my dove, do you think?"

"No, no; who cares about a dove just now?"

"Nell, I really do care, and my cage is most beautiful and clean. I put in fresh seed and water only this morning; wasn't it lucky?"

"Well, the dove hasn't come," said Nell; "you know it was 'perhaps' about the dove, and about the pony, and about all the jolly things--you're always forgetting that it was 'perhaps.' There, go and eat your lobster, and come back to me when you have done; don't drink too much champagne, or maybe you'll turn giddy. I'll wait here by this window."

Boris, looking decidedly depressed, hesitated for a moment; then seeing that Nell was resolute, he decided that, even if disappointment were in store, he could all the rest of his life reflect that he had sat up late and eaten lobster salad for supper. He accordingly sidled away in the direction of the supper-room, and Nell, with a light movement, sprang on one of the benches and then into the deep recess of a window. Here, with her cloudy hair all about her, her little face as white as her dress, her eyes big and spiritual in the trouble which vaguely stirred her sensitive soul, she looked out into the night. Her large wings shielded her little form, and nobody noticed that one fairy was not joining in the revels.

"I did see him," murmured Nell; "I saw his face just for a minute; he pressed it up against the pane and looked in; his hair was all ruffled, and his eyes, his eyes--oh, the thought of his eyes makes me ache so badly. Why doesn't he come in? What is he doing out in the garden? I know he has come back. I know he's not in London; he has come back and he is in the garden, and we are all so jolly, and he so sad. What is the matter? Oh, I know quite well; it's **perhaps**; and the pony, and the dove, and the rabbits have not come home. Wings--I thought I'd be so happy when I had wings, but I'm just mis'ribble I'm just mis'ribble."

There was a little noise behind Nell; she turned her head to see Boris scrambling up into the seat by her side.

"I had two plates of salad," he began; "'twasn't so very nice, not so nice as--why, what's the matter, Nell?"

"Come," said Nell, taking his hand, "quick, jump down, he's under the oak tree, just where the shadow is thickest; I saw him move; that's him; let's go to him, Boris; take my hand; let's run to him."

Boris's hot hand clutched Nell's. They ran quickly along by the comparatively empty space near the wall, reached the entrance, and flew swiftly across the moonlit grass.

CHAPTER XVII.
FAIRY AND BROWNIE.

Perhaps it was not the first time that the moon had looked down on a fairy and a brownie running across that old, old lawn. No one could say anything for certain on this point. We all of us have a sort of undying belief in fairies, so perhaps they did exist once, before our hearts had grown too cold and our natures too worldly to understand them. Children know most about them, but even children don't quite believe in them now, in the good old-fashioned way of long ago.

A very pretty fairy and brownie were out now. The moon silvered Nell's wings and put a sort of unearthly radiance into her hair, and Boris, with his bright locks standing almost upright on his head, in his quaint little costume, with his upturned toes and ruffled hands, looked quite like a true denizen of fairy land. Certain it is that the man who stood under the shadow of the oak gave a perceptible start when he saw the fairy and brownie. For a moment the old belief of his early childhood flashed through his brain, then he recognised Nell and Boris, and coming to meet them, he took a hand of each.

"What is it, father?" exclaimed Boris; "what are you standing out of doors for? I know it's a very warm night, but we want you dreadfully, dreadfully, in the house."

Boris rubbed himself against his father's knee as he spoke. Nell clutched Squire Lorrimer's other hand, and raising it to her lips, kissed it passionately. Nell did not speak at all.

"Come in, father, come in," repeated Boris; "and where's mother, and what are you doing out here under the oak tree?"

"Looking at you little people; you make a gay sight," said the Squire.

In spite of himself, his voice was quite hollow.

"But why don't you come in?"

"I'm not coming in; I'm going back to London again to-night."

"Why, father?" asked Nell, opening her lips for the first time, and looking at him with great intentness.

The Squire stooped and lifted Nell into his arms.

"I did not want you to see me," he said. "I knew you were having your big party to-night, and I had to come to the Towers on--on business. What are you trembling for, Nell? You ought not to be out; you must run back to the house at once; why, you are cold, child."

"I'm **not** cold, and I **will** stay and kiss you."

Nell's arms were pressed tightly round the Squire's neck. Her little soft lips pressed kiss after kiss on his somewhat grisly cheek.

Boris, standing on the ground, and looking up at Nell in her fathers arms, thoroughly realised for the first time that he had gone to useless trouble in cleaning the dove's cage.

"Now, Nell, you must be sensible," said her father. "I was obliged to come to the Towers to-night to--to fetch something. I knew from Molly's letters that you were going to have a big ball. I thought I'd like to see how the ball-room looked. We have not had a ball, a very big ball, in that room since the days of my great-grandmother. My grandmother has told me about that ball, and about the very window where my great-grandfather stood when he asked my great-grandmother to be his wife. He asked her to marry him at that ball, so of course she never could forget it; and the story of the green dress she wore--apple green--with her golden locks falling over her shoulders, and the story of the window where he proposed to her, have been handed down in the family ever since. To-night, in that same window, the little great-great-grandchild sat, and looked out, and I saw her; now, you must run back, Nell. Boris, you run back, too; run and enjoy yourselves; be happy--God, God bless you."

"Why don't you come in, father?" asked Boris.

Nell felt as if she could not say a word. There was so much meaning in fathers words; there was so much that he said with his eyes, and with the tight pressure of his arms, which the rather commonplace words he uttered seemed to have nothing to do with. Nell understood, and her heart ached so, she seemed to be turned dumb.

The Squire put Nell firmly on the grass.

"Run in, both of you," he said. "I must go back to the railway station at once, or I shall miss my train. I am returning to town to-night. Say nothing of this to anyone until the ball is over, then you may tell Molly, if you like, that she will probably see her mother to-morrow. Good night, chicks."

"Won't we see you to-morrow, father?"

But the Squire's only reply was to stride softly away under the trees.

"Why, he's gone," exclaimed Boris with a little cry.

"Yes. Didn't you know he was going, Boris? What is the use of making a fuss?" said Nell. She found she could speak quite well again now. "Take my hand and come back to the house; let's do what he said."

"Do you think he's put out about anything?" asked Boris. "He seemed dumpy, like; I couldn't say anything about the dove; I knew it hadn't come. Do you think father was sad about anything, Nell?"

"He didn't say he was, did he?" asked Nell.

"No."

"Well, let's come back and dance, or people will miss us. Father said we weren't to say anything until the ball was over, and then only to Molly."

"But if Molly goes back to the Grange?"

"She mustn't; she must stay here. I'll dance with you now, Boris, if you like."

The time had sped faster than the children had any idea of while they were out. But the dancing still continued and went on until a late hour. Then the moment when expectation must yield to a delightful reality arrived. Towards the end of one of the prettiest figures of the cotillion, the fairies and brownies assumed new characters. Either a fairy or a brownie conducted one of the many personages who figured in the fancy ball up to the fairy queen, who, assisted by a number of satellites, bestowed upon each a gift carefully selected in advance to meet the requirements of the special child in question. Each child was expected to drop on one knee to receive the fairy queen's benediction with her gift; they then filed one by one into the supper-room, where refreshments of a particularly ethereal, grateful character awaited them. This scene really ended the never-to-be-forgotten fancy ball. Hasty departures followed. Carriages rolled away with many sleepy and happy little folk, and at last the two carriages which were to convey Sir John Thornton and his party back to the Grange, appeared.

Nora was to return with them, and Annie Forest had arranged to specially attend to her comforts. Molly, who intended to come back to the Towers in a day or two, was also wrapping a white shawl round her shoulders preparatory to departure, when a brownie rushed quickly from one of the ante-rooms, flung his arms round her neck, and whispered in her ear.

"Oh, Molly, what are you waiting for?" exclaimed Nan. "We're all perfectly dead with sleep, Boris, you naughty boy; you know you have nothing whatever to say; what are you keeping Molly for now?"

"I have something to say," replied Boris. "Something most 'portant, I can tell you." His face flushed with anger; he dragged Molly into the ante-room.

"There she is, Nell," he exclaimed; "now you can tell her."

"What is the matter, Nell, darling?" exclaimed Molly, struck by the expression on her little sisters face.

"Molly, Molly," exclaimed Nell, with a sort of gasp in her voice.

"What is it, Nell, dear? Do speak; they're all waiting for me and I must go."

"Oh, must you go? Do stay, do stay; I have something very important to say; its a message."

"A message!" exclaimed Molly; anxiety stealing quickly into her voice; "is it anything about--about father and mother?"

"Yes, yes; and nobody else is to know; you will stay?"

"Yes, I'll stay. Wait there a minute, and I'll be back with you."

Molly ran up to Hester, who was waiting for her in the entrance hall.

"Good-bye, Hetty," she said, kissing her; "I'm not going back with you."

"What in the world do you mean, Molly?" exclaimed Hester. "You know you have promised to stay with us for another day or two, and I want you to know more of Mrs. Willis, and--why, what's the matter, dear?"

"Nell is not quite well, I think," replied Molly; "anyhow, I must stay here tonight; don't say anything to make Nora anxious; good-night."

"I am afraid, Hester, that we must not keep the horses waiting any longer," said Sir John in his most measured tones. "Good-night, Molly, we shall be pleased to see you at the Grange to-morrow if you can tear yourself away from domestic cares."

Hester went away, the carriage door was shut, and a moment later the last of the visitors had departed.

Molly rushed back for one moment to Nell.

"I am here," she said, "but if you have a secret to tell me, I can't talk to you for the present without exciting the curiosity of the whole house. Go upstairs and get into bed, and I'll be with you as soon as I can. I daresay my bed is not ready for me, so I'll sleep with you to-night."

A ghost of a smile of pleasure flitted across Nell's face as she glided away.

Molly went back to the rest of her brothers and sisters. Jane Macalister, still true to her Minerva costume, was seated at the supper table, eating a large slice of cold game pie.

"I am famished," she said; "it was the most fatiguing thing I ever did, and the dressmaker has made the sleeves of this horrid dress a great deal too tight, and the neck chokes me. Now, I hope this is the last folly of the kind that we shall have here for many a long day. I, for one, refuse to be laced up in this heathen mythology style again. Now then, my dears, all of you to bed. Molly, what in the world are you stay-ing here for? We didn't expect you, and your room isn't ready."

"Oh, I'll sleep with Nell," replied Molly.

"Very inconsiderate indeed," replied poor Minerva. "Nell's bed is only large enough for herself, and she's like a feathers weight--with those dark circles under her eyes too. I saw her flying about and absolutely going out on to the lawn this evening. Nell is a great deal too excitable, and certainly her sleep ought not to be disturbed."

"I promise not to disturb it," replied Molly; "you know, Jane, I'm not an excit-ing sort of person."

"No more you are, my dear; but it frets me to have my arrangements put out by fads. However, off with you to bed now. Dear me, I am famished. If Minerva felt as I do, I pity her, poor soul. I'll have a glass of stout; there's nothing like it when you're worn out. Good night, Molly."

Molly ran eagerly away. She was waylaid by more than one brother and sister on her way upstairs, but at last she found herself in Nell's room.

Nell was sitting on the side of the bed; she had not attempted to undress.

"Oh, come, this will never do," said the practical Molly; "why, you're ready to drop with fatigue, you poor mite. Here, let me undress you, and you can talk while

I'm doing it. Now, what's the trouble?"

"It's about father."

"What about him?"

"He came back to-night; he stood under the oak tree at the end of the lawn. I saw him first, because he pressed his face up against one of the windows and looked in, and afterwards he stood under the oak tree; Boris and I ran out to him."

"Yes, yes; go on, Nell."

Molly's fingers were trembling now, but they did not cease their busy task of unfastening Nell's clothes.

"Go on," she said; "what did he say, and why, *why* didn't you call me?"

"Boris tried to catch you up, but you would dance with Hugh Pierson. We ran out to father and he talked to us. The 'perhaps' has come true, Molly; oh, Molly, the 'perhaps' has come quite true."

"How do you know, Nell? Don't tremble so, Nell, dear."

"Father wouldn't come in," continued Nell, making a brave effort to recover herself. "He told us about our great-great-grandmother and her apple-green dress, and he said that he had come back to fetch something, and that he must return to London to-night; and then he said,'God--God bless you,' and his voice shook just a tiny bit, and he said that mother would be home to-morrow, and----"

"Yes, Nell, and----"

"Boris said 'Will you come home?' and--but----"

"What did he say to that?"

"He said nothing to that; he walked away very soft and quick. Molly, what does it mean?"

"I don't know," said Molly. "Now, Nell, you must get into bed. You are quite cold and shivery. I am going downstairs to fetch you a little hot wine and water, and then I'll put my arms round you until you sleep."

Nell was glad to submit to Molly's most comforting ministrations.

"But I think I do know what it means," murmured the elder girl as she listened to the gentle breathing of her little sister by-and-by.

CHAPTER XVIII.
THE LORRIMERS OF THE TOWERS.

The morning post brought a letter from Mrs. Lorrimer, which set all curiosity at rest. This letter was addressed to Jane Macalister, who read it through first, with feverish haste and brows drawn darkly together, then again straight from the beginning more slowly, and then a third time, during which she surreptitiously wiped her eyes, and hoped the children had not seen her do so.

Jane was seated before the tea equipage at the head of the long breakfast table. Molly was helping her brothers and sisters to porridge, cups of milk, and bread and jam, in her usual deft fashion. Jane raised her eyes and encountered the brown ones of Molly.

"Well, Jane," said the young girl in a steady voice; "what is the news?"

"It's for you all to know, my dears," said Jane Macalister in a steady voice. "Your mother has asked me to break it to you all. It's just a question whether you shall all hear it together, or whether Molly shall hear it by herself first. I think Molly must decide that point."

"I'll hear it with the others," said Molly.

As she spoke she went and sat down in a vacant chair near Nell.

"Perhaps it is not such news to Nell and me as you think," she said. "Anyhow, we are prepared to hear it."

"It's 'perhaps' come true," said Nell in a faint voice, looking at Molly with the ghost of a smile.

"Dear, dear," exclaimed Kitty, "whatever it is, let's out with it. I don't suppose we are a set of cowards, any of us. I'm going to guess what it is beforehand; it's that father's mare has broken her knees; that's about the worst thing that ***could*** happen. Father sent for the mare to London a week ago; don't you remember, Guy, and when he was riding her in the park she fell and broke her knees; that's it, you bet."

"Do shut up," exclaimed Guy.

"You bet I'm right," replied Kitty, flushed and defiant.

Under no other possible circumstances would Kitty have dared to say "you bet" in the presence of Jane Macalister.

"Well, my dears," said poor Jane, looking round at all the eager faces. "I'd better read your mother's letter aloud. I've read it three times to myself, and have got over the choky business; so now I can read it aloud without breaking down. This is what your mother says, children. If I stand up, my loves, you'll all hear it better."

Jane Macalister stood up at the end of the long table. All the children dropped their spoons, and knives, and forks, as they listened to her.

MY DEAR JANE," she began.

Here she paused.

"Your mother and I," she said, "have been Jane and Lucy to each other ever since we were children."

"Who cares about that rot now?" murmured angry Kitty. Harry gave her a pinch which make her scream.

"You shut up," she said back to him. "I must say something or I'll 'splode."

"MY DEAR JANE," continued the governess,

"I must ask you to break the news as you best can to the poor children. The Squire and I have done all that lay in the power of mortals to avert the blow. But it has been God's will that we should not succeed. You can tell Molly by-and-by how it is that her dear father has got into such terrible money difficulties, but now the all-important thing for the children to know is this.... The Towers is sold, and we must all go away from the dear home we have loved so long. The Squire is terribly upset, and cannot bring himself to come back just at once, but I am returning to-morrow. There is nothing for us now but to bear up and make the best of things. It is not so hard on any of us as it is on the Squire.--Believe me, dear Jane, your affectionate friend,

"LUCY LORRIMER."

There was dead silence after the letter had been read. Then quite suddenly the terrible and unexpected sound of Nell's weeping filled the room.

"Oh, father," sobbed Nell. "Oh, father's face; oh, father's face."

She hid her head on Molly's shoulder and moaned in the most broken-hearted way. Boris, too, looked very pale. He remembered the pressure of the hand which had held his the night before. He heard the words which were commonplace enough, once again, and he saw the haggard lines round the lips and round the kindly eyes.

Boris slipped away from his own side of the table. He went up to Nell and began to kiss her.

"I know," he said. "I understand. I saw him, too; but he'll be all right by-and-by. It's like a big battle, but he'll not flinch; father's made of the stuff that soldiers have in them. He'll be all right by-and-by."

"I wish you'd let me look at that letter, Jane Macalister," said Guy.

Guy was the heir of the Towers. It was his property and all his future, which that letter seemed suddenly to deprive him of. He was the last boy in the world to think first of himself; but now his head did feel a little dizzy. If, it seemed to him up to this moment, there was a solid fact in all the world, it was that in due time he should step into his father's shoes and become Squire Lorrimer of the Towers.

Molly instantly understood the tone of Guy's voice. She started up, and going to Jane took the letter; then she went to Guy, and put her arm round his neck.

"Let's come into the garden and read it together," she said.

He stumbled up and went with her as if he were blind. They went out through the open window and down the lawn, and Molly read the letter aloud once again.

"Well, it's all up," she said when she had finished. "I have been expecting it for a long time--a long time; haven't you, Guy?"

"No," answered Guy. "That's the awful part to me; it's such a sudden blow. I knew, of course, there were money difficulties; but, then, somehow or other, most fellows' fathers seem to have got them; and I was so busy with my books and keeping ahead of the other fellows in form that I didn't fret specially. I never wanted to think of myself specially; but sometimes the thought used to cross my mind that there might be a difficulty about my going to Cambridge by-and-by, and, of course, I knew that Eton was quite out of the question; but that was the worst, the very worst, that I thought could happen to me, and now--now."

"Poor Guy," said Molly. "You'll never be Squire Lorrimer of the Towers."

"Oh, of course, that doesn't matter," said Guy, in a would-be careless tone. "They can never take my real birthright from me. I'm the son of a gentleman, and I come of the real old stock. It's thinking of father that floors me, though, Molly. Why, this will just kill him."

"I'm awfully anxious about him," said Molly.

"How did he contrive to get into a scrape of this sort? I'm sure we never were extravagant; we didn't care a bit what we wore nor what we ate; and I know the grammar school at Nortonbury is cheap enough, and I really don't think Jane Macalister gets ten pounds a year. I'm sure she never has a new rag to her back; and as to you girls, of course I'm not blind; but if you were dressed like other fellows' sisters, you and Nora would look far and away the prettiest girls in the place."

"No, no, that's humbug," said downright Molly. "I'm not a bit pretty, and what's more I don't want to be. Of course, Nora is different. I acknowledge that she has a beautiful face."

"And you acknowledge another thing," said Guy; "that very little money has been spent. How in the world has father got into this scrape?"

"Well, of course, we can't understand that," said Molly; "only I think I can guess a little bit. Of course, these are bad times for all landlords, and half the farmers don't pay their rents properly; and you remember, Guy, last autumn the lease of the Sunny Side farm fell in, and father hasn't been able to let it since, because the whole place is so fearfully out of repair that no one will take it until it is put in order; but the real thing which has made it necessary to sell the Towers is, that father went security a long time ago for a very large sum of money, and all the other sureties have died or lost their money, and so father has to pay. I know there was a great fear of that, because mother told me of it more than a year ago. She said that father always intended, if the worst came, to try and borrow the money. I suppose he has failed to do so, and that must be the reason why the Towers has to be sold."

"It's a bad business," said Guy, "and I can't realise it a bit yet; of course we young ones must be as plucky as we can about it, that goes without saying, but I can't take it in yet. I'm glad it's holiday time, and I needn't go to school. I couldn't face the other fellows just for a bit."

"I know you'll be splendid about it, Guy darling," said Molly looking affectionately at her brother; "and now do you mind coming with me to the Grange, for, of course, poor Nonie must be told? We won't stay there long, for we must do what we can to help mother when she comes home."

"Yes, I'll come with you," said Guy; "we'd best start at once, it's not too early."

"Stay where you are, then, for a moment," said Molly. "I'll run into the house and tell them we are going."

She went back to the breakfast-room, where an animated conversation was going on.

Nell was lying on a sofa with a shawl over her, and Jane Macalister was sitting by her side and holding her hand. Harry, Boris, and Kitty were standing in a little knot by the open window eagerly discussing a subject which was causing them intense pain, and obliging them to use many bickering words. They were feverishly anxious about the removal of their several pets.

"I know the big rabbit will die," exclaimed Boris. "Unless we can take the hutch which is built into the wall he'll die. He never will sleep anywhere except in that one corner of his hutch. It makes him ill, I know it does, to sleep anywhere else. He'll die if he's moved."

"No he won't die," said Kitty roundly; "rabbits have got no souls, and you can't be affectionate and fond of a thing if you haven't got a soul."

"Oh, what a lie," interrupted Harry; "and you mean to tell me that my dormice aren't fond of me, and that they don't prefer me to you--you clumsy monkey."

Kitty looked nonplussed for a moment.

"That's only because you feed them," she said then. "If you didn't feed them, they'd love me just as well. Ah, yah; who's right? You can't answer me now, can you? It's only cupboard-love animals have got, and that proves that they have no souls."

"It seems to me," said Harry, in a would-be sarcastic voice, "that very much the same thing may be said of some girls. Who caught you stealing a peach a week ago? Ha, ha, Miss Kitty."

"Oh, for pity's sake, children, don't quarrel," exclaimed Molly.

"That's what I'm telling 'em," said Boris in a tearful voice; "and I think my big rabbit *has* a soul, and I'm awful 'feared it will kill him if he leaves his corner of the hutch."

"Jane," interrupted Molly, "Guy and I are going over to the Grange to tell poor Nora about mother's letter, but we'll both be home before mother returns."

"Very well, my dear," replied Jane Macalister. "You'd better not have Nora back, though, Molly, for she's quite certain not to be sensible about matters, and that's the only thing left to us now. For heaven's sake, I say, let us keep our senses and not give way to sentiment at a crisis like this. Go, my dear; tell her that she must take it in a quiet, matter-of-fact way, and not consider herself in the very least. The Squire and your mother, and Guy are the three victims; the rest of us are of no consequence; go, Molly."

Jane blew her nose very hard after uttering this oration, and there were suspicious red rims round her eyes.

Molly joined Guy, and they started on their walk to the Grange.

Guy had now quite got over the stunned feeling which oppressed him. There was a great deal of grit in all the Lorrimers, and Guy and Molly had both even a larger amount of this most valuable quality than the younger children. The ground, therefore, no longer swam under the brave boy's feet, and Molly, now that she was obliged to act, and now that she knew exactly what was going to happen, felt really less unhappy than before the blow had fallen.

It was little after ten o clock when the children reached the Grange. They found Hester and Annie out in the garden picking flowers, and Nora, looking very happy and very pretty in her new pink cambric, was lying under a shady tree on the lawn.

"Hullo, what have you come over so early for?" she asked of the two, as, dusty and hot, they came up to her side. Mrs. Willis was sitting near Nora, and reading aloud to her. Nora felt immensely flattered by her attentions, and yet at the same time not absolutely at home with her. Mrs. Willis could read character at a glance. She had taken an immense fancy to Molly, and pitied Nora without admiring her.

"She is a shallow little thing," she murmured to herself. "Pretty, of course, but nothing will ever make her either great or wise. Sweet Molly is one of the angels of the world."

She rose now to greet the brother and sister as they approached. The trouble round Guy's handsome eyes was not lost upon her. Poor Molly looked untidy, and quite worn and old.

"Oh, how the ball has fagged you!" exclaimed Nora; "see how fresh I am, and kind Mrs. Willis is reading me a charming story."

"I won't read any more at present, my dear," said Mrs. Willis, "as no doubt your brother and sister want to talk to you."

"Oh, I'm sure they don't," said Nora; "they can't have anything at all particular to say, and I am so immensely interested. I want to know how Lucile conquered her difficulties with the French grammar. I have such a fellow feeling for her, for I always detest grammar. Please, Mrs. Willis, don't go away."

"I'll come back presently," said Mrs. Willis; she crossed the lawn as she spoke, leaving the fascinating book open on Nora's sofa.

"How tiresome of you both to come and interrupt," said Nora in her crossest tone. "Molly, you look positively dishevelled; and Guy, you needn't wear those worn-out tennis shoes when you come to the Grange. You really, neither of you, have the least idea of what is due to our position."

"Our position be hanged," growled Guy. "Look here, we have come to say something, and as it's particularly unpleasant, you had better listen as quietly as you can."

"Then I'm sure I don't want to hear it; I hate and detest unpleasant things. You know I do, don't you, Molly?"

"Yes, darling," said Molly, kneeling down by her; "but sometimes bad things must come and we must be brave and bear them."

She knelt down by Nora as she spoke, and laid her hot, and not too clean hand, on Nora's pretty fresh sleeve.

"I do think its unkind of you to rumple up my frock like that," said Nora; "if you don't care to look nice, I do, and if you've got unpleasant news, you shouldn't tell it to me; for the doctor says that I'm not to be worried at present. I'm getting well nicely, but I'll be thrown back awfully if I'm worried."

"That can't be helped," said Guy in a firm voice. "Sometimes unpleasant things have to be borne. It's no worse for you than for the others."

"Oh, Nonie, Nonie," sobbed Molly, burying her head on her sister's shoulder; "it's this, it's this: Guy, you mustn't be cruel; remember she is weak. Nora, darling, we wouldn't tell you if we could help it, but you must know, because everyone else will know. The Towers is sold. The dear old home is ours no longer. We are not the Lorrimers of the Towers any more."

CHAPTER XIX.
TOPSY-TURVEY.

While Guy and Molly were in vain endeavouring to comfort Nora, who, after uttering shriek after shriek, closed her eyes and lay perfectly still, so much so, that Molly thought for a moment that she had fainted, Sir John Thornton left his own private study, where he had been busily writing letters, and stepping out on the lawn, approached the spot where Hester and Annie, in their cool white dresses, were picking flowers to replenish the vases in the different sitting-rooms. The girls made a pretty picture, and Sir John always admired beauty in any form and under any guise.

"Really, Hester is becoming quite distinguished looking," he said to himself; "she inherits a good deal of her mother's grace, and although she will never be exactly pretty, she is very aristocratic in appearance. She has a good figure, too--graceful and lithe. Even beside Miss Forest, who is a regular beauty of the piquant gipsy order, she quite shows to advantage. Presently we may be able to get her presented, and, if necessary, we must have a house in town for three months in the season. (I shall detest it, but Laura says it is inevitable.) Yes, I'm sure I have done right. Hester is such a sensible girl that she will probably be glad of my news; yes, it is evidently my duty to take Hester into society, and Laura is just the woman to take all the care and worry off my hands. I should never have thought of marrying again if it were not for Hester and Nan, but no one can say that I shirk a father's duties. Now I must break it to Hetty, for Laura says she will be here on Saturday. I would rather she did not bring her daughter with her, but she evidently has not the least intention of coming anywhere without Antonia. Dear, dear, I hope Hester will be sensible. I don't want a bad quarter of an hour."

Sir John had now reached the two girls. He had quite forgotten his dislike to

Annie, and smiling at her, asked her in his gracious way why she did not offer him a rosebud.

She picked one at once, and he got her to place it in his button-hole

"Thank you," he said with a smile; "your taste is admirable, and now I have a favour to ask of you."

"Granted, of course," said Annie with a smile.

"I want to deprive you of Hetty's company for a quarter of an hour. I have some domestic matters to discuss with my fair housekeeper."

"You can arrange the flowers, Annie," called Hester, dropping her basket as she spoke, and going up to her fathers side.

He drew her hand through his arm and they walked across the lawn together.

"I have just been admiring you and your friend," he said. "Do you know, Hester, that you really grow very nice looking."

Hester flushed with a strange mingling of irritation and elation.

To be praised by her fastidious father was something to be remembered, but she always shrank from having her personal appearance commented upon.

Sir John turned round now and smiled into her blushing face.

"Come down this shady walk with me," he said. "I have a good deal to talk over with you. Hester, you and Nan have always found me a kind, indulgent father, have you not?"

"You have been very good to us," replied Hester.

"Oh, perhaps not so good as some fathers, but good according to my lights, eh?"

"You have been very good to us," repeated Hester.

"And you are a good, dear daughter," replied Sir John, with almost enthusiasm; "you never complain of the dull life I give you at the Grange."

"The life is not dull, father."

"My dear, my dear," Sir John patted Hester's long slim fingers as they rested on his arm, "I was young once myself and I know what youth wants, and I have seen other girls, and I know what my girl requires. Hester, I am not unmindful of you; and the step--the step I am about to take is taken not wholly, but mainly, on your account and Nan's."

Hester suddenly withdrew her hand from Sir John's arm. A kind of intuition told her what was coming. Like a flash a sword seemed to pierce right through her heart. She had a memory of her mother, of the loving eyes now closed--the voice so full of sympathy now silent. Was her mother to be supplanted and because of her? For once passion got the upper hand of prudence.

"Do it," she said, suddenly flashing round upon Sir John; "do it, certainly, if you wish, but do not do it for Nan's sake and mine. Nothing in all the wide world could pain us more."

Sir John looked as astonished as if Hester had suddenly slapped him in the face.

"Your words are extremely vigorous, my dear," he said in a voice of ice; "and I am not aware that I have yet told you what I mean to do."

"Oh, I know, I know," answered Hester; "you are going to marry again. Oh, don't do it for our sakes; that is all I have to say."

Sir John was quite silent for nearly a minute. Then he said quietly: "As you have been so clever as to guess my intention, you have of course saved me the trouble of breaking my news to you. Young girls sometimes resent the presence of a stepmother, but as a rule they appreciate the advantage of one when once they have become accustomed to the change. The lady who has honoured me by promising to accept my hand is Mrs. Bernard Temple. She is about my own age and has one daughter of seventeen--your age, Hester--whose name is Antonia. I have not yet seen Antonia, but I am told that she is a most charming, ladylike girl. Mrs. Bernard Temple has written to me to say she will come here on a visit on Saturday with Antonia. This is Thursday, and I expect you, Hester, in the meantime, to break the news to Nan, and to get everything ready for the honoured guests who will then arrive. I expect this is a surprise to you, my dear, so I forgive the excited words you have just made use of. You will doubtless have reason to rejoice yet at my decision. You are too young to be at the head of a great establishment like this, Hetty. I am doing wisely in removing such a burden from such young shoulders."

"I have never felt it a burden," said Hester in a choked voice.

"No; you have been good, very good, and now you will reap your reward. My marriage will probably take place in October, and my wife and I will return to the Grange for Christmas. Next season we shall probably have a house in town, when my dear Laura will present you and Antonia at one of the drawing-rooms."

Hester made no remark.

"I think that is all, my love," said Sir John; "you can now return to your friends.

I have several letters to attend to."

"May I tell Mrs. Willis, and--and the others?" asked Hester.

"You may tell everyone; it is no secret."

Sir John took out his cigar case as he spoke, and Hester, with a sinking heart, turned away.

Annie, full of trouble on her account, dreading inexpressibly the moment when Mrs. Willis should ask her for the ring, was sauntering up and down, lost in anxious thought in front of the house.

She caught sight of Hester coming slowly towards her.

"Good gracious, Hetty, whatever is the matter?" she exclaimed. "I never saw your pale face with peonies on it before, and your eyes look as if you had been crying. I cannot imagine what has come to everyone," continued Annie; "the whole place seems to be in a ferment. Nora, I know, has been crying about something, and Molly's face looks positively blotchy."

"Oh, I should like to see Molly; is she here?" exclaimed Hester.

"Yes, she's on the lawn talking to Nora, and Guy is with them, and Mrs. Willis joined them half an hour ago. I was running up to them, but Nora shrieked out to me to keep away. What can be the matter? There seems to be an earthquake everywhere."

"So there is as far as I am concerned," replied Hester. "There is an awful earthquake, and I don't know at the present moment whether I am standing on my head or my heels."

"Dear me, you are on your heels," replied Annie; "but you look rather top-heavy, so do be careful."

"My father is going to marry again in October," continued Hester, "and my future stepmother is coming here on Saturday, and there is a girl called Antonia coming with her--her daughter, and--and Antonia will live at the Grange in the future, and Annie, I cannot realise it; oh, Annie, I cannot bear it."

"You poor darling," said Annie. She put her arm round Hester's neck and kissed her hot cheeks.

"What a horrid old man Sir John is," murmured Annie to herself; "what in the world is he making a goose of himself for?"

Aloud she said in a faint voice, "Oh, I am bitterly sorry for you. I don't know what I'd do to my dear old rough-and-ready father if he dared to give me another mother. And Hetty, Hetty, if these new people are coming on Saturday, must I go away?"

"No, of course not, Annie; it would make me much more wretched even than I am now not to have you in the house; oh, I really don't know how I dare tell Nan; she is so excitable, and Mrs. Martin has put her against stepmothers already."

"It doesn't matter half as much for her," said Annie, "for she will be at school most of the time. Would you like me to tackle her? I think I can get her to behave with outward propriety at least."

"I wish you would tell her," said Hester.

"Very well, I'll search for her right away; and shall I send Molly to you?"

"Dear Molly; yes, I'd rather see her than anyone."

"I'll fly round and tell her you're here," replied Annie.

She had now a reason for joining the group on the lawn, which not even Nora's frantic wavings of the hand to her to keep away could prevent her attending to.

"Molly," she said, not coming too near, but shouting from a little distance; "Hester is on the lawn at the back of the house and wants particularly to see you for a minute or two."

Molly stood up and shook out her crumpled holland frock.

"Very well," she said, "I'll go to her."

"Stay here, Guy," she continued, laying her hand on her brother's shoulder. "I won't stay long with Hetty, but she would think it unkind if I did not tell her. I wonder if she has heard anything. I won't be long away, for we must go back to the Towers before lunch, in order to be sure to be in time to meet mother."

Molly went slowly away, her poor dejected little figure showing only too plainly the weight of sad care which filled her heart.

Hester Thornton was, however, for once so self-centred that she could think of no sorrow but her own. She noticed nothing particular in Molly's lagging step, and guessed of no special sorrow in her tear-dimmed brown eyes.

Hester ran up to Molly and clutched her arm with feverish force.

"Oh, Molly," she gasped, "how can I bear it? my worst, worst fears are realised. My father is going to marry again."

These words gave Molly a shock; she turned quite white for a moment.

"Hester," she said, "oh, Hester, and I remember your mother, your sweet mother. I was only a very little girl when I saw her last. She was ill at the time and she died soon afterwards, but I cannot forget her face nor her words; she seemed something like an angel."

"So she was," said Hester. "A beautiful, dear angel--too good for this world."

Hester's courage gave way; she began to sob brokenly.

"Come into the field at the back of the house," said Molly; "we'll be quite alone there, and then you can tell me everything and I can tell you everything."

"Oh, have you bad news too?" said Hester. "Annie seemed to think you had; she said your face was blotchy, and that Nora had been crying. Oh, Molly dear, Molly dear, how selfish I am; I have been absolutely swallowed up in this dark cloud, and can think of no one but myself. I notice now how red your eyes are, and how sad your mouth. Poor, dear Molly, what is it? Is Nell really ill? Was that why you did not come back with us last night?"

"It isn't Nell," said Molly in a trembling voice; "it's--Hester--it's what we feared. We had a letter from mother this morning, and it's all over--it's all over, Hetty--the Towers is sold."

"And my father is going to marry again," said Hester; "it seems to me as if the world were turning topsy-turvy. Oh, Molly, what are we both to do?"

"Jane Macalister would say that we are not to think of ourselves," said Molly with a wan attempt at a smile, "but somehow I don't feel like following her advice just at present."

"Nor I either," replied Hester; "I never, never in the whole course of my life felt more horrid and wicked, and rebellious, and selfish."

CHAPTER XX.
THE NEW OWNERS.

It is surprising how soon, at least when we are young, the greater number of us get accustomed to things. The news of the sale of the Towers, and of Sir John Thornton's approaching marriage, had electrified the Lorrimers and the Thorntons on Thursday. Had electrified them to such a degree that even the common observances of life seemed queer and out of place. It seemed wrong to eat when one was hungry; inhuman to smile; and even when one was sleepy, it seemed necessary to go to bed with a sort of apology. Nevertheless, the hungry people had to be fed, smiles had now and then to chase away tears, and in youthful slumber sorrow was for a time forgotten.

By Saturday life was going on much as usual in the two households. The Lorrimers were not to leave the Towers for six weeks. There was no immediate necessity, therefore, for the younger members of the household to think about moving the pets. Six weeks seemed something like for ever to them. The anxious consultations of the elders were not shared by them. Mother had come home, and mother kissed them just as tenderly as ever at night, and petted them just as much in the morning, and coddled them just as persistently when there was the least scrap of anything the matter. Whenever they went away, mother would go with them, and that, after all, was the main thing. In their secret hearts, they became rather excited about the move, the packing, and the new home. Boris, it is true, sometimes woke at night with a start and a hot remembrance of the clutch the Squire had given his hand when he stood under the oak tree, and Nell sobbed out piteously once or twice, "Oh, father's face, oh, father's face;" but father was not with them and mother was, and the sun rose and set as usual, and the fruit ripened in great plenty, and the pets were all well, and it was holiday time, and mother earth was specially tranquilising and kind. By Saturday, Boris, Kitty, and Nell were to all appearance just as they were before, and even the elder members of the family behaved, as Jane Macalister expressed it, "like sensible Christians."

In the Thornton household, too, the first overwhelming shock of Sir John's approaching marriage had passed by. Nan had stormed and raged, and flung her arms round nurse's neck, and sobbed herself at last to sleep on her breast, but Nan's passion was over now, and she was even a little curious to see what sort of woman Mrs. Bernard Temple was, and what sort of girl Antonia would be. Hester, whether her heart was heavy or light, was forced to attend to many household cares, and Annie was happy once more, for Mrs. Willis had not yet asked her for the ring. Mrs. Willis had yielded to Hester's strong entreaties to remain at the Grange until Monday. She was deeply interested in the Lorrimers, and was most anxious to help Molly in any way in her power; she was also desirous of seeing Hetty through the difficult ordeal of her first introduction to her future stepmother; she resolved, therefore, at some personal sacrifice, to prolong her visit at the Grange for a few days. No events less absorbing would have made her forget the ring. The exciting events of Thursday had, however, put it completely out of her head. On Friday, it is true, she did think of it, but Annie was not present at the time, and she now resolved not to trouble herself to have the ring copied, but to buy another present for her ex-pupil.

Annie knew nothing of this intention, but delay had made her bold, and, as usual, she had great faith in her own good luck.

On Saturday morning Sir John contributed vastly to the excitement and interest of the party by a certain piece of news which he read aloud to them from a letter he had just received from Mrs. Bernard Temple.

"My dear Hester," he said, looking down the length of the table at his daughter, "did not you once tell me that you had a schoolfellow at Lavender House of the name of Susan Drummond?"

"Sleepy Susy," exclaimed Hester with a smile. "I had almost forgotten her, although she managed to worry me a good deal at school. She was my room-mate for the first couple of terms. Oh, dear, oh, dear, shall I ever forget the trouble we used to have to wake her?"

"She left Lavender House a good many years ago; what of her?" exclaimed Mrs. Willis; "the fact is, I have quite lost sight of her."

"And so have I," said Hester; "frankly, I did not care about remembering her."

"Well, whether you like it or not, you are likely to hear a good deal more of her now," said Sir John, "for Susan's father is the new owner of the Towers, and Mrs. Bernard Temple wants to know if she may bring Susan as well as Antonia to-day, as Susan is naturally most anxious to see her new home. Have we a vacant bedroom, Hester?"

"Oh, yes," replied Hester, "but it seems----"

"What, my dear?"

"Nothing, father--only--but----"

"But me no buts," replied Sir John in a tone of irritation. "Nothing can be more natural than a young girl's wish to see her future home. I shall telegraph to Mrs. Bernard Temple to let her know that we shall be pleased to give Miss Drummond a hearty welcome."

Sir John rose from his chair as he spoke, and a moment later left the room.

"Poor Nora," exclaimed Hester, when the door had closed behind him. "Susy is certain to say something to hurt her dreadfully, for unless she has tremendously altered, I never saw a creature with less tact."

"We must hope for the best," said Mrs. Willis. "I am rather glad, my dear," she added, "that I am here, for I think Miss Susy will be on her best behaviour in my presence."

"Well, I think it's the most awful thing that ever happened," exclaimed Nan. "Fancy having a sleepy thing like that at the Towers, instead of Nell and Kitty and Boris."

The girls discussed the matter a little further, and then Hester went away to attend to Nora.

The shock of Molly's intelligence had really affected Nora to an almost painful degree. Her nerves had been terribly shaken by her serious fall, and she was so restless and miserable for the first twenty-four hours after the stunning blow had been given to her that the beloved Towers was no longer her home, that a doctor had to be sent for, who ordered her a soothing draught, and said that she ought to be kept extremely quiet.

By this time, however, Nora was not only better, but much interested in the strange new outlook. She had found her life often dull enough in the dear old home-

-for it was by this term she now invariably spoke of the Towers--she had longed to flutter her little wings in a larger and gayer world--she had fancied the small triumphs which might be hers, and had believed much in the charms of her own pretty face. She had dreamed dreams of herself in society, and felt sure that the fact of her being a Lorrimer of the Towers would insure her a passport into any circle. Now, of course, matters would be different, but still the new life must be, at least, more interesting than the old. It would be impossible any longer to have nothing to do in the day except to learn rather old-fashioned lessons under the tutorship of Jane Macalister, to contrive to dress out of almost nothing at all, and to listen for ever to Molly's slow talk about ways and means, and the children's chatter over their pets. Nora looked ahead with interest. She was sorry for Hester, of course, but she thought it would be very delightful to meet Mrs. Bernard Temple and Antonia, and even the news that Susan Drummond was coming, and that Susy's father was now the owner of the Towers, scarcely disturbed her equanimity.

"It's very kind of you to break it to me, Hetty," she said; "but of course I knew that someone had bought the Towers, and why not Mr. Drummond as well as another?"

"Why not, truly," replied Hester; "I am glad you are so sensible, Nora. I'll send Annie to you as soon as ever I can. Now I must run away, as there is a great deal to be done."

"How pale you look," said Nora, touched with a feeling of compunction at an indescribable something in Hester's face and voice. "Are you really, really fretting?"

"No, I hope not," replied Hester; "but I am really, really fighting, and that is hard work; now I must be off."

She left the room in a hurry, and as she went away to interview the house-keeper, some tears gathered in her eyes.

"Dear, dear Molly," she murmured to herself; "how very different she is from Nora; oh, how I wish Susy was not going to be settled at the Towers, it seems to be quite the last straw. 'As well Mr. Drummond as another,' says Nora; ah, but she would not say that if she really knew Susy."

The remaining hours which were to intervene before the arrival of the guests passed swiftly by. Sir John went alone in the landau to Nortonbury to meet them. An omnibus was sent for the luggage and for Mrs. Bernard Temple's and Miss

Drummond's maids. Nan, flushed, excited, and defiant, stood in her white dress on the steps; Hester, also in white, stood by her little sister and held her hand with a firm pressure.

"Keep quiet, Nan--do keep quiet, for my sake," she whispered once in an emphatic voice.

"I'll vent it on Susy Drummond," exclaimed Nan: "she's the safety valve; I'm glad she's coming."

"Here they are," said Hester. She felt herself turning very pale, and laid her other hand on Nan's shoulder. The sound of wheels was distinctly audible, and the next moment the landau with its four occupants bowled rapidly up to the door. Mrs. Bernard Temple was all smiles and bows. She was a graceful, well-preserved woman, handsomely and fashionably dressed. Although the same age as Sir John, she looked years younger. Antonia was a dark-eyed, sallow-faced girl, difficult to say anything about at the first glance, and Susy Drummond was the well-known Susy Drummond of Lavender House. A little taller, a little fatter, a little more sleepy-looking, if that were possible, than she used to be in the old days, but still the Susy whom Hester had detested, and whose departure from the school was hailed with relief by everyone.

Before anyone else could speak she now raised her full, light blue eyes, fixed them on Hester, and drawled out, "Who would have thought of seeing you again, Prunes and Prism?"

Hester ran down the steps accompanied by Nan. There was a confused murmur of greeting and introduction. Mrs. Bernard Temple kissed Hester on her forehead, called her "dear child," and looked into her eyes in a way which made Hester long to shut them, patted Nan on her shoulder and hoped she was a good, obliging little girl, and then, followed by Antonia and Susy, who dropped a succession of wraps the whole way, entered one of the drawing rooms.

"My dear John, what a perfectly *charming* room," exclaimed Mrs. Bernard Temple, turning to her future husband and glancing down the long room with a critical eye. "Furniture just a *little* out of date--not enough Chippendale--old-fashioned, but not antique--we'll soon put that right, however. Antonia has a wonderful eye for colour. You see, she has been trained in an atelier in Paris."

The faintest perceptible frown might have been seen between Sir John's eyebrows. He took no special notice of Mrs. Bernard Temple's remark, but walking up the long and exquisitely proportioned room flung open some French windows which led into a flower garden, gay with every imaginable flower. There was a distant and very lovely view from this window.

"I think you will admire the landscape from this window," he said, turning and speaking with an air of great deference to his distinguished guest.

"In one moment, my love," she replied. "Antonia, what do you think of old gold curtains, and one of those dark olive-green papers for the walls? This light decoration is absolutely inadmissible."

"Old gold is quite out of date," replied Antonia, opening her lips for the first time. "I'm sick of old gold, it's not *chic* now. I'll look through some of my antique designs and sketch my idea of a drawing-room for you presently, mother; now pray attend to Sir John."

Mrs. Bernard Temple favoured her daughter with a glance which was returned in a very frank and determined manner by that young lady. She then sailed slowly up the room and condescended to admire the view pointed out by Sir John.

Hester was standing near one of the windows talking to Susy, who had already sunk into an easy chair, and was fanning herself with an enormous black fan which hung at her girdle. Antonia, after a moment's hesitation, came up to Hester.

"I'm very sorry we have come," she said, "but it really is not my fault. Mother is in a state of flutter at having caught Sir John. I'm disgusted about it all. I don't want a stepfather any more than you want a stepmother. I'm to be turned into a fine lady now, and I hate being a fine lady. I have a soul for art. I adore art. I'm all art. Art is sacred; it shouldn't be talked about the way mother speaks of it. When I was in Paris I was in my element. I wore a linen blouse all over paint; ah, that blouse-- those happy days."

"Oh, Tony," suddenly burst from Susy's lips, "for pity's sake don't go off into a trance; you'll put Hester into a fit. Her face at the present moment is enough to kill anyone. For goodness sake, Hester, don't look like that; you'll make me laugh, and if I laugh immoderately it always wakes me up. I was looking out for a little nap before tea--forty winks, you know--I can't live without my forty winks, and now if you put on that killingly tragic face, I'll scream with laughter, I know I shall. Oh, dear, oh, dear, you must learn once for all never to mind a single thing Tony says;

she's the oddest, most irrational creature--a genius of course--her pictures are simply monstrosities, which is a sure sign of genius."

"Would you like me to take you to your room?" said Hester, turning to Antonia when Susy had given her a moment of time to open her lips. "I'm sure you must be tired after your long journey."

"What should tire me?" asked Antonia, opening her big brown eyes in astonishment. "I travelled first-class from London, and drove out here in a landau; the whole journey was nothing short of effeminate. When I was in Paris I rose at four in the morning, and worked at my easel standing for five hours at a stretch; that was something like work. No, I'm not the least tired, thank you, and I don't want to be bothered tidying myself, for I may as well say frankly that I don't care twopence how I look."

"Tea will be ready in half an hour," said Hester. "Will you come out into the garden, then, for a stroll?"

"If you don't hate me too much to walk with me; but pray consider your own feelings if you do, for I don't in the least object to strolling about alone."

Hester and Antonia had now stepped out on the velvet lawn. They each gazed fully at the other.

"No," said Hester, speaking with a sudden swift intuition; "I don't hate you; I rather like you. I am glad you are frank."

"Oh, I hate pretence," said Antonia, with a shudder. "Fancy a priestess of art stooping to pretence. Well, if you don't detest me, let us walk about for a little. Have you no wild, uncultured spot to show me, which the hand of man has not defaced? My whole soul recoils from a velvet lawn."

"Oh, Tony, Tony, you're too killing to live," shrieked Susy from the other side of the window.

Antonia and Hester moved slowly away together; Hester was trying to think of some portion of the grounds which might be sufficiently full of weeds and thorns to satisfy the priestess of high art, and Susy lay back in her chair and wiped her eyes.

"This is rich," she murmured to herself. "To think of poor Prunes and Prism being thrown with Tony--to think of Tony as a sort of sister to Prunes and Prism. Well, this is a delicious lark. Hullo! is that you, Nan? Come along and speak to me at once, you pert puss. Why, do you know you've grown?"

"Well, I don't suppose I've stood still for the last five years," replied Nan, who could be intensely pert when she pleased. "I'm too busy to stay with you now, Susy; Nora wants me."

"Nora; who is Nora?"

"Nora Lorrimer."

"Nora Lorrimer, is she one of the Tower Lorrimers?"

"Yes; she wants me in a hurry; I must fly to her."

"Stay a moment, my dear child," Susy absolutely rose from her chair in her strong interest. "If this girl is one of the Tower Lorrimers, I had better know her at once; you had better bring her to me and I'll question her."

"I can't bring her to you; she has had a fall and is lying on her back she can't walk."

"Dear me, what a nuisance; well, I'll go to her, then. Come along, Nancy. show me the way this minute."

"But really, really, Susy," began Nan, raising blue, imploring eyes. "Really, it is very sad about the Towers, you know."

"Sad; good heavens, are the drains wrong?"

"It's sad about the Lorrimers," continued Nan, stamping her foot and growing red with anger; "we love the Lorrimers; they are our dearest, our very, very dearest friends, and we hate their leaving the Towers. Perhaps Nora doesn't want to see you, Susy."

"Come along," said Susy in a firm voice; "I want to see her. What sentimental folly you talk, Nan. Squire Lorrimer was very glad indeed to find such a purchaser as my father for his tumbledown old place."

"The Towers tumbledown!" exclaimed Nan, "the beautiful, lovely, darling Towers! Susy, I hate you--I hate and detest you; I won't show you the way to Nora's room, so there!"

Nan pulled her frock out of Susy's detaining hand and rushed away.

Miss Drummond stood quite still for a moment where she had been left. Then she put up her hand to smooth her brow.

"This sort of thing would be ruffling to most people," she murmured, 'but I really don't mind. Now, shall I have my forty winks before tea, or shall I poke round by myself until I find this blessed aggrieved Nora? That horrid little piece of impertinence has quite woke me up, so it's scarcely worth while to get soothed down again; I think I'll find Nora and ask for some information which I am anxious to write to father about, then after tea I can have a snooze until it is time to dress for dinner. Dear, dear, they might have the politeness to have tea ready on one's arrival. I expect my stay here will be precious slow, with their old-fashioned, prim ideas; if it weren't for Tony I'd die, but she'd really make a cat laugh; it will be better than a play to watch her at dinner to-night with Sir John. Now, then, for a search for the tearful Nora."

Susy, accordingly, in her usual ponderous, somewhat heavy mode of progress, wandered from one room to another until at last the sound of voices guided her to the pretty little boudoir, where Annie Forest and Nora had taken shelter, and where Nan was now standing, pouring out her tale of woe. A slight creak which the door made caused the girls to turn their heads, and there stood Susy, shedding articles of her wardrobe, as usual, as she walked. Her flaxen hair was partly unpinned and lay in a rough coil on her fat neck. She came with elephantine weight into the room, and ignoring Annie Forest altogether, held out a hand to Nora.

"Here I am," she said. "I'm Susy Drummond. 'Miss Susan Drummond, the Towers,' will soon be on my visiting cards. Isn't the place very ramshackle? Doesn't it want to be put into repair a good bit? I'm just dying to hear all about it. Oh, and here's an American swinging-chair--I just adore them. You don't mind if I see-saw gently while you talk to me. Nan, I bear no malice; fetch me a footstool, love, and let me know when tea is brought into the drawing-room. Annie, how do? I hope the female dragon is very well." Annie flushed crimson. Only a startled look on Nora's pretty face enabled her to control herself. She walked to the window and looked out.

Susy blinked her sleepy eyes after her.

"Never mind," she said, winking at Nora, "it's an old feud which I buried--I'm the most forgiving creature in Christendom--but if she chooses to dig up the hatchet, I can't help her. I always called that detestable Mrs. Willis the she-dragon. You don't know her, I suppose? You're in luck, I can tell you. Thank you, Nan, for the footstool. Now, this is most comfortable. You'll begin to tell me all you can about the Towers, won't you?" she continued, bending slightly forward and laying her fat hand on Nora's slim white arm; "and so you really are a Lorrimer? How profoundly interesting."

Nora fidgeted restlessly on her sofa.

"I'm a Lorrimer," she said at last in a steady voice. "I--I don't think I can tell you about the Towers; you'll probably go and see the place for yourself, either to-morrow or Monday."

"I shall certainly go to-morrow, and at an early hour, too; my father is most anxious to get my opinion on it."

"Well, then, you'll see it for yourself."

"So I shall--quite true, little Miss Rosebud; but, nevertheless, there is such a thing as curiosity, which, doubtless, you can gratify. Now, let's begin. I'm nothing if I'm not practical. How many bedrooms are there?"

"I don't know."

"You don't know? Are you simple? Have not you lived there all your life?"

"I have, but I don't really know. Perhaps if I count I can tell you. First, in the Tower, there's Jane Macalister's room, and Boris sleeps near her, and then there's Kitty--she has a room to herself--it's rather small, but she's immensely proud of it, and there's Nell and--"

Susy suddenly clapped her hands to her ears.

"For goodness sake stop," she exclaimed. "What do I care for your Macalisters, and Boris's, and Kittys? I want to know how many bedrooms there are--ten, twelve, twenty, thirty? Can't you count?"

"Yes, perfectly," replied Nora with spirit; "but I never troubled myself to count the number of bedrooms at the Towers; you can do so for yourself when you go to see it to-morrow."

"Thanks for nothing. If I'm anything I'm practical, and I shall not only count the bedrooms to-morrow, but measure them also. I shall take a measuring tape with me, and my maid Linette and a foot measure."

"How pleasant for Linette to be sandwiched between a measuring tape and a foot measure," exclaimed Annie, turning round from her position at the window and speaking for the first time.

Susy favoured her with a slow glance of intense dislike. Slightly turning her back she proceeded with her catechism of Nora.

"At least you can say something about the drawing-rooms. How many feet long is the principal drawing-room?"

Before poor Nora could reply, the door of the room was slowly opened and Mrs. Willis, with her usual calm, strong face, entered.

Susy Drummond gave such a start of dismayed surprise that Annie forgave her a good many of her sins on the spot.

Mrs. Willis came up to her and held out her hand.

"How do you do?" she said. "Sir John Thornton told us this morning at breakfast that we might have the pleasure of meeting you here. Are you well?"

"Oh, yes, I'm--I'm quite well, ma'am," replied Susy, stammering out her words in hopeless confusion.

"Nora, dear, you are looking very tired," continued Mrs. Willis. "I propose to have tea with you here alone, and to read to you for a little afterwards. Annie, will you take Miss Drummond to the drawing-room? I saw the tea equipage being taken in as I passed."

Susy shambled out of the room in Annie's wake.

CHAPTER XXI.
HESTER SPEAKS HER MIND.

The next day was Sunday, and Susy, notwithstanding her strong inclinations, was forced to submit to Sir John Thornton's decree that she should not visit the Towers that day. Hester had sent a hurried note to Molly apprizing her of Susy's arrival, and begging of her, if she valued her peace of mind, not to come near the Grange on this dreadful Sunday.

It passed somehow. Poor Hester always, during the remainder of her life, looked back upon it as a day of hopeless worry and confusion of brain. Everyone seemed to be playing the game of cross-purposes with everyone else. Sir John kept on assuring himself that he was the happiest man in existence, while Mrs. Bernard Temple and Antonia evidently trod on his corns at each step he took. Susy, in her moments of wakefulness, was sly and watchful. Antonia was absolutely indifferent to everything but high art. Mrs. Bernard Temple was busy as busy could be making hay while the sun shone. She guessed shrewdly--perhaps her experiences with the late Mr. Bernard Temple helped her--that it was during the time of courtship when most of her wishes would be carried out. She insisted, therefore, on going carefully into the many alterations which she proposed to make in the Grange, and Sir John, notwithstanding his innate aversion to fuss of any kind, was forced to listen to her demands, and, as he was really attached to her, she soon got him to say yes to her different proposals.

Nan and Hester, Annie and Nora, kept as much together as possible. This was made easy for them by kind Mrs. Willis, who not only kept Susy in considerable awe, but contrived to interest Antonia by allowing her to talk art to her by the hour. Antonia used a jargon which Mrs. Willis did not in the least understand, but even Antonia was not proof against the gracious sympathy of this high-minded woman.

The girls had, therefore, plenty of time for self-pity. Annie was the very soul of sympathy, and it was a comfort to poor Nora and Hester to pour out their sorrows in her affectionate ears. As for Nan, she took refuge a good part of the time with Mrs. Martin, who shook her fists, when Nan was not looking, at the backs of Sir John and Mrs. Bernard Temple as they walked down one of the lawns side by side.

"She's his match!" murmured the old woman. "She'll give it to him; now he'll know what a selfish wife means! He have 'ad his turn of the other kind, and now he'll know what the selfish sort is. Serve him right, I say; serve him well right!"

At last the weary Sunday came to an end and on Monday, after breakfast, Susy announced her intention of going over to the Towers.

"I suppose I can have a carriage?" she said, turning to Sir John, who paused in his exit from the dining-room to give her his polite attention.

"I suppose I can have a carriage?" she repeated.

Annie interrupted--

"The Towers is scarcely a mile away across the fields," she said.

"I don't think I can walk a mile," replied Susy; "my muscles are awfully weak--I dare not strain them."

"You can have a carriage with pleasure," said Sir John. "I will order one to be round at whatever hour you wish to name."

"At once, please," said Susy; "there's a good deal to be done. I've to measure all the rooms for carpets and druggets."

"You surely won't cover the rooms with carpets?" exclaimed Antonia. "I never heard of anything so Philistine. Oak parquetry, with rugs that slip about, is the only thing admissible. Better bare boards than carpets--carpets are simply atrocious!"

When Antonia began to speak, Sir John was heard to slam the door behind him; he had had quite enough of this young lady.

An eager discussion followed his departure, and it was finally decided that Susy, Hester, and Antonia, accompanied by Annie Forest, should drive over to the Towers.

"My part in the expedition will be this," exclaimed Annie, taking Hester aside for a moment. "I'll collect every single Lorrimer child I can lay hold of and carry them away to the most remote part of the grounds I can find, to be out of the reach of that detestable Susy and the torture she means to inflict. I should recommend you, Hester, to come with us."

"I'd like to very much," replied Hester, with a faint smile; "but I think I must stay with Mrs. Lorrimer and Molly. I don't know that I shall be the least comfort to them, but somehow I can't desert them."

A few moments later the little party drove off, and in the course of half-an-hour they arrived at the Towers. There was a winding and rather steep beech avenue, leading up to the older part of the mansion. Owing to the sad state of Squire Lorrimer's finances, this avenue was by no means in a state of complete repair. Hester turned her fleet little ponies--for she was driving--into it. They were spirited, but always well-behaved; on this occasion, however, they started violently, for Antonia was heard to utter a piercing shriek of rapture.

"Oh, those briars," she exclaimed--"those heavenly, heavenly, artistic briars! Stop the carriage, I beg of you, Miss Thornton! I must cut some without a moment's delay!"

"We can't stop on the side of a hill, Antonia," said Susy. "The ponies are fretting already, and nothing would induce them to stand still. You don't want us to be killed, I suppose, for the sake of an odious briar?"

The only answer Antonia made was to press her bony right hand with unnecessary force on Susy's right arm and vault from the carriage.

"Go on," she said, waving her hand to Hester; "I'll follow you presently. You don't suppose I'm going to lose a chance of this kind! I have brought my colour-box with me, and I mean to make a study of those briars before I go another step."

Suiting her action to her words, Antonia had already seated herself on a steep bank and was unfastening her portfolio.

"What a show she'll be when she does arrive," exclaimed Susy. "She'll probably bring three or four enormous briars into the house with her; but we may be thankful to be rid of her for a little, for she is so painfully positive. I place the greatest faith, of course, in her opinions, for she really is a magnificently ugly artist, and ugly art is, of course, the only correct thing now; but I do think we might have the bedrooms comfortable, don't you, Hester? With my tendency to forty winks at odd moments, I think it is scarcely safe to have every room covered with oak parquetry and rugs that slip about. The doctor says I am very deficient in muscle, and if I fell I might break a bone rather badly--don't you think so, Hester?"

"Yes, I do!" said Hester. "I think you had better furnish the Towers exactly as you please, and not take any opinions from Antonia!"

They had reached the brow of the hill now, and Hester was resting her ponies for a moment.

"How fiercely you speak," said Susy in an aggrieved tone. "Aren't you really interested in me and my future? Coming to the Towers is a very important step for me. I shall be the mistress, and in a position of great distinction. Father says I must entertain, and I hate entertaining, for it rouses one up so dreadfully; but I do think that you, as an old schoolfellow, might take a little interest in me."

"Listen to me for a moment," said Hester; "I want to say something."

"Oh, how appallingly solemn you are! I wish I had a lollipop to stop your mouth with."

"You must listen," said Hester in a firm voice; "I'm not joking. Times come in all lives when one cannot joke. I did not love you as my schoolfellow, Susy, and, frankly, I do not love you now; but, when you come to the Towers, I'll do everything in my power to help you, not because I like to do this, but because it's right. I can help you in many ways, for you don't know anything of county society; and, coming after such an old and popular family as the Lorrimers, people will be very apt to cut you if you are not careful. My father and I know everyone in the place, and we can get them to be kind to you if--if you deserve it; but that depends altogether on how you treat the Lorrimers now."

"Bravo," burst from Annie, who was sitting in the back seat, but who overheard Hester's words.

"Don't interrupt me, Annie, please," said Hester.

"The Lorrimers are my dearest friends," continued Hester. "Molly Lorrimer, whom you have not yet seen, and Annie, here, are the two greatest girl friends I have in the world. It is a great, great sorrow to the Lorrimers to leave the home where they and their people have lived before them for hundreds of years, and until they leave the place you ought not to talk before them of the way you mean to furnish the Towers when you are in possession. You ought to regard their feelings; and if you wish to please me, and if you wish me to help you by-and-by, you will. Remember, you are not in possession yet. The Towers is not your place yet."

"Well, I never!" exclaimed Susy. "Why, you've turned into an orator;" but Hester's words had subdued her a good deal, for if she had one source of envy, it was the envy which *parvenus* like her give to the old county people, and if there was an ambition in her stagnant soul, it was to be considered a county person herself.

Accordingly, when the party entered one of the drawing-rooms of the Towers, and Molly, looking pale and anxious, came forward, and Mrs. Lorrimer received Susy with that gentle kindness which always characterised her, the young lady had not a word to say. She sank down on an ottoman in the centre of the room and gazed vacantly around her.

A whoop from Boris was heard outside. Annie rushed to the door to be greeted by him and the other children, and carried away in their midst.

Mrs. Lorrimer asked Susy if she would like to see over the house.

"Yes, please," replied Susy; "I have brought the tapes and measures."

She stopped, for Hester had given her a heavy frown.

"If its really inconvenient, I needn't do anything to-day," she said, sinking back into her seat.

Mrs. Lorrimer looked puzzled, and Molly opened her brown eyes very wide.

Just then there came an interruption, in the shape of two individuals who entered the drawing-room by separate doors. One of them was Jane Macalister, who carried a duster in her hand, and had a large smut on her forehead. The other was Antonia, whose hat had fallen off, and who trailed two enormous briars behind her.

The priestess of high art and the priestess of domestic economy, met almost in the centre of the room.

"Good gracious me," exclaimed Jane Macalister, "who in the world are you, my dear, and what, in the name of all that's orderly, are you bringing those abominable briars into the house for?"

"Abominable?" exclaimed Antonia; "these briars abominable? Oh, what crass ignorance one comes across in this benighted land. My name is Antonia Bernard Temple, and I am an art student. I claim nothing higher. I shall be an art student as long as I breathe."

"And my name is Jane Macalister," replied poor Jane, her whole face growing scarlet with vexation, "and I claim nothing higher than the love of order and decent neatness. Give me those briars, child, and don't lumber the room with such messes."

Before Antonia could utter a word of remonstrance, Jane had whipped her duster round the briars and had rushed out of the room with them.

For a moment Antonia felt inclined to pursue her; but as she was preparing to move, her large gaze was attracted by a couple of huge Chinese dragons which were reposing under one of the tables.

"Oh, you loves! you darlings! you adorables!" she shrieked. "Here, indeed, is a prize."

She made a rush to the objects of her worship, and kneeling down on the floor opposite to them, whipped out her sketching materials preparatory to work.

"Tony, you must at least allow me to introduce you to Mrs. Lorrimer before you begin to sketch," said Susy, who had perfectly recovered her own equanimity in the amusement which Antonia's conduct afforded her.

"Yes, yes, anything," muttered Antonia "Oh, these dragons are a prize; they are a prize. Yes, Susy, what is it you want?"

"Get up," said Susy, "and come and be introduced."

She pulled Antonia by her sleeve, who rose in a sort of dream and approached Mrs. Lorrimer, looking like a person in a trance.

"This is my friend, Antonia Bernard Temple," exclaimed Susy, addressing Mrs. Lorrimer.

"I am glad to see you, my dear," said Mrs. Lorrimer in her sweet voice; "and I am pleased to find that you appreciate the old china."

"The dragons? Superb; Ruskinesque," exclaimed Antonia. "You don't mind if I go back to them? I must seize the opportunity of transferring them to my note book. Oh, what a heavenly room this is! Old, disorderly, worn, dim with the hue of ages. An artist might grovel in this room--grovel with delight!"

"Well, go back and grovel over the dragons," exclaimed Susy, giving her friend a playful poke.

Antonia hurried to obey. Her work instantly absorbed her; she saw nothing else.

"Isn't she killing?" exclaimed Susy, addressing poor surprised Mrs. Lorrimer. "She's to be a sort of sister to Hester in the future; she's to live at the Grange. She's the daughter of Sir John Thornton's *fiancee*. Don't you love the word *fiancee?* I do. Did you know that at school we called Hetty Prunes and Prism? Fancy Prunes and Prism and the Priestess together. Its almost too killing."

Mrs. Lorrimer, gentle as she was, was also the soul of quiet dignity. She made no reply whatever to Susy's outburst with regard to Antonia, but gently led the conversation to matters of every-day interest.

"This is our largest drawing-room," she said, "but we have two others leading into it. The farthest drawing-room takes you into the dining-room, and that again into the library and morning-room. All our reception-rooms open one into the other. You will notice that they are built round the central hall, which is almost octagon in shape. I am sure you would like to see the house, and I do not at all object to showing it to you. Ah! here comes Jane Macalister. I'm sure she will have great pleasure in taking you round. Jane, dear, come here."

Jane came up at once. She still wore her smut, but the duster was gone.

"Jane, let me introduce you to Miss Drummond. Her father is the new owner of the Towers; Miss Drummond would like to see over the house, if it would not trouble you too much to show her round."

"Trouble me," exclaimed Jane; "*that* doesn't trouble me. Come, child, this way. I'll go in front and you can follow. This is the smaller drawing-room. It was here that Charles the Second passed a night in the year of grace--"

"Oh, for heaven's sake," exclaimed Susy, stopping her ears, "don't go into dates; the whole thing is confusing enough without dates."

Jane favoured her with a quick, contemptuous glance.

"I shan't dream of instructing you if you don't wish it, my dear," she said. "Those who like ignorance, in ignorance they shall remain, as far as Jane Macalister is concerned. Well, then, here's a room with three windows and four walls and a ceiling and a floor. The furniture won't belong to you, so you needn't look at it. Now come on. This room we also use as a drawing-room, but *you* needn't unless you like."

"Do stop, pray!" exclaimed Susy. "I can't rush through the place like this. You are not a Lorrimer, are you?"

"No, I'm a Macalister, of the clan of----"

"Oh, please, I don't want to hear about the clan. What I wanted to say was this, that I have got the tapes and measures in my pocket; Hester tells me I mustn't use them on account of paining the Lorrimers, but as you are not one, of course you won't mind. I see you have got carpets on all the floors."

"Yes, why not? Carpets are put on most floors--at least they used to be when I was young."

"But Antonia says that we ought to have parquetry and slippery rugs."

"And do you mean to tell me," exclaimed Jane, "that you are going to heed the words of that poor daft lassie? It's nothing to me what you do, of course, but that poor girl has not got her proper wits, and if I were you I would try to follow someone with a grain of sense."

Susy laughed heartily.

"Antonia is as right as anyone else," she said "only she has a passion for art."

"Preserve me from such a craze," exclaimed Jane. "How much longer are we to stand in the middle of this floor while we talk about tapes and measurements and that silly girl?"

"But may I measure?"

"You may do anything you please, provided you don't injure the furniture."

"And it won't hurt your feelings?"

"No, you couldn't touch 'em. I'll sit here and wait till you have done."

Jane flung herself on a hard chair as she spoke, and drawing a long stocking out of her pocket, began to knit furiously.

Susy, who had about as much idea of measuring a room as she had of turning the heel of a stocking took her tapes out of her pocket and began an impossible task.

Jane watched her in silence for a moment or two, but Susy's futile attempts were too much for this deft, managing creature.

"Why don't you foot it?" she exclaimed. "My word, I never saw such a way to set to work. Here, you want the length of the room. I'll do it for you. Take your pencil and paper and jot down what I say. You haven't got any? That's a nice way of doing business. Well, then, I hope you have a good memory. I always measure a yard as I walk. Now, then, you count. Here I begin--one, two, three--are you counting?"

"No," said Susy; "I'm greatly obliged, but you confuse me awfully. I won't do any more measuring to-day; I shouldn't sleep for a week if I had to keep all that in my head. Some men must come down from Liberty's or Morris's. Antonia prefers Morris, she says he's the most *chic*."

"I don't know what you mean by chick," said Jane Macalister, "unless you allude in some mysterious way to the fowls; but I am glad you've got sense enough not to undertake what Providence has given you no aptitude for. Now, do you or do you not want to see the rest of the house? To a person like you, it's just like any other house, only nothing like so modern and nothing like so comfortable. There's a ghost in the tower----"

"A ghost," shrieked Susy; "I tremble at ghosts, I'm in terror at them; I won't go near the tower."

"I don't want to drag you there against your will. It's my private opinion that the ghost is made up of rats, but be that as it may, there's an awful scrimmage in the old tower at night. Now, then, will you see it, or will you not?"

"I think I won't," said Susy. "The Towers seems to be, from what you say, much like any other place. I hope my father has not been induced to pay too much for it."

"Hoots! he has got a place that mere money couldn't purchase unless the Lorrimers had come to grief. Don't you talk of what you know nothing about, child. The Towers is the Towers, sacred with memory and beautiful----; do you know why the Towers is beautiful, Miss Susy Drummond?"

"No, I'm sure I don't," said Susy, staring in astonishment at Jane, who had stalked up to her now and was staring her full in the face.

"Well, then, perhaps I'd better tell you, if it is for the last time. The Towers is beautiful because for hundreds of years brave men have been born here and gentle noble women have lived here, and their influence has got somehow into the walls and into the furniture, and it pervades the rooms inside and out. It's bad to go against that kind of spirit and you and your father had better be careful when you come here, or you may rake up ghosts that you won't much care about. Now, if you'll have the goodness to go back to the others--you'll find them in the front drawing room. I'll return to my duties, which at the present moment consist of shelling peas and chucking raspberries. That's your way, Miss Susan Drummond, through that door, and if you're wise you'll remember my words."

CHAPTER XXII.
ANTONIA'S GIFT.

When Susan returned to the drawing room she saw no one there but Antonia, who, squatting on the floor, was absorbed heart and soul in copying her Chinese dragons. Susy was not in a humour to talk to Antonia, she therefore proceeded to go further afield. She was anxious to find Hester and Annie. The Towers, with its old-fashioned rooms and old-world furniture, had much disappointed her. It needs the sort of education which nothing could ever give to Susy Drummond, to appreciate a place like the Towers. Hester and Jane Macalister had also between them contrived to depress her, and it was a subdued and rather crestfallen Susy who now crossed the magnificent octagon hall in pursuit of the rest of her party.

Antonia meanwhile worked at her dragons with a will. If Susy were out of her element, Antonia was absolutely steeped in hers. The faded furniture, the subdued light, the rich colour of the magnificent china filled her really artistic nature with a sense of rejoicing. Behind all her affectations, Antonia had a soul. It had never been awakened yet. All her life hitherto poor Antonia had spent her time with the most empty-headed and frivolous people. Only art seemed great and glorious and satisfying. She loved it sincerely, and for itself alone; she had no ambitions with regard to it, ambition was not a part of her queer nature; she would all her life be a humble votary at a lofty shrine. She did not imagine that there could be anything greater than art in the whole world. As yet her soul had not been really aroused, but the time of awakening was near.

Having made a rough, and, in truth, a very distorted sketch of the dragons, she gathered up her colours and portfolio, and prepared to search farther afield for objects on which to expend her genius. She followed Susy into the octagon hall, but, seeing the wide front doors open, went out, and, crossing a by no means well-kept field, entered the paddock, where the colts, Joe and Robin, had disported themselves before their sale. The paddock was skirted by a copse of small fir-trees, and Antonia sniffed the air as she walked towards it. Antonia was in a rusty black dress, with very little material in the skirt, and an extremely long train, which she never held up. She had just got to the edge of the copse of young trees, and was preparing to make a sketch of their straight trunks with the delicate sunlight shining across them, when a strange noise attracted her attention. She dropped her colour box, uttered one of her affected little shrieks, and then dropped on her knees beside a child who was lying face downwards on the grass. The child's dark hair completely covered her face, but the sobs which shook her slender little frame were too violent to be inaudible. Whatever ailed the child, she was prostrated by such a tempest of grief that Antonia forgot high art in an honest wish to comfort human misery.

"Who are you?" she asked. "Can I do anything for you? What can be the matter with you? Have you lost your colour box?"

Antonia could understand grief at such a loss, hence her inquiry.

Nell turned a little when she was spoken to; dabbed her pocket-handkerchief into each eye, and then looked up at Antonia.

"I wish you'd go away," she said. "I don't want you. I have come away here to hide. I wish, I wish you'd go away!"

"I don't wish to trouble you in any way," replied Antonia, "but I can't go away, for I've come here to sketch. Your sobs don't disturb me now that I know there's nothing very serious the matter, so perhaps my presence won't disturb you. I'll sit here and not take the least notice of you. I must imprison that sunshine before it goes. You can sob away, I won't listen."

But to be told that you can sob as long as you like has generally the effect of stopping tears, and Nell, astonished at Antonia's appearance and words, presently sat up on the grass, and, flinging back her heavy mane of hair, watched the priestess of art with great interest. How could Antonia imprison a sunbeam? It sounded interesting! Nell blinked her eyes and looked at her solemnly.

"Well, child," said Antonia, pausing in her work, and giving her one of her slow glances, "I'm glad you're better; I never heard such distressing sobs. It's a great pity for you to cry so much, for you disfigure yourself; but I wish now that you are here you'd sit still, for I'd like to sketch you with that woebegone look. I never saw such a perfect ideal of true artistic beauty before."

"Beauty?" said Nell, with a little laugh. "But I'm called 'the ugly duckling'!"

"Charming!" exclaimed Antonia. "I'll immortalise this 'ugly duckling.' She shall be the foreground for these pine trees, and the imprisoned sunbeams can light her up from behind."

Notwithstanding her sorrow, Nell found it intensely interesting to be made the foreground of a picture. She wondered how the imprisoned sunbeams would like their office of always shining round her head. Nell was by no means vain. She honestly believed herself to be a hideous little girl, but it was refreshing once, as a change, to be spoken of as a true artistic beauty. She thought that she would learn the phrase, and repeat it over when she looked at herself in the glass, or when Kitty and Harry became more than usually aggravating about her personal appearance.

Meanwhile, the artist dashed in her colours with fiery speed. Nell sat perfectly still, and gazed straight at Antonia. Suddenly a flood of colour spread itself all over her face. Was Antonia the new owner of the Towers? If so, *she* was the cause of poor Nell's heart-broken sobs.

The younger members of the Lorrimer household had solemnly vowed an undying feud against the new owner of the Towers. They had established this feud with the solemnity of a sacred rite. They had made a bonfire and stood round it in a circle and joined hands, and declared the following awful formula:--

"Neither I, nor my children, nor my grandchildren, nor any of my descendants, will ever speak a friendly word to the new owner of my ancestral home. I wish the ghost of my ancestor, Hugh Lorrimer, who died in the Wars of the Roses, to haunt the new owner and his family; and I solemnly declare that I never will have part or lot with him or his."

This jargon had been made up by Harry, but each member of the feud, as they termed themselves, had solemnly repeated it, even down to little two-year-old Philip.

Suppose this wonderful, queer lady, who was making a sketch of Nell, was the new owner. In that case, it was Nell's duty to leave her at once.

"I want to ask you a question," said Nell.

"Yes--don't stir, please--ask me anything you like."

"Are you the new owner of my home?"

"I the new owner?" exclaimed Antonia. "Heavens! no! I own nothing except this"--she clasped her colour-box and looked up with a face of ecstacy. "I only want this," she said, "*and this*," she continued, waving her hand with an impressive sweep which was meant to include both earth and sky.

She claimed a good deal, Nell thought; but, after all, that did not matter, as she had nothing to do with the feud.

"I'm glad you are not the owner," said Nell, "for, if you were, I should have been obliged to leave you."

"Why so?"

"I and the others have sworn it solemnly round a bonfire."

The words were so unusual that Antonia was greatly amused.

"You don't like to leave the Towers, then?" she said.

"Like it?" replied Nell. "Would you, if you had lived here ever since the tenth century?"

"Mercy, child! how venerable I'd be!" exclaimed Antonia. She smiled in quite a tragic way--it was quite a new thing to see a smile on Antonia's face.

Nell looked at her very gravely. Her own sweet grey eyes grew full of tears.

"It will kill father," she said suddenly, in a smothered voice.

She swayed herself backwards and forwards as she spoke, in an ecstasy of pain. Strange to say, she seemed to understand Antonia, and, still stranger, Antonia understood her.

The priestess of art dropped her palette.

"Tell me about your father," she said, quickly; "tell me about yourself. You and your people have lived here for years--centuries--and it breaks your hearts to go? It's wonderfully artistic--it savours of mediaeval romance. And you go for a creature like Susan Drummond--shallow as a plate--no soul anywhere about her? She gets your rooms replete with memories, and your dear briary avenues and your fir trees, and this uncultured waste?"

"It's a paddock," interrupted Nell, who could not quite follow Antonia's imagery.

"It's a waste," said Miss Bernard Temple, with fire. "The Towers is untrammelled by man's vulgar restraint. Child, I do not even know your name, but I think

I understand your grief."

"You cannot," said Nell, with gentle dignity--"you are not a Lorrimer. But I'm glad I didn't vow to hate you round the bonfire. Now I'm afraid I must go."

"One minute first," said Antonia. "Did you say that leaving this place would kill your father?"

"I'm afraid it will," said Nell. "He won't come home--mother can't get him to come back. He came the night he had sold the Towers, and Boris and I saw him; but I don't think he'll ever come back again. I think his heart is broken. But I cannot speak of it any longer, please--it hurts me so dreadfully here."

Nell had risen from the grass--she stood tall and thin and pale by Antonia's side. When she uttered the last words, she pressed her hand against her heart.

"Good-bye," she said solemnly. "Jane Macalister said I was to be in at twelve o'clock to help her with some darning. Good-bye."

Antonia held out one of her very long, very bony hands. She slipped it round Nell's waist, and drawing her close, kissed her gently between her eyebrows, then she let her go.

Nell left the paddock; but Antonia did not attempt to finish her interrupted sketch. She sat on, lost in a world of musing. At last she uttered some emphatic words aloud.

"I'm not much use," she said to herself; "nobody cares about me, and I care for no one. I love art with a divine passion; but art does not need such a poor, feeble disciple. Art can still exist and be glorious without Antonia. I am ugly I know, and I have no genius; but I have got one power--I can get my own way. All my life long, through a queer kind of persistence which is in me, I have got my way. I do not get it because people love me, for I don't honestly think a soul in the wide world loves me, but I get it because--because of something which I don't myself understand. It's a power I've got; it's my one gift. Did mother want me to study art in Paris? No; still I went. Did mother wish me to become grotesque, and to wear a dress like this? No; still I wear it. Did mother intend me to come with her on Saturday to the Grange? No, a thousand times no; still I came. I can twist mother round this finger. She appeals to me; I counsel her; she asks my advice; she is obliged to take it whether she likes or not. Mother is completely under my thumb. So it was with the professor who taught me; so it was with the students who worked with me; so it will be in the future with Hester, if I still wish it; and with Sir John Thornton, if I ordain it. They think very little of Antonia now; but wait until they feel my power; wait until I choose to direct them, and--hey, presto--they walk in my paths, not their own. Now I have made up my mind on one point. I have not the faintest idea how it is to be managed; but managed it shall be. Susan Drummond and her father are not to desecrate the Towers with their commonplaceness, their shallowness, and vulgarity. The Lorrimers are still to live here; and Nell's heart is not to be broken. For the sake of the ugly duckling I do this. How, I know not; but I turn all the power that is in me in that one direction from this hour forward.

"Poor, ugly duckling with the pathetic eyes. I do believe Antonia loves you."

CHAPTER XXIII.
TRUTH AND FIDELITY.

Hester and her party returned to the Grange in time for lunch. All the way back Antonia was silent. They drove home by another road; they passed a bog of extreme desolation, and some larger and wilder briars than ever; they skirted a melancholy common, but Antonia never made an observation; her whole gaze was turned inward; she was looking so intently at the picture of a sorrowful child, that she was blind to everything else. Susy was decidedly in a bad temper; Hester's brave heart was full of aches, doubts, and fears; and Annie was again going back to that unsolved problem of how she was to get back the ring for Mrs. Willis.

The return party was, therefore, a dull one; although no one noticed the other's dulness, each being so occupied with her own thoughts.

Mrs. Willis was to leave the Grange immediately after lunch, and Hester and Annie were to accompany her to Nortonbury in the landau.

Just as the carriage drove up to the house, Mrs. Willis remembered the ring and spoke to Annie.

"My dear," she said with a smile, "I am leaving the house without my ring. It is too late now to send it to Paris to be copied; but as I see you never wear it, I may as well take it back with me to Lavender House. You know, my love, how much I value that ring. I feel quite lonely without it."

Annie's pretty face turned pink.

"But I should like to wear it before I go back to school," she said, "and you promised that I might have it during the holidays."

"So I did; well, I will say nothing more. Be sure you take good care of it and give it back to me on the day of your return to Lavender House."

Annie promised with a light heart. The holidays were to last for another week, and what might not happen in a week? She laughed quite gaily, and springing lightly into the carriage, seated herself by Hester's side. As she did so, her eyes encountered the grave dark ones of Antonia fixed fully upon her. There was a curious expression round Antonia's mouth which puzzled Annie and gave her a momentary sense of discomfort.

The drive, however, through the pleasant summer air revived her spirits, and on the way home she had so much to talk over with Hester that she naturally forgot the ring and her anxieties with regard to it.

When the girls returned to the Grange they found the whole party out of doors enjoying afternoon tea on one of the lawns. Susy was swinging backwards and forwards in a large American chair. Nora was lying on a low couch slowly fanning herself. Mrs. Bernard Temple, looking very handsome and stately, was pouring out tea for the rest of the party and looking down at Sir John, who was lounging on the grass. Antonia was sitting with her back straight up against an oak tree her eyes were half shut, and a very full cup of tea was on her lap--the tea was in extreme danger of being spilt, but Antonia cared nothing for any of these things.

As soon as ever Annie and Hester appeared in view Miss Bernard Temple sprang suddenly to her feet. Of course the cup of tea came to instant grief. Sir John uttered an exclamation of decided annoyance; Nora exclaimed, "Oh, Miss Bernard Temple, what a mess you have made of your dress!" and Susy roused herself sufficiently to shake a playful finger at Antonia.

"Oh, Tony, Tony, how killing you are," she said; Mrs. Bernard Temple looked aggrieved but said nothing, she knew Antonia too well.

"How am I killing?" exclaimed Antonia; "this will shake off: that is the good of a shabby black dress--it stands anything. Miss Forest, I particularly want to speak to you; I am glad you have come home."

She went straight up to Annie and tucked one bony hand through her arm. "Come," she said, "let us retire somewhere--I am anxious to talk to you."

"But I want my tea first," said Annie. "I am really very thirsty."

"How material," exclaimed Antonia; "well, I'll wait--be quick."

She marched a step or two away, and leant against the wide trunk of the oak tree.

Annie felt provoked. Antonia's queer glance returned uncomfortably to her memory.

She took her tea, therefore, in greater haste than usual and then, going up to Miss Bernard Temple, told her she was ready to listen to anything she had to say.

"Come, then," said Antonia; "we must have solitude. Where is the most solitary spot?"

"We can walk up this rise," said Annie--"here, where the path is. There is a summer-house at the top of this hill, where we can sit. But I cannot imagine what you have to say to me."

"It's simple enough," said Antonia; "I wish just to inform you that I know something."

"I expect you do," said Annie, with a light laugh; "several things, most probably."

"Something about you," pursued Antonia, in a firm, hard voice.

"Indeed? How interesting!" Annie's tone was not quite so comfortable now.

"I'll tell you what it is," continued Antonia, standing still, facing round and turning her melancholy gaze full on Annie: "you have not got the ring."

"What ring? What do you mean?"

"The ring Mrs. Willis asked you to return to her. You did not return it, because you had not got it You would have returned it if you had it--you are not the girl to care enough about rings just to keep it for the sake of wearing it. I know what has happened--you have sold or pawned the ring."

"How can you know?" exclaimed Annie, in a voice almost of fear; "how is it possible for you to tell? You don't know anything whatever about me--how can you tell?"

"Intuition," replied Antonia, in a light voice. "I can see farther than most people when I choose to see. Intuition and experience. Do you imagine that I, in my chequered career, have never had to part with a jewel. Once, when in Paris, I sold my hair. I had no money to buy canvas and colours, so I went to a barber, and he cut it quite short and gave me a napoleon for it. Ah! that nap, that darling nap, how I loved it!"

"You are a very queer girl," said Annie.

"That's neither here nor there," replied Antonia. "I didn't take you away from the others to speak of myself. I have watched you since I came here, and I can see that you are a very bright, clever girl; also, that you are pretty, according to modern ideas. You are not true art, by any means; but what of that? I know that you are in trouble about that ring, so you may as well confide in me."

"But will you tell?" asked Annie.

"Tell!" said Antonia, with scorn. "I don't ask for confidences to repeat them again--that is not Antonia Bernard Temple. Art is my mistress--art exacts both truth and fidelity from her disciples. You need not fear that I will tell."

"You are a queer girl," replied Annie. "I'm sure you will not tell. Yes, I am in trouble about the ring, and I don't mind confiding the trouble to you."

"Sit down here, then, on the bank," said Antonia, flinging herself on the grass as she spoke, "and state the case as briefly as possible. Where and when did you pawn the ring?"

"Oh, I didn't pawn it--it wasn't done by me; and, as things have turned out, it wasn't really pawned at all. This is the story."

Annie told it in a few forcible words; Antonia listened attentively, taking in all the facts.

"And thirty-two shillings would get you out of this scrape?" she said, in conclusion, looking fixedly at Annie.

"Oh, yes, indeed. If I had thirty-two shillings, I would pay Mrs. Martin and get the ring back, and when I return to Lavender House I would tell everything to Mrs. Willis. I would tell her what I have done, and how badly I have acted. At present there is a cloud between us; and she is my best, my kindest, my most valued friend. What I cannot bear to do--what I cannot stand--is to have to tell her that I pawned what was not my own, and at the same time not to be able to give her back the ring."

"I partly understand," said Antonia in a slow voice; "I partly grasp your meaning. The pawning of the jewel is to me a mere nothing. I have had chequered times when the tea-pot and even the coffee-pot have been sold for the sake of a quarter of a cake of cobalt or of rose-madder, but then the tea-pot and the coffee-pot and the hair which grew on my head were undoubtedly my own. I cannot understand your taking another's property, nor your being deceitful about it. The paths of deceit are shut doors to me, naturally, who am a disciple of the great and divine Art. I mention this as an incident, but whether I understand you or not scarcely affects the case.

I am willing to help you if you will help me. I can manage to get you thirty-two shillings, perhaps not to-day and perhaps not to-morrow, but certainly before you return to your school."

"Oh, you are good!" exclaimed Annie, whose pretty cheeks were like peonies, for Antonia had managed to make her feel terribly small and contemptible.

"No, I am not good," replied Miss Bernard Temple, "and I am not doing this in any sense for you. I do it because I wish to be in your confidence, as I think you can be a useful ally. I have a delicate mission before me, and I see that you may be very useful."

"A mission?" said Annie, looking up in surprise.

"Yes; there is a great deal at stake, but I believe that, difficult as the undertaking is, I may be permitted to succeed. I want to wrest the Towers from the hand of the Philistines."

"What *do* you mean?" exclaimed Annie.

"In other words," continued Miss Bernard Temple, "I want to keep the Lorrimers in the home of their ancestors and to make those shallow Drummonds stay in their own place."

"I suppose we all want that," said Annie; "but how can you possibly do it? You have no power."

"So you think, but you are mistaken; I have a great deal of power. Now, will you help me?"

"To do this? Yes. With all my heart and soul."

"That is good. I don't wish to say anything to Hester Thornton nor to Nora Lorrimer, nor to any of the Lorrimers, nor least of all to Susan Drummond. I think I can manage Susy, for I am up to some of her pretty little vagaries. I can also manage mother, and mother has a good deal of influence in a certain quarter just now. You are a sort of outsider, and yet you are very friendly with everybody, so you can render me very important help; but, of course, you clearly understand that fidelity is my motto, and you know also that your mission will be one of extreme delicacy."

"I have plenty of tact," said Annie. "I most faithfully promise to reveal nothing, and I will do everything in my power for you. I begin to believe in you. I think you are a wonderful girl."

"Don't say that," said Antonia, with solemn impressiveness; "if there is one thing more than another that gives me intense pain, it is praise. I am but the meanest disciple of great Art. I am doing this in the cause of Art. Now, I am not going to tell you what my plan of campaign is, at least, not to-day, but I want you to make certain inquiries for me. I want you to try and discover all you can from Hester with regard to her father's wealth, and all you can from Molly with regard to the Lorrimers' difficulties; and you are somehow or other to get the address in London where Squire Lorrimer is now staying. Have all this information ready for me by to-morrow morning. Now you can return to the others; I am going back to the house."

CHAPTER XXIV.
A WET SPONGE.

Antonia walked slowly in the direction of the house, trailing her long skirt behind her. She entered by a side door, and went straight up to her own room. The bedroom set apart for Miss Bernard Temple opened into the large and stately bedroom occupied by the future mistress of the Grange. Both rooms were dainty and fresh in the extreme. Mrs. Bernard Temple's maid was now sitting in Antonia's room mending a long rent in that young lady's brown Liberty velveteen evening dress.

"You have made an awfully jagged rent, Miss Antonia," said the girl.

"Have I?" said Antonia; "why mend it, then? I never expect to have my clothes mended. Of course, if you are good enough to occupy your time over me, Pinkerton, I am much obliged to you, but I don't expect your services, so clearly understand the position."

"Lor'!" answered Pinkerton, who had a round, country face and a somewhat brusque manner, "what a show you'd be, Miss Antonia, if someone didn't make you and mend you."

Antonia went over to the open window, and, flopping herself down on her knees, leant her two elbows on the window-sill and looked out.

"I wish you'd let me know if Miss Drummond is having forty winks in her room," she said suddenly. "She generally does go to her own room about this hour, does she not?"

"I believe so, miss. I'll inquire if she's there now."

Pinkerton soon returned with the information that Miss Drummond's door was locked, that she could not see her maid anywhere, but that she heard sounds proceeding from within the room which led her to infer that the forty winks were being enjoyed.

"But there's no use in your going to her, Miss Antonia," said Pinkerton, "for she won't hear you however hard you knock."

"I'll see about that," said Antonia. "Do you happen to know, Pinkerton, if Miss Drummond's window is open?"

"Sure to be, miss; every window in the house is kept open during this sultry weather."

"There's no time to be lost," murmured Antonia; "I must scale the wall."

She left her own bedroom in a hurry, and ran downstairs.

"Nan," she shouted, catching sight of Nan's white frock in the distance, "come here."

Nan ran up to her rather unwillingly. Antonia was detestable in her eyes as belonging to the dreadful new stepmother.

"Why do you frown at me like that, child?" said Antonia; "it isn't pretty."

"Tell-tale tit," answered Nan rudely; "you'll be making up stories of me in the future, won't you?"

"I?" said Antonia, with a careless rise of her brows. "No; I shan't have time. Now, can you tell me if there's a ladder about?"

"No, I can't," answered Nan.

"Are there no ladders to be found in this benighted and over-cultivated region?"

"Plenty; but I can't tell you where they are."

Antonia knitted her brows. Nan gazed at her curiously. It was really interesting to have something to do with a person who wanted a ladder. What was she going to do with it?

"I must climb without," said Antonia. "I wonder are there creepers."

"What do you want with it?" said Nan in quite a friendly tone.

"I want to get into Susan Drummond's room by her window."

"Oh, dear, what fun!" Nan's eyes danced.

"She is sound asleep," pursued Antonia, "and I propose to use the wet sponge with effect."

"They did that at school," replied Nan. "How lovely! Oh, how perfectly lovely! I'm sure I can help you to find a ladder. Come round with me to the farmyard."

Nan held out her hand, which Antonia grasped. They rushed across the lawn helter-skelter, and in an incredibly short space of time a ladder was leaning up against Susy's window. Nan held it from below while Antonia climbed. The next moment she had entered the room.

"Thank you heartily, Nan," she called to the little girl.

She made a good deal of noise, but Susy, lying on her back in the centre of the big bed, was impervious to sound. Antonia filled the sponge with cold water, and, standing at the foot of the bed, dashed it at Susy. The first application only made the sleeper groan and snore heavily, but at the second she opened her eyes, and at the third she sat up.

"Now, what is the matter?" she exclaimed. "Am I back at that detestable school with the she-dragon once more? Oh, Antonia, what in the world are you doing here?"

"Sponging you," said Antonia. "I have something to say, so wake up."

"Wake up?" replied Susy. "I should think I am awake. Who could stand such barbarous treatment? I was so comfortable, and I had locked the door to make all things perfectly safe. How in the world did you get into the room?"

"By a ladder, through the open window. Now pray don't waste any more time over trivial details. I have come here to have a serious talk with you."

"Why serious, Tony? You know how I hate grave subjects."

"I have come to have a quiet talk with you about the Towers; you can sit there, just where you are. Don't dry your hair, or you'll get sleepy again. I'll keep a basin of cold water near me and sponge you whenever you wink an eyelid. Now then, what do you think of the Towers?"

"I have scarcely seen it yet."

"You must have a first impression; what is it?"

"Really, Tony, you needn't have awakened me and gone to the trouble of a ladder, and an open window, and a sponge, for the sake of hearing my first impressions."

"That's neither here nor there," answered Antonia. "What do you think of the Towers?"

"Oh, it's well enough; it seems to be a very old place."

"Didn't it strike you that the rooms were musty?"

"Well, yes; now that you mention it, I thought they were decidedly musty."

"It will be impossible," said Antonia, "for you to turn the Towers into a proper Moresque or Libertyesque house."

"I thought you liked the place; you seemed so delighted with the briars."

"The briars are well enough, and so is the china; it's the rooms I complain of; they never can be reduced to high art--your sort of high art, I mean, Susy But now, tell me, did you do much measuring?"

"No, I didn't; a dreadful woman came with me; she quite frightened me, and spoke a lot about the Lorrimers, and a ghost in the tower."

"Well, of course there'd be a ghost in the tower," continued Antonia; "an old place like that couldn't exist without its ghost."

"I don't believe a bit in ghosts," said Susy. "No sensible people believe in them; there are no such things. You know that, of course, Antonia."

Susy looked uncomfortable while she spoke, and Antonia knew well that she was an arrant coward.

"You don't believe in ghosts either," continued Susy; "do you now, Tony?"

"Oh, but I do," answered Antonia; "I believe in them profoundly. I have Shakespeare for my authority on the subject."

"And you really think that--that the Towers is haunted?"

"No doubt whatever on the subject. If you don't want to be convinced against your will, you must choose a bedroom in the most modern part of the house, and avoid the old tower, with its funny, quaint little rooms. Frankly, I am disappointed in the Towers as a place for *you*--the rooms are not your sort--you want great, lofty, bright, modern rooms. I don't like that musty smell either; it points to damp somewhere. Then, it is scarcely likely that the water supply is perfect; those old wells are full of danger, and you once had typhoid, don't you remember? Your father will have to spend a lot on the place before he makes it anything like what your sort of high art requires; and when all is said and done, you'd be lonely there. You know I'm perfectly frank; you know that well, don't you?"

"Yes, Tony," answered poor Susy in a most melancholy voice. "Oh, please don't throw any more sponges at me; I am quite shivering, and your words make me feel so melancholy. But why should I be lonely at the Towers; there are plenty of neighbours all around?"

"That is true, but I don't believe you'll care for them, nor they for you: they are the Lorrimer sort, and the Miss Macalister sort, and the Hester Thornton sort. You know you don't care for those sorts of people, do you?"

"I'm sure I don't. I hate them. I wish father hadn't bought the Towers without consulting me."

"Can't he back out of it?"

"Back out of his bargain? What do you mean?"

"I mean what I say; can't he get out of it? The Towers isn't a bit the sort of place for you; it isn't even healthy for a girl like you. There's a ghost there, and ground damp, and bad water, and the neighbours aren't sociable, and you'll be moped to death."

"How perfectly miserable you make me, Tony, but I won't be quite friendless, for you'll be here most of the time now, won't you?"

"Not I; I am going back to my atelier in Paris. Do you think I'd live in a poky corner of the world like this?"

"What shall I do?" echoed Susy. "I think you're very unkind to make me so wretched and to depress me in the way you are doing. The Towers is bought now, and we must make the best of it."

"I only hope you won't suffer the consequences of this piece of folly," retorted Antonia with spirit. "The Towers is not the place for you, and you ought to persuade your father to get out of that bargain. Let him take a nice cheerful villa at Richmond; that's where you ought to live."

"I wish he would," said Susy; "but it's a great deal too late, a great deal too late to draw back now. Besides, we did so want to be county people."

"You'll never be county people, whatever that jargon means--that is, you'll never be like the Lorrimers and the Thorntons. You don't want to be, do you?"

"Good gracious, no; they are a depressing set."

"Then that's what county people are, so why should you kill yourself to be one of them? Aren't you going to write to your father to tell him what you think of the Towers?"

"Shall I?"

"I would if I were you. You might suggest----"

"Yes; do you think it would be any use?"

"There is no saying--it's your own affair. If you choose to die of *ennui*, don't tell me that I haven't warned you. Now I see you are wide awake, so you may dry your hair and get up."

"Oh, dear, oh, dear," sighed Susy after Antonia had swung herself out of the room, "I'm chilled to the bone and every scrap of spirit taken out of me. I hate that awful Towers--*why* did father buy it?"

One of Antonia's great ideas was on all occasions to strike while the iron is hot. It was her plan to leap over obstacles or to push them vigorously aside. She had no respect for people's corns. Their preconceived prejudices were nothing to her. Having succeeded in disturbing Susy, she now went straight to her mother's room. Mrs. Bernard Temple was seated in an easy chair by the open window, enjoying a quiet ten minutes for thought and rest before It was time for her to dress for dinner. Pinkerton was moving about putting the different accessories for her mistress's toilet in order. Antonia pushed her almost rudely aside as she swept across the room.

"Go away, Pinkerton," she said, "I want to speak to mother by herself."

"Oh, really, not at present, Antonia," said Mrs. Bernard Temple, with a look of alarm spreading over her high-class features. "I have gone through a great deal to-day and am quite tired, and I shall have to begin to dress for dinner in a few minutes. Sir John is very particular about my appearance, and I wish Pinkerton to try the effect of arranging my hair in a new manner. I thought, Pinkerton, that you might pile it up high on a sort of cushion--it has a very old-picture effect."

"You ought to wear a cap," said Antonia, standing in front of her parent; "it would be much more suitable and appropriate, and would save you a lot of trouble."

"A cap!" almost screamed Mrs. Bernard Temple. "To hear you speak, Antonia, one would think that I was advanced in years."

"As it's only I who think that, it doesn't matter, mother," said Antonia. "You shall wear your hair any way you please, only I really must have a little talk with you first. The sooner I begin my talk the sooner it will be over, so please go away at once, Pinkerton."

Pinkerton knew Antonia too well to dream of disobeying her. She left the room, slamming the door behind her, and Mrs. Bernard Temple looked up at her resolute daughter with a frown between her brows.

"Now, out with it, whatever it is," she said. "You have got something at the back of your head, and you can say it in ten words as well as twenty. What do you want me to do?"

"You have great influence with Sir John Thornton, haven't you, mother?" asked Antonia, kneeling down as she spoke by the open window, and leaning one pointed elbow on the sill. Mrs. Bernard Temple permitted herself to smile agreeably.

"A man's *fiancee* has generally influence over him," she said in a sentimental voice.

"That's what I thought," said Antonia. "I'll never be anybody's *fiancee*--the mere thought would make me ill--but that's neither here nor there. Granted that you have influence over Sir John, I want you to use it in my way--now, do you understand?"

"Really, Antonia, really,"--Mrs. Bernard Temple looked quite alarmed--"Sir John cannot bear erratic people, he tells me so from morning to night. I am afraid you have managed to displease him very seriously, my dear. When you spilt your tea in the garden this evening, he acknowledged, when I pressed him on the subject, that it gave him quite a sense of nausea. You see, Antonia, how careful you ought to be. The comforts of the home I have provided for you may be jeopardised if you are too erratic. You know I did not wish you to come to the Grange until after my wedding. The fact is, Sir John is very much annoyed about you. He has spoken to me most seriously on the subject of your extraordinary manners, and has asked me why I permit you to do the things you do. When I tell him that I have not the smallest scrap of influence over you, he simply does not believe me; and then he has such an aggravating way of drawing comparisons between you and that icy-mannered girl, Hester."

"Oh, I'm not a patch upon Hester," said Antonia; "she is a very nice, well-bred, English young lady. I'm Bohemian of the Bohemians. I'm nobody--nobody at all. I extinguish myself at the shrine of great Art. I love to extinguish myself. I adore being a shadow."

"I think, Antonia, you are quite mad."

"Think it away, my dearest mother, only grant my request; influence Sir John in my way."

"Oh, you terrible, terrible child! Well, what do you want me to do?"

"Now you're becoming reasonable," said Antonia, "and I really won't keep you from your hair a moment longer than I can help. I went to the Towers this morning, mother; it's really a heavenly old place; quite steeped in the best sort of mediaeval art. In the house, old china and low ceilings; out of doors, nature untrammelled. Think of a place like the Towers in the possession of Susy Drummond and her father, the ex-coal-merchant. Mother, it is not to be."

"My dear Antonia, I can't listen to you another moment." Mrs. Bernard Temple rose as she spoke. "Pinkerton, come at once," she called.

Pinkerton turned the handle of the door.

"Go away, Pinkerton!" shouted Antonia. "Now, mother, sit down; there's oceans of time."

"Really, really, my dear! Oh, what a trial one's children sometimes are. The Drummonds have bought the Towers. The whole thing is an accomplished fact."

"It is not too late," pursued Antonia. "I have been giving a spice of my mind to Susy, and she hates and detests the place, and will do what she can to get her father to back out of his bargain. Well, the Lorrimers are almost dying at the thought of going. The ugly duckling told me the whole story to-day, and I never listened to anything more piteous; and Squire Lorrimer is hiding in London because of his poor feelings. In short, the moment for strong measures has arrived; and if you won't speak to Sir John, I will."

Mrs. Bernard Temple turned white. "If *you* speak to him, Antonia," she said, "he will break off the match, and we shall be ruined--ruined."

"Very well, mother; you must have a conversation with him. One or other of us must have it, that is certain."

"Oh, you most terrible child! What am I to say to him?"

"Say this, and say it firmly. Say that you won't marry him unless he goes to see Squire Lorrimer, and makes an arrangement to lend him sufficient money to stay on at the Towers. The Drummonds will be delighted to get out of their bargain, and the Lorrimers will be saved. That's the plan of campaign. Either I undertake to see it through, mother, or you do. Now, which is it to be?"

"You must give me until to-morrow morning to think over your wild words. Really, my poor head is splitting."

Antonia went up and kissed her mother.

"You can come now, Pinkerton," she called out.

CHAPTER XXV.
MOLLY'S SORROW.

Hester was a good deal astonished that same day, when, just before dinner, Annie Forest came up to her with a request.

"I don't want to dine here to-night," she said. "I want to go to the Towers to have a good long talk with Molly."

"But, really, Annie," replied Hester, "is it necessary for you to go to-night? I did not know--I mean I did not think that--that you and Molly----"

"That we were special friends?" interrupted Annie. "Oh, yes, we are quite friendly enough for the little talk I mean to have. You'll spare me, won't you, Hetty, and if Molly offers me a bed, I'll sleep there and be back quite early in the morning."

"I can't refuse you, of course," said Hester, "but that won't prevent my missing you. It will be rather a dreadful dinner party, with only Mrs. Bernard Temple and Antonia and that dreadful, sleepy Susy. You are so full of tact and so bright, Annie, that you generally make matters go off fairly well. But to-night there won't be anyone to stem the current. Oh, dear, I do trust that Antonia won't talk *too* much high art."

As Hester spoke, she looked at her friend with an expression of great anxiety on her face. Under ordinary circumstances this look would have completely overmastered Annie, who would immediately have yielded up her own wishes to please Hester, but now she remained quite obdurate.

"I am sure you will manage very well," she said, in an almost hard voice for her. "You know, Hetty, you won't always have me, and you will have Mrs. Bernard Temple and Antonia."

"It is too dreadful," sighed Hester. "When my father thought of marrying again, why did he not think of someone more congenial?"

"I suppose Mrs. Bernard Temple is congenial to him," replied Annie, "and that he doubtless considers of the first importance. After all, Hetty, I'm sure she will let you have your own way in everything, and I don't really think that Antonia is half bad. If I were you I would try and make friends with her."

"It is not in my nature to make friends easily," replied Hester.

She was standing in her pretty bedroom as she spoke, and Annie was leaning by the open window, swinging her garden hat in her hand.

"Hester," she said, suddenly, "forgive me if I ask you rather a rude question. Is your father a very rich man?"

Hester looked surprised.

"I suppose so," she answered; "to tell the truth, I have never thought about it. Oh, yes, I conclude that he is quite well off."

"But I want him to be more than well off. Is he rich--very rich? so rich that he would not miss a lot of money if he had suddenly to--to lose it?"

"What a very queer question to ask me, Annie," replied Hester. "I am really afraid I cannot reply to it. I think my father must be rich, but I don't know if he is rich enough to be able to afford to lose a lot of money--I don't think anyone is rich enough for that."

"Oh, yes, some people are," answered Annie. "Well, good-bye, Hetty keep up your heart. I'll be back early to-morrow morning."

"I must get that question of Sir John Thornton's wealth clearly answered some-how or other," thought Annie, "for there is no manner of use in Antonia stirring up a lot of mischief if there is no money to be found. I wonder if nursey could help me. I think I'll just have a word with her before I go to the Towers."

Mrs. Martin was alone when Annie entered the room.

"Well, my dear, and why ain't you at dinner?" asked the old woman. She was still fond of Annie, whom she invariably spoke of as "a winsome young body," but recent events had soured her considerably, and as she herself expressed it, the keen-est pleasure now left to her in life was to "mope and mutter."

"Moping and muttering eases the mind," she said; "it's a wonderful relief not to have to sit up straight and smiling when you feel crooked and all of a frown."

Accordingly Mrs. Martin received Annie Forest with brief displeasure.

"I have no heart for dinner," said Annie, who took her cue at once from the old woman's face. "I know you are miserable, Nurse Martin, but you need not look at me so scornfully, for I am trying to mend matters."

"You," exclaimed nurse, "a child like you! Now, Miss Annie, I would try and talk sensibly, I would, really."

"Well, I'm going off to the Towers for the night," said Annie, "and if you weren't so cross I'd like to say good-bye and give you a kiss before I started."

"Eh, dear," replied nurse, her countenance visibly softening however; "kisses, however sweet they be, don't heal sore places."

"But you'll take one, won't you, nursey?"

"Eh, my bairn, you have a winsome way, but don't you come canoodling me now, when my heart is like to break about my own dear children; and the young ladies at the Towers, too, in such a muck of trouble."

"Dear nursey," exclaimed Annie; "dear, loving, faithful, true-hearted nursey."

She stroked the old woman's brow and rubbed her soft cheek against hers.

"Out with it now, my pet," said Nurse Martin. "What is it you want me to do? If it's the pawn-shop again--once for all, no, I won't."

"It isn't the pawn-shop," said Annie; "it's just to ask you a simple question. I asked Hester, but she couldn't tell me. Is Sir John Thornton a rich man?"

"Is he rich?" echoed nurse; "do you think *she'd* be after him if he wasn't?"

"I don't know. Is he rich, nursey?"

"Yes, he's rich," replied nurse.

"Very, very rich? Dear Nurse Martin, please say yes."

"He's rich," replied nurse in an emphatic voice. "He has got his gold and his lands, and not a debt anywhere, and small expenses compared to his means. Yes, he's rich. More shame to him for taking the money from Miss Hester and Miss Nan to provide a new wife and an outlandish stepdaughter."

"If he lost a lot of money, a great lot, would he be a beggar?" pursued Annie.

"Well, really, Miss Annie, it isn't for me to say; but I think it would be a very big sum that would beggar Sir John. What are you after, Miss? I don't understand you at all."

"I'm thinking of the outlandish stepdaughter," replied Annie.

"Oh, Miss Annie Forest, don't name her to me. She turns my heart sick. Its in an asylum she should be. The messes she carries about with her, and the dress she wears, and the whole look of her! It isn't fit for Miss Hester and Miss Nan to have anything to do with her."

"You don't know her yet," replied Annie. "She has beautiful thoughts and grand resolves."

"Preserve me from 'em," said nurse. "There, now, miss, if you re going, you'd better go. I don't want to hear anything more about that girl, for lady she ain't."

"Good-bye, nurse," said Annie. "I am glad you are certain that Sir John Thornton is rich."

"I'd be glad if I was as certain that Miss Hester and Miss Nan were going to be happy," replied the old woman.

Annie blew a kiss to her and ran away.

The task Antonia had set her was quite to her heart. If, in addition to helping the Lorrimers, she could by this means get out of her own scrape, why, so much the better. It was one of Annie's gifts to be able to discriminate character with great nicety; and while Antonia spoke to her, she acknowledged a sudden respect and even admiration for the power which this queer girl possessed.

It was almost night when Annie set off on her walk across the fields to the Towers. She could not help singing to herself as she skipped lightly over the ground. She felt somehow, she could scarcely tell why, as if a great load had been lifted off her mind. One part of Antonia's mission she had already accomplished. She had found out from a very trustworthy source that Sir John Thornton was really a rich man. The second half of her task, the discovery of the present address of Squire Lorrimer, would surely not be impossible of fulfilment.

The Lorrimer children were out as usual. Whenever was a Lorrimer within doors, when he or she could be out? When Annie approached they were dismally employed, for Harry had inaugurated weekly meetings of the feud during the remainder of their stay at the Towers; and the children were now dancing solemnly round the bonfire, and repeating the solemn dirge which was to work evil consequences to the new-comers. Harry was spokesman on the occasion. He repeated the words to a sort of chanting air, and all the others repeated them after him with immense unction and smacking of lips. Kitty said afterwards that the dirge made her feel nearly as bloodthirsty as a Red Indian, and Boris openly wished that he could live in a wigwam and wear scalps.

Annie's appearance on the scene diverted the whole party, and Boris eagerly asked her if she would like to become a member of the feud.

"I would immensely," replied Annie; "but it wouldn't be of any use, as I'm not a Lorrimer."

"I could marry you, and then you'd be one," said Boris, looking up at her with a great shining light in his eyes.

"So you could, you sweet," said Annie, bending down and kissing him, "and the day I marry you I faithfully promise to join the feud; but I must run off now to find Molly."

"She's somewhere in the tower packing books," screamed Kitty after her.

Accordingly Annie pursued her way round to that part of the house.

The tower was at least two hundred years older than the rest of the mansion, and, as Annie ran up the spiral stairs, she had to feel her way through thick darkness, for the Lorrimers never thought of spending money on illuminating the stairs and passages of this ancient building.

A dim light in the distance presently guided her steps, and she soon found herself standing, out of breath and a good deal blown, in the presence of Molly and Jane Macalister. They were both clothed from head to foot in long brown-holland aprons. Jane was vigorously dusting and brushing a heap of dilapidated books, which Molly was arranging in orderly piles on the floor. Jane looked up when she saw Annie and uttered a little scream.

"Now, what have you come about?" she said; "you see we are quite up to our eyes in work."

"Delightful," said Annie; "I'll help. Toss me an apron, Molly, do."

Off went Annie's hat, on went the brown-holland apron, and Jane found that she had secured a valuable assistant in the matter of dusting and brushing.

The work went on for two or three minutes in silence, then Molly said, "I hope there's nothing the matter with Nora, Annie? It seems so very late for you to come to pay us a visit."

"I have come here to stay for the night, if I may," replied Annie.

"Hoots! I don't know if that will be possible," interrupted Jane.

"Oh, I'll sleep anywhere; I'm not a bit particular. I want to talk to you, Molly; I've a great deal to say."

"There's no use in girls wasting their time with silly havering when work has to be done," snapped Jane. "I'm willing to grant that a heavy misfortune has come to this house, but come rain or sunshine the daily round *must* go on. Pass me that clean duster, Molly. These books have to be sorted and put in boxes before we either of us lie down to-night."

"But three pairs of hands make lighter work than two," rejoined Annie. "I'm willing to help; I mean to help; I am helping. Molly, pass me a duster, too. I'll talk to you, Molly, when the work is over."

"That's the time for sleep," said Jane.

"Oh, come, Jane, if Annie wants to talk to me, she must," said Molly in an almost fretful tone. "There's plenty of room for you in my bed, Annie, so that matter is settled; now let us fly along with the books."

Jane did not utter another word of remonstrance. In her inmost heart she had a great admiration for Annie, whom she always spoke of as a "bonny, capable lassie." The books were all sorted and packed in a little over an hour, and then the girls went downstairs to supper in the great hall. Supper consisted of porridge and milk, followed by great dishes of stewed fruit. The children all sat round a table, and Mrs. Lorrimer, with the air of a royal matron, dispensed the simple food.

Immediately afterwards, Annie slipped her hand through Molly's arm, and drew her out of doors on to the moonlit lawn.

"I can't wait another moment," she said. "I've oceans of things to ask you."

"I suppose you have come over on some special business," replied Molly. "Has Hester sent me a message?"

"No; Hester has had nothing to do with it. I came over because I really want a talk with you all by myself. I cannot tell you what I thought to-day when that dreadful Susy Drummond came with her sort of 'take possession' style into the house."

"And do you really imagine," answered Molly, "that Miss Drummond annoyed us in any way? for if you do you are greatly mistaken. We are in great trouble just now about father, and about dear Guy being cut out of his rightful inheritance, and naturally we shall all feel leaving the Towers, but if you think that girl makes any difference one way or other, you are quite wrong."

Annie was silent for a moment. Then she said in a low voice, "I'm glad you don't mind her; she would try me a good bit. How soon have you got to leave, Molly?"

"Mother would like us to be out in a month," replied Molly. "Mr. Drummond does not take possession for over five weeks, but mother thinks that when a very painful thing has to be done, the sooner it is over the better. And she has almost taken a roomy old cottage on the edge of Sharsted Common. She says the children must not be cooped up in a town house, and they will have plenty of room to run about on the common, and as Nortonbury is only a mile away, Guy and Harry can still go to school there."

"And will you still stay at home, Molly?"

"I don't know, all the future is a complete blank. I am not educated according to modern ideas, and I love my own people so deeply that it would be agony to leave them. At the same time, I know some of us must go away, for we shall be very poor; we'll have no money at all except the income from mother's little fortune, and that will go a small way. I have asked mother to let us do without a servant, for I quite love housework. But really, Annie, everything at present is simply in chaos."

"It is good of you to tell me," said Annie, in her caressing voice. "You know I am poor myself, and I dearly love poor people; they are fifty times more interesting than rich ones. Fancy what zest is added to life when you have to contrive and scrape, and patch and fit every one of your dresses."

"As to that," replied Molly, "I don't in the least care what I wear; but I must frankly say that patched and contrived dresses are, as a rule, very ugly. Now shall we come into the house?"

"Not yet," replied Annie; "it is lovely out. Let us take another turn just here in the moonlight. Have you heard anything about the Squire lately, Molly? Is he likely to come back to the Towers soon?"

"No; I'm afraid he won't come at all. The sudden necessity which obliged him to sell the old home has had the strangest effect upon him. We are very anxious about him--very, very unhappy. The state of his health is our keenest grief."

"And do you know where he is?"

"Oh, yes, in London. Mother writes to him to his club."

"It seems a great pity that he should be alone there," said Annie. "I wonder your mother likes to leave him."

"Mother is only carrying out his wishes. He has absolutely refused to come back to the Towers. He says he may come after we have all gone, but not before. I cannot tell you, Annie, how miserable we are about him. He is completely altered. He used to be the tenderest, the most unselfish of fathers, and now the whole burden of everything is put on poor mother's shoulders."

"What is the name of his club?" asked Annie.

"The Carlton."

"Have none of you any influence over him?"

"Nell has the most. She is a strange child, and has a way of seeing down into the very heart of things. Where her interests are aroused, she has such intense sympathy that it gives her wonderful tact. If father were at home, I believe Nell could manage him; but where is the use of talking? He is away, and we none of us can move him by letter or otherwise. Mother hopes that when we are really settled at the cottage, he will return; but oh, dear--oh, dear--I believe the changed life will shorten his days. There, Annie, I never thought to confide in you, but you see I have done so. Now let us come indoors."

CHAPTER XXVI.
PLOT THICKENS.

Mother," said Antonia, two days after the events mentioned in the last chapter, "I think we have been quite long enough at the Grange." Mrs. Bernard Temple was taking a walk by herself round one of the lawns when Antonia swept up to her and made this remark.

"I thought you would be saying something erratic of this sort," replied her parent, a good deal of annoyance in her tone. "We have not been at the Grange a week yet and, as it is to be the future home of both of us, it does not seem at all inconsistent to spend a fortnight here now, particularly when we are enjoying ourselves so much."

"Pray speak for yourself with regard to the enjoyment, mother," responded Miss Bernard Temple. "I must say that dreariness is no word for this place as far as I am concerned. These trim *parterres*, those undulating velvet lawns are abhorrence to me; but I am not thinking of myself at all when I say that I think it would be well for us to return to our rooms in town. I wish to do so for quite another motive. In the first place, I have got to take care of you, mother; you must not make yourself too cheap."

"Oh, my dear Antonia, what a horrid expression! I hope I understand what is due to my own dignity."

"Frankly, mother, you don't--not on all occasions; but now to revert to the more important business. I am anxious to be back in town because I want this matter with regard to the Towers to be carried into effect as soon as possible. By the way, have you spoken to Sir John Thornton on the subject?"

"Yes, oh, yes! for goodness sake don't you interfere, my dear."

"Of course I won't if you have done your duty. What did you say?"

"Oh, just what I thought necessary! I think I made up quite a moving story. Sir John listened attentively. Said he had the greatest possible respect for Squire Lorrimer; that it gave him considerable pain to feel that *parvenus*, like the Drummonds should reside at the Towers; but he said, further, that he could not quite tell how he was to interfere."

"Oh, I dare say!" answered Antonia. "I know enough of him to be certain that every step of the path to the rescue must be made clear by others. Did he give you to understand, mother, that he would be willing to help Squire Lorrimer if the occasion arose?"

"Well, my dear, I gathered that he would not be averse to doing so; but, really, the matter is one of extreme delicacy, and one which it is quite impossible for me to say much about."

"But I have not the least objection to talking about it," said Antonia. "It is one of my failings not to feel delicacy except with regard to art. I can talk to him if you like. I should recommend extreme bluntness. These obtuse people never see things unless they are put right up in front of their eyes."

"Really, Antonia, in addition to being eccentric, you are now becoming positively vulgar. What have I done to be afflicted with a daughter like you? I beg and beseech of you not to say a word to Sir John on the subject."

"All right, mother, I won't, if you will promise without fail to return to London to-morrow."

"Oh, dear, dear, it will be most inconvenient."

"But you'll come?"

"I--really----"

"I see Sir John in the distance; he is smoking a cigarette, which will soothe him while I talk. If I talk to him, you needn't go to London so soon. Which shall it be?"

"Oh, London, London--anything better than that you should worry poor Sir John. Was there ever a woman so worried? You had better send Pinkerton to me."

"That's a good mother," said Antonia, bestowing one of her rare and wonderfully sweet smiles upon her parent. She rushed away to the house in her headlong style; met Hester in one of the corridors; stopped her to exclaim, "Cheer up, Hetty, the incubus is leaving by the first train in the morning," and then finding Pinkerton, despatched her for orders to Mrs. Bernard Temple.

A few moments later, Antonia had forced her way into Susy's presence.

"Mother and I leave to-morrow," she said. "I don't know if you feel inclined to stay here much longer?"

"I? No, I'm sure I don't," answered Susy. "I am sick of the place; they are all such a lot of slow coaches."

"County people, you know," said Antonia with a slight sneer, "are always a little slow to us *parvenus*; we're so wonderfully fresh, you know; not worn out like the poor county folk."

"You can call yourself a *parvenu* if you like," said Susy in a rage, "but I decline to allow the name to be applied to me; however, I think I'll go back to father to-morrow, and I may as well take advantage of your escort."

"That's what I thought. Get your maid to pack your things, for we shall be off by the first train, remember. By the way, did you hear from your father with regard to your letter?"

"Yes, I heard this morning."

"Well, what did he say?"

"He says he is sorry I don't like the Towers, but he doesn't see how he is to get out of the purchase now. He is to take possession in a little over a month."

"What a horrible future for you," said Antonia. "That musty old place--the ghost in the tower--the family feud----"

"What do you mean by the family feud?"

"Oh, a little arrangement lately entered into by the younger Lorrimers for your benefit. I'm not bound to repeat it, but I can truly say I shouldn't like the little formula they have made up to be chanted nightly about me. Frankly, Susy, I pity you. You must hate the idea of going to the Towers."

"Yes, I loathe it," said Susy.

"The best thing you can do is to see your father, and have a very serious talk. Its settled that you come back with us to-morrow. That's right. Ta-ta for the present."

Antonia left the room.

She stood for a moment by herself in one of the passages.

"Who would have thought," she murmured to herself, "that I, Antonia Bernard Temple, would devote myself to anything except the services of high Art. Here am I absolutely wearing myself out and devising the most horrible plots and stratagems, all for the sake of an ugly duckling. Shall I succeed? Yes, I think so. Matters move in the right direction. Susy hates going to the Towers; the Lorrimers hate leaving the Towers. Sir John Thornton has more money than he knows what to do with. Surely some scheme can be suggested to keep the old family in the old place. When we are in town, we can soon get to know Squire Lorrimer. Hurrah! I have an idea. Annie Forest and Nora shall both come up to town with us to-morrow. Annie is a capital kind of girl, although she did behave with want of fidelity as regards that ring. I must get it back for her somehow before we leave. Annie we must have, for she's a perfect jewel of tact, and so sweetly pretty, just like a red rose, while I'm a fierce--very fierce--tiger lily. Nora must come, too, because, of course, Squire Lorrimer will visit us for the sake of seeing his child. Mother shall propose to Sir John Thornton, and he will further suggest to Mrs. Lorrimer, that Nora would be the better for the best surgical advice. Hey presto! the thing is delightfully managed. Antonia, my dear, you begin to see daylight, don't you?"

Antonia skipped away in high good humour, and, wonderful to relate, her different little schemes for collecting a party to accompany her mother and herself to town were all carried out without hitch or difficulty. Annie, of course, was only too delighted to spend her last few days of holiday in London, and Nora, who had never been there, quite forgave Mrs. Bernard Temple for becoming Hester's stepmother when she heard that she was going to take her to the "Heart of the World," as she termed the great metropolis. On the evening of that same day Antonia, having concluded, as she considered, an arduous campaign, stood for a moment in earnest contemplation. "There's only the ring," she said to herself. "I must get the ring for poor Annie before I go. Now, who will lend me thirty shillings? I'll try Pinkerton first."

She swept into the room where the tired maid was completing her somewhat laborious packing, for Mrs. Bernard Temple invariably carried nearly a houseful of dresses about with her.

"Well, Miss Antonia, what now?" said the maid. "I wish you'd take off that evening dress, miss, and let me lay it just over the others here in in this box."

"I can stuff it into my Gladstone bag," said Antonia; "don't trouble about it. Pinkerton, when were you paid your wages last?"

"Oh, wages, indeed!" said Pinkerton, with a sniff. "Don't talk of em, Miss Antonia. It's months and months I'm owed, but I suppose it will be all right when your ma is married to this rich gentleman."

"You haven't got about thirty-two shillings you could spare me?" said Antonia.

"I couldn't oblige you with thirty-two pence, miss."

Antonia drummed with her fingers on a chest of drawers near which she was leaning. "And it's such a paltry sum," she muttered--"not worth a fuss. You ought to have your wages, Pinkerton--it's a shame! I must speak to mother about them when my mind is a little less burdened. I have a good deal to think of just now, so good-night!"

"What about that dress, miss?"

"I can't give it to you at present. I'll stow it away somewhere. Good-night!"

Antonia closed the door behind her and ran downstairs. She must get the thirty-two shillings from somewhere. To whom could she apply? She suddenly found herself face to face with Sir John Thornton. An inspiration seized her. She rushed up to him and took one of his hands. He shuddered, but had the strength of mind to remain perfectly still.

"Can you lend me thirty-two shillings?" said Antonia. "You're as rich as Croesus, so you won't mind. I'll pay it back to you a shilling a week out of my dress allowance. Will you lend it? Say yes or no in a hurry, please."

"Yes," said Sir John, "... with pleasure." He moved back a step or two. "Here are two sovereigns," he said. "Pray don't mind the change. The change doesn't matter, I assure you. Oh, any time, of course, as regards repayment. I am happy to oblige you." He dropped the sovereigns into Antonia's large palm and prepared to fly.

"You are happy to oblige me?" she said with a sort of gasp. "Oh, do stay just a single moment. You have made me very happy. Thirty-two shillings must go for a special purpose, but eight blessed shillings remain. Don't you really want the change? May I really borrow the change?"

"Most certainly. I am rather in a hurry."

"I'd kiss you, but you wouldn't like it," said Antonia. "These eight shillings mean--do you know what they mean?"

"If they make you happy, my dear young lady, that is enough for me."

"They do, they do! Cobalt ... Indian red ... rose madder ... burnt sienna ... canvasses ... a new flat brush for the skies ... some drawing pins--Oh, he's gone! Dear old man. What an affliction I was to him; but how triumphant I feel!"

CHAPTER XXVII.
NELL IS IN TROUBLE.

All Antonia's plans were carried into effect. She paid Mrs. Martin thirty-two shillings and gave the old woman her address in town, begging of her to forward the ring there without an hour's delay. In due course it arrived, and Annie had it once more in her possession. Poor Annie turned pale when Antonia put the little box which contained it into her hand.

"I could cry as well as laugh," she said, looking at Antonia with tears springing to her eyes. "I have not behaved well about this ring, and I ought not to have it back like this. I ought to be properly punished. It does not seem fair that I should have the ring returned to me again in this easy manner."

"Undoubtedly you have been deceitful," replied Antonia, "and your conscience must feel ruffled. I can stand most things, but a ruffled conscience, I confess, is too much for me. I suppose you will soothe it in the only possible way?"

"What do you mean?" asked Annie.

"Confession is good for the soul," replied Antonia, in a sing-song voice. She went to the window as she spoke and looked out into the sunlit street.

The two girls were standing in the room which Antonia was pleased to call her studio. It was an attic at the top of the house, and had a dormer window with a north light. The dormer window had sides which were curtained with green. In Annie's opinion this room was simply hideous. Huge canvasses covered with great daubs of colour occupied the walls. A skeleton stood in one corner, and one or two draped figures were in others. Antonia had lured Annie up here for the purpose of taking her likeness in a white kerchief. Antonia was fired with an idea that Annie would look well as Marie Antoinette on her way to execution. She was not quite sure whether to make her Charlotte Corday or Marie Antoinette; but, on reflection, decided that the latter character would suit her best, as she did not think that Annie could ever get sufficient tragedy into her eyes for the former.

"I am going to paint myself some day for Charlotte," exclaimed Antonia. "I'll study before the glass whenever I've an odd moment, and I believe I shall do the fixity of purpose stare after another week of hard practice. Now, do stand still Annie-- the bother of the ring is at an end, so you can forget it. Just turn your head a little to the left, I want to get a peep at your ear--you have got a good ear, quite shell-like. Now, for mercy's sake look tragical! Think of the guillotine, and the crowd looking on, and La Belle France and the Tuileries, and the horrid feeling when your head is separated from your trunk. Now, then, realise it--get it into your eyes. Are you realising it?"

"Frankly, I'm not," replied Annie. "I can't sit for Marie Antoinette any longer to-day. I really can't, Antonia. This room is so stiflingly hot, and I want to go out. I want to get into one of the parks. Are there any near this?"

"Oh, yes! Hyde Park is quite close; but you'll find it as dry as chips. Remember, it is September now. Hyde Park is not pretty in September."

"I wonder anyone can live in London," replied Annie.

"Do you? I don't. I hate this poky little house in the centre of detestable fashion; but if I could have an atelier, or a studio, I ought to say, in Gower Street, it would be nearly as good as Paris. Well, if you won't sit any longer, I suppose you won't. Now let us come downstairs."

The girls left the studio and entered the drawing-room. Here they found Mrs. Bernard Temple and Nora. Nora was lying on a sofa looking tired and pale, and Mrs. Bernard Temple was moving about the room in a bustling sort of fashion arranging flowers. The drawing-room was small and crowded with knick-knacks. Antonia seldom swept across this room without knocking a table over or flicking a paper on to the floor.

"Now, my dear, be careful!" exclaimed her parent. "That papier-mache table on which I have just arranged these lovely late roses, sent to me by dear Sir John, will not stand one of your lunges. I cannot imagine how you have got that peculiar walk, Antonia; its exactly as if you were on board ship."

Antonia lounged towards a chair, into which she flung herself.

"Dear me, it is hot!" she exclaimed, pushing back her thick black hair from her forehead. "Never mind about my walk, mother; let me hear the news. What did Sir Henry Fraser say of Nora?"

Mrs. Bernard Temple sank into another chair.

"The dear child!" she exclaimed. "She had a trying morning."

"Pray don't talk of it!" exclaimed Nora from her sofa. "It was too desperate."

"Why, did he hurt you?" exclaimed Antonia.

"Oh, no! he was kindness itself; but we had to wait so long before we saw him."

"Pooh!" answered Antonia. "Was that the dreadful part? Tell me what he said when you did see him? Are you likely soon to be quite well again?"

"With care," interrupted Mrs. Bernard Temple, "dear Nora will recover perfectly. Her back is still very weak, but there is no injury. She may walk a little daily, but must lie down a good deal."

"You're quite sure he wasn't anxious about you?" asked Antonia, fixing her eyes on Nora.

Nora started.

"No; what do you mean?" she said. "You quite startle me. Why should he be anxious?"

"Well, I almost wish he were. It would suit my purpose to have him anxious for a day or two. However, if he isn't, he isn't, and there's an end of it. Nora, don't you want to see your father very badly?"

"Oh, yes!" replied Nora. Her face grew pink and red. "Of course I'd like to see him, but I have not an idea where he is."

"He's in London, close to you, you goose."

"Antonia!" interrupted Mrs. Bernard Temple.

"Mother, she is a goose not to remember that Squire Lorrimer is in town. You ought to write to him, Nora, and ask him to come to see you."

"If he's in London I don't know his address," answered Nora.

"You can write to his club--the Carlton. Here, I'll find you paper and pen, or, if you are too tired to write after the doctor's examination, you can dictate a letter to me. Here, what do you want to say? I'm not a good hand at letter-writing, but you must know the sort of thing. You had better ask him to dinner to-night; there's not an hour to be lost."

"You forget that we are going to the theatre to-night," said Mrs. Bernard Temple.

"Oh, what does that matter. Nora can't go, with her weak back."

"Yes she can. I have taken a box, and she shall have my air-cushion to lean against."

"And I want to go to a theatre awfully," said Nora.

"Well, well, so much for filial affection. Ask him to come to lunch to-morrow. Write any way--show that you're a daughter, a loving daughter."

"Of course I'm a loving daughter, but I----"

"For goodness sake don't have any more buts. Write or dictate, whichever you please."

"I'll write if I must, but really--I don't suppose father will care to come."

"Doesn't he care for you, then?"

"Care for me? What a thing to say. Of course he cares for me."

"Then he'll come. Now, I give you five minutes. Write the letter, and I'll take it out and post it."

Nora muttered and grumbled, but Antonia's perfectly motionless figure, as she sat in an easy chair facing her, was too much to be resisted. She took up a pen, dipped it in ink, and began to write.

"Do it lovingly," said Antonia; "put heart into it; show that you're a daughter."

Mrs. Bernard Temple motioned Annie to come and sit near her.

"Really," she said in a whisper, "poor Antonia becomes more peculiar and trying each day. She simply bullies us all. Look at that poor dear little Nora, submitting to her caprice as gently as a lamb. I don't know why she wants Squire Lorrimer to come here. I am not acquainted with him, and it will be really painful for me to see him in his present afflicted condition. I am a very cheerful person by nature, and hate depressing circumstances."

"I am sorry you are not sympathetic," answered Annie.

Mrs. Bernard Temple raised her brows.

"Sympathetic," she exclaimed; "my dear, I'm the soul--the very soul of sympathy; but where's the use of wasting emotion? I can do nothing for Squire Lorrimer, and it will only pain poor Nora to see him. Really, really, Antonia is beyond anything afflicting. Now, my love, where are you going?"

The latter part of this speech was addressed to Miss Bernard Temple, who was leaving the room. "Where are you going, Antonia, my love?" repeated her mother.

"Out, mother; to post this letter."

"I beg of you to do nothing of the kind. I can send it by William, when next he goes for a message."

William was a very diminutive, and much overworked, page-boy.

"Thanks," said Antonia; "but I prefer to go myself."

She left the room, shutting the door rather noisily; and Mrs. Bernard Temple looked for sympathy to the two girls.

"Is not she trying?" she repeated. "With my mind so preoccupied with thoughts of my approaching marriage, and of dear Sir John, and those sweet girls, Hester and Nan; it is really too much to be worried by Antonia's whims."

"Oh, but she means everything splendidly," said Annie. "I admire her beyond anything. If you will let me, Mrs. Bernard Temple, I will go out with her."

"Oh, certainly, my dear. I see you are under her spell, so I have nothing to say. Dear Nora and I will try to make ourselves happy together."

Annie left the room, and met Antonia in the hall.

"Wait one moment, Antonia," she said; "I'll go with you."

She ran upstairs, fetched her hat and gloves, and joined Antonia. The two girls went into the street.

"I'm determined that no pranks shall be played with this letter," said Antonia; "so I intend not to post it, but to take it to the Carlton myself."

"Antonia, is that right?"

"Right--what can there be wrong in it? There is no one who will eat me at the Carlton. I shall simply give the letter to the hall-porter, and desire him to put it into Mr. Lorrimer's hands the moment he appears. Now, come on, if you are coming. You can stay in the street while I interview the porter."

"But the post seems safer and easier," said Annie.

"Well, I don't think so. Come, come; what are you loitering for?"

As was universally the case, Antonia's strong will prevailed.

She knew London thoroughly, and followed by the somewhat breathless Annie, in due course reached the Carlton Club.

She had run up the steps, entered the hall, interviewed the porter, delivered her letter, and once more joined Annie, when the latter said to her in a voice of suppressed excitement--

"There is Squire Lorrimer; that man with the bent head and hat pushed over his eyes. He passed the club while you were within. There he is, just turning the corner."

"Run after him and stop him," exclaimed Antonia. "Quick, quick--I'll fetch the letter out while you're catching him up."

"Oh, I don't like to," said Annie.

"What a goose you are--then I'll do it--he'll be lost to view if we wait another instant arguing. Is it that rather old man who walks slowly? Yes, yes, I see him. Stay where you are and I'll bring him back to you."

Before Annie could interfere, Antonia had hastened forward with long strides, which she soon quickened into a run. She reached Mr. Lorrimer, and gave one of his coat sleeves a fierce tug.

He started, took off his hat instinctively, and then stared in amazement at the wild-looking girl, whose face was completely unknown to him.

"Oh, yes, you think I'm mad," said Antonia, "but I'm not. I'm about as sane as anyone in England. You are Mr. Lorrimer, and you're afraid to go home, and your family are in dreadful trouble. I'm Antonia Bernard Temple; yes, it's a long unwieldy sort of name, but I have the misfortune to own it. If I'm a diamond at all, I'm a rough sort; very rough and uncouth, but I mean well. My mother is engaged to Sir John Thornton, and we have been staying at the Grange, and I have seen your magnificent untrammelled old place, with its briars, and dragon china, and I, in short--I have seen Nell. Nell is in trouble, and my heart has gone out to her; and Nora is in town staying with us, with my mother and me, and she wants to see you, naturally; so please come home with me now. Please turn round and come to the Carlton first. There's a letter there for you from Nora. Come and see her, and hear about Nell and Molly."

There was the queerest mixture of every sort of emotion in Antonia's wild, disjointed speech; but above it all was an overpowering earnestness, which somehow attracted the poor, forlorn-looking Squire.

"You are a very queer young lady," he said.

"Oh, they all say that," exclaimed Antonia clasping her hands. "I beg of you not to be commonplace; do come home with me."

"But somehow you seem to know all about my people," he continued. "Is it possible that Nora is in town? Yes, I'll go and see her. Where is she?"

"Come with me and I'll take you to the house. It's in a most poky, fashionable part--an odious locality, where poor Art hides her head. Just walk back with me to meet Annie Forest, and to get your letter. You know Annie Forest, don't you?"

"I have met her."

"Well, she's waiting close to the Carlton Club for us both; and we can't leave her there, you know; come quickly."

The Squire turned.

His step was slow. The look of depression on his face was painful; his grizzled hair was nearly white, and his once keen, hawk-like blue eyes were now dim and dull. Antonia had never seen him before, but Annie started when he held out his hand to her.

He walked in almost silence back with the two girls, and in a little more than half an hour, Antonia had the pleasure of introducing him to her mother and Nora, who were enjoying afternoon tea together in great contentment and peace of mind. Nora uttered a little shriek when she saw her father. He took her in his arms and kissed her tenderly. Annie did not follow the Squire into the drawing-room.

"Come, mother," said Antonia, going up to her parent.

"Where?" asked Mrs. Bernard Temple in astonishment.

"Out of the room--come."

CHAPTER XXVIII.
THE LION AND MOUSE.

No one could be in a more terrible state of complete collapse than poor Mr. Lorrimer. The blow he had most dreaded had overtaken him. He had been as plucky an English gentleman as ever walked. As true-hearted and affectionate a husband and father, as kind and considerate a landlord--as honourable as man could be in all his dealings--a keen sportsman, a lover of horses--in short, an ideal squire of the old school; but the Towers had been his backbone; now that circumstances for which he was scarcely to blame deprived him of the home of his fathers, he found himself unable to stand up against the blow. He had made a gallant fight up to the last moment, but when he saw plainly that the tide had set in dead against him, he ceased to fight and allowed himself to drift. He made up his mind that his last memory of the Towers should be that evening when the old ball-room was full of light and movement, and when two little fairy-like figures had flitted across the lawn to greet him. That fairy and that brownie had comforted him on that night of keen desolation, and their memory lingered with him still. He lived in cheap lodgings near his club, ate what was put before him, read nothing, moped away the long hours, and was fast reaching a stage when serious breakdown of some sort or other was imminent. He desired all letters to be sent to him to the Carlton, and not only refused to allow his wife to come to him, but would not let her know where he was lodging. He promised, however, to join his family when the move from the Towers had been made.

On the day when Antonia met him, he was feeling more wretched even than usual. He had never hitherto been a weak or undecided man, but now he was completely limp--there was no other word to describe his condition. Antonia's firmness compelled him to obey her, and he found himself against his will in Nora's company. Nora was not his favourite child; she was not like Molly to him, nor like Nell and Boris, still she was one of his children, and his heart throbbed with a great wave of pain when he saw her.

"My poor little girl," he said, kissing her tenderly, "my poor dear little girl. I have been a bad father to you, my little Nora."

"Oh, no, no, father," said Nora, sobbing now, and much overcome "No, no, dear, darling father; I'm so delighted, so delighted to see you again."

The Squire sat down on the sofa near Nora, and putting his arm round her, drew her pretty head to rest on his breast.

"So you are staying in town," he said, "quite close to me; and how--how are the others, my dear?"

"Quite well," replied Nora "only fretting about you."

"About me? They needn't do that--I'm not worth it. You're sure your mother is quite well, Nora?"

"Yes."

"And Molly?"

"Yes, quite well."

"And the young 'uns, Nell and Boris?"

"Oh, they're well, only Nell frets a good bit."

"Poor child, poor child; bless her, she's a loving little soul. I suppose Guy is awfully cut up, eh, Nonie?"

"Oh, father, indeed he's not. Guy is too much of a man--he's splendid, he is, really. I wish you'd go back again, father, that's all they want. It's you they want, not the Towers--you are more to them than the Towers."

"You're a good child to say so," said the Squire; "but I can't go back at present. When I think of that place going out of the family, I feel like an unfaithful steward. It was committed to me to keep and to hand on intact to my boy, and I've lost him his inheritance. You none of you know what it means; but I can't go back--not at present."

"May I write and tell mother where you are?"

"No; she writes to me to the Carlton--I'm all right; don't you worry about me, pet."

"You don't look all right--you look very ill."

"See here, Nora, don't you write home and tell them that--promise."

The Squire's manner grew quite fierce. He looked at Nora out of his bloodshot eyes. "Promise," he said. "I won't have it done--do you hear?"

"No, father, of course I won't if it vexes you."

"It does, my child, it does," the Squire's manner became tenderer than ever. "I'm worried and in trouble at present, and I am best alone; I am best all by myself for a bit. God knows, I suppose I shall pull round after a bit, and face you all--that poor boy whom I've ruined, and the rest of you--but I must get time--that's only reasonable--I must get time. Now I'm off; I'm glad to see you looking well, Nora."

"But you'll come and see me again, father; you promise, do promise that you'll come and see me again."

"Yes, my child, if you wish it."

"To-morrow; promise you'll come to-morrow. Antonia made me write to ask you to come to lunch, and I sent the letter to the Carlton. Will you come to lunch to-morrow?"

"No; I can't do that, but I'll look in some day. Good-bye, Nora, good-bye, my pet."

The Squire put his arms again round Nora, kissed her on her lips and brow, and left the house.

Antonia, who was trying to keep her mother quiet in the dismal dining-room, heard him slam the hall door after him, and rushed to the window to watch him down the street.

Mrs. Bernard Temple went and peeped over her daughter's shoulder.

"I am glad he has gone," she said. "It's so trying to be turned out of one's drawing-room. He's very seedy about his clothes, but he has an aristocratic walk. I suppose I may go back now, Antonia, to finish my cup of tea."

"Oh, yes, mother, all in good time. What does tea signify when you see a man broken with an awful grief of that sort? Why, he looks like a captive lion. Mother, cant you get enthusiastic on the subject? Can't you try?"

"I'm sure, my dear, I have tried, but I cannot really see that it will injure the Lorrimers for me to finish my tea. With all I am undergoing on my own account at present--but of course, Antonia, you have no sympathy for your mother."

"Oh, yes, I have when you need it, but you don't just now; you are perfectly happy. However, you must of course have your tea, and I won't worry you any more after you have sent off the telegram."

"The telegram! Oh, you erratic, perverse child; what next?"

"You have to telegraph to Sir John, mother, to beg of him to come here immediately. Things have gone much farther with Squire Lorrimer than I had the least idea of. He must be put out of his pain as quickly as possible or something bad will happen. We must get my new father that is to be on the spot to-night, and if you don't telegraph for him I shall myself take the next train to Nortonbury, and tackle him on the subject. I don't in the least mind which it is, but one or other must be done directly."

"Antonia, you quite terrify me. Sir John will be seriously angry."

"What of that. Let him be angry."

"But I assure you, my dear, he is not a man to be trifled with."

"Oh, I'll manage him, mother, if you're nervous."

"I really think you must. I have not the courage to make or meddle in this matter; in short, I wash my hands of it."

Antonia clapped hers.

"Hurrah!" she said. "I can manage much better all by myself. All I ask you now, dear, good mother, is to trust me. Be sure that nothing whatever will happen to injure you, and simply give me leave to say, when I am telegraphing, that you would like to see Sir John."

"Well, naturally, I always like to see him, dear, devoted fellow."

"That's all right. Now you shall go back to your tea, and I'll be as mum as a mouse for the rest of the day."

Mrs. Bernard Temple left the room, relieved at any sort of truce with her troublesome daughter. Antonia addressed the telegraph form to ... ***Sir John Thornton, The Grange, Nortonbury***, and filled in the following words:--

"Mother wants to see you without fail this evening. Take next   train. Important. Antonia. Reply paid."

The words went hard with the enthusiastic girl, for her precious eight shillings were nearly exhausted, and she knew that she must deny herself some sadly-needed cobalt if she sent that telegram.

"Never mind," she said, as she let herself out of the house, and rushed off to the nearest post-office. "You must do without that background of blue sky which I so wanted for your picture, Marie Antoinette. It is odd, but I never did think that I would allow Art to suffer in the cause of an ugly duckling."

Antonia sent off her telegram and watched anxiously for the reply. It came in the course of an hour and a half, and was addressed to her mother.

"Expect me by the train which reaches Waterloo at nine o'clock," wired the gallant Sir John.

"There, now, Antonia," said Mrs. Bernard Temple, "you have only yourself to blame. What is to be done? We shall be at the theatre at nine o'clock."

"Nothing could possibly be better, mother; I shan't go. I shall wait here for Sir John; we'll have a nice quiet time."

"My dear, I'm afraid he'll be terribly offended."

"No, mother, he won't; at least, not with you. Now, do go the theatre and be happy. Take Annie and Nora, and let them enjoy themselves. I promise you that you shall have serene skies on your return. Can't you trust me? Did you ever find me fail you yet when I promised you anything?"

"No, I never did, you queer, queer creature."

Mrs. Bernard Temple was restored to good humour. Dinner passed off pleasantly, and immediately afterwards a cab conveyed three of the party to the Lyceum.

Antonia had donned her rusty brown velveteen dress, and sat with her hands folded in front of her in a deep armchair.

Her black hair was combed high over her forehead; her eyes were bright. Anxiety had brought a slight colour into her cheeks; she looked almost handsome.

At about twenty minutes past nine a cab was heard to stop at the door, and a moment later Sir John Thornton was ushered into the drawing-room.

"How do you do?" he said, in a stiff voice, to Antonia. "Where is your mother? Her telegram has startled me a good deal."

"It was my telegram," said Antonia, in a calm voice.

"Well, that does not matter. Will you have the goodness to inform your mother that I am here?"

"I can't very well at the present moment, for she is enjoying herself at the Lyceum."

Sir John's face grew scarlet. He drew himself up to his stiffest attitude, and compressed his lips firmly together.

"Perhaps you feel annoyed," said Antonia, "and I don't think I am surprised. Will you sit down and let me explain matters?"

"Pray do nothing of the kind. I can wait until Mrs. Bernard Temple comes home. When is the play likely to be over?"

"I expect mother and Annie and Nora back about half-past eleven. It is now half-past nine. Have you had dinner?"

"No."

"Will you come downstairs, and let me give you something to eat?"

"No, thank you. As your mother is not at home, I shall dine at my club, and come back later on."

"No, you won't," said Antonia.

She started up, and placed herself between Sir John and the door. He felt himself groaning inwardly. Was that awful girl mad? What did her strange telegram mean? And why, if Mrs. Bernard Temple sent for him in a hurry, had she not the civility to wait at home to see him? This was really taking matters with a free-and-easy hand with a vengeance. The proud Sir John had never felt more thoroughly angry in his life. He stalked up to Antonia now, and endeavoured to pass her, but she dodged him successfully.

"I know you are a gentleman," she said; "and a gentleman always listens to what a lady has got to say, even when he is angry with her. I'm an awful personage in your eyes, but if you will listen to me to-night, I will promise to be as good and unobtrusive as girl can be in the future. I'll even wear ordinary dresses when I come to visit you, and I won't talk of my sacred Art when you are in the room. There, can girl promise more?--can she?"

"Will you have the goodness to let me pass?" said Sir John.

"I will in a moment or two. You shall go and dine at your club after you have heard why I sent for you."

"Why *you* sent for me?" exclaimed Sir John.

"Oh, yes; it was all my doing."

"But the message certainly came in your mother's name."

"Yes, because you would not have come otherwise. It was I, Antonia, who really sent for you. You have come up to town in this violent hurry on my account.

Now, will you come down to eat a very nice little dinner which has been prepared, and which the cook is waiting to send upstairs, and let me talk to you while you are enjoying it? Or will you listen to me here, and then go afterwards to your club? You must do one or other, unless you are rude enough to take me by main force and move me away from the door."

Sir John Thornton might be very angry, but he was the pink of propriety, and the idea of lifting the bony Antonia from the neighbourhood of the door was too repellent even to be thought of for a moment.

"You have got me into a trap," he said, "and I am deeply offended. Your mother must explain the position of affairs to me when she chooses to return home. I suppose I must listen to you, whether I wish it or not. I only beg of you to be brief."

"Now you are delightful," said Antonia. "Won't you sit down?"

"I prefer to stand."

"Well, I'll sit, if you don't mind, for I've a good deal to say."

"I must again beg of you to be brief."

"Very well; I'll put it into a few words, but they'll be strong, I promise you."

Sir John made no response. He folded his arms and looked down at Antonia. His face looked very cold and satirical; his lips were so tightly shut as to appear like a straight line. Antonia's face, all enthusiasm and fire, gazed up at him.

"Can I melt that iceberg?" she said inwardly. "Now for the tug of war."

"This is the heart and kernel of my reason for wishing to see you," she said. "I have taken up the cause of the Lorrimers. The Lorrimers are leaving the Towers because Squire Lorrimer has got into money difficulties. I don't know how, and I don't know why. He is obliged to sell the beautiful and noble home of his ancestors to clear himself of these difficulties. The children are all sorry to go--Molly loses the freshness of her youth when she leaves the Towers; Guy loses his rightful inheritance; the younger children are embittered by an unnatural feud which I need not trouble you about, but which will sour their characters; Nell is not strong, and simple grief may shorten her days; and the Squire, the Squire himself is so cut up, so heart-broken, that he cannot bring himself to say good-bye to the old place. He is in town, here, close to us; he is hiding somewhere near us because his proud old heart is broken. His hair is white ... his head is bowed and his eyes are dim."

"What does all this mean?" interrupted Sir John.

"What does it mean?" exclaimed Antonia, springing like a young lioness from her chair. "It means that you are to come to the rescue. Why should all that family be made wretched? and why should the Towers go to strangers when you can put things right? Take your money out of the bank, or wherever you have placed it--it will be the finest deed you ever did in your life--and buy back the Towers and give it to Squire Lorrimer and to Guy for their own place again. Yours is the talent buried in the ground. Take it out and save the Squire, and you'll be so happy you won't know yourself. Why, you'll be all on fire and alive with gladness. There, that's what I telegraphed to you for; you know now. You'll do it ... of course you'll do it. I have spoken now. You know what I want."

Antonia sank down into her chair again. She was trembling visibly through all her slender figure. Sir John gazed at her in amazement. Her eyes met his fully, and then her heart gave a leap in her breast. He was not angry. She guessed then that she had won her cause.

"You certainly are a queer girl," he said, sitting down near her. "You amaze me. I never heard of a girl who would take up a thing in this way ... and the Lorrimers are not even your friends. Oh, no! I am not angry ... not now. Hester frets morning, noon, and night, at the thought of parting with Molly; but Hester never thought of this. It is fine of you--quite impossible, of course; but I always admire real bravery when I see it."

"Never mind praising me," said Antonia; "tell me why you call it impossible."

"My dear young lady, do you think for a single moment Squire Lorrimer would accept a gift of this sort from me? Do you think the Towers would be of the least value to him won back in such a way? *Noblesse oblige* would prevent his accepting such an offer."

"I have thought of all that," said Antonia. "I guessed that there would be a good deal of pride to overcome. Fortunately I am not bothered with *noblesse oblige*; but I guessed that you county people would worry over it. We art lovers never think of it; we rise above it; we go back to the old, old, *old*, times, when those who loved each other had all things in common."

"As long as we live in the world," said Sir John, "the men of the world must adhere to its usages. It is not the custom for one man to present another with the sort of gift you propose that I should favour Squire Lorrimer with."

"Then you must not give it in the form of a gift. You must go to your solicitor and consult him about the matter. I happen to know that Susy Drummond hates the Towers, so I am quite sure that Mr. Drummond would be very glad to be out of his bargain. The Squire wants a certain sum of money; you must lend it to him on very easy terms. Oh! of course you know how to manage! You must make it possible for him to stay at the Towers whatever happens. Oh! I know you'll do it! I know you'll be clever enough and kind enough to do it. You'll think of a way, and in all the world no man will ever have a more faithful daughter than I'll be to you. Dear me! how dead tired I am! Are you going out to your club to dinner? If so, I'll go to bed."

CHAPTER XXIX
GOD BLESS ANTONIA.

Mrs. Bernard Temple waited up for Sir John that night; but he did not appear. When he left Antonia he went straight to his club, ordered dinner, and ate it with his usual refined and somewhat languid appetite. He then went up to his room, and being tired thought he would go early to bed. He did go to bed--he even went to the length of shutting his eyes, preparatory for a peaceful night's slumber. Up to that point he was the Sir John of old. The calculating, reserved, cold-natured Englishman; but beyond that point he was different, altogether different from what he had been before. Between him and his accustomed night's rest came the eager face and passionate words of a girl--a lanky, untidy, and, in his opinion, most disagreeable girl. Still, she had roused him as he had never yet been roused. She had absolutely awakened a sort of conscience in him. For the first time in his whole existence, he carefully considered the question, who is my neighbour?

Certainly Squire Lorrimer was his neighbour. Their estates joined; they had been good friends from boyhood upward; they had been lads at the same school, and afterwards men of the same college. His children and Squire Lorrimer's children loved each other dearly. He had noticed of late how often Hester's eyes had been red as if with tears. She had been very good about his own proposed marriage, but she had cried when the Lorrimers were mentioned Nan had been sulky and disagreeable and defiant, and this was also on account of the Lorrimers. He was very sorry for his children, and very sorry also for the Lorrimers, but never until to-night had it entered into his head to help the Lorrimers out of their trouble.

He could do so, of course--he was a very rich man--he was also a careful man, never living up to his large yearly income. By no means extravagant in his tastes, not specially fond of hoarding money, but being really possessed of more than his wants required. He lay awake, and thought and thought, and after an early breakfast the next morning he did adopt Antonia's suggestion, and went to see his solicitor. From there he wrote a brief note to Mrs. Bernard Temple.

"As she had not, after all, required his presence in town," he wrote, "he would not come to see her. He happened to be particularly engaged, and wanted to return to the Grange that evening."

This letter was delivered at Mrs. Bernard Temple's house by a Commissionaire. It made that good lady very uneasy, but when Antonia read it she proceeded to skip up and down the drawing-room with such energy that two papier-mache tables were knocked over and a valuable china cup and saucer smashed.

"Don't speak to me, mother," she exclaimed. "I have nothing whatever to say, only if I don't give vent to my feelings in some sort of exercise I shall go mad."

The next day or two passed without anything special occurring, but on the third day Mrs. Bernard Temple received a letter which astonished her very much.

It was from Sir John, begging of her to come back to the Grange, and especially asking that Antonia should accompany her.

"Dear old man," murmured Antonia when she received this message. "I knew he'd rise to it; I knew he would. Mother, which is the most fashionable shop in London?"

"For what, my dear?"

"For an up-to-date costume. I must go at once and be rigged up. You had better order a hansom--never mind the extravagance--it will be untold torture, but it is a promise, and it must be done. Annie, love, you are exquisite on the subject of dress; come and see Antonia made fashionable."

"Yes, go with her, Annie," said Mrs. Bernard Temple. "I cannot imagine what this queer thing portends, but anything to make Antonia look like an ordinary girl I willingly agree to. Don't be extravagant, my love, for my purse is not too heavy; but anything under ten pounds I will willingly spend to make you presentable."

"It's appalling to think of the waste of money," said Antonia. "Oh, what would not ten pounds do in the cause of Art? But a promise is a promise. Come along, Annie, we'll go to Regent Street and choose."

Five minutes later, the two girls set off. Antonia's face was wreathed with wonderful smiles, but she was mute as to the subject of her thoughts, even to Annie.

"I suppose I must have a respectable hat," she said, suddenly; "and I suppose it must sit in the correct way on my head; therefore, the first thing is to go to a hairdresser's. I must be fringed, and curled, and frizzed."

"Oh, Antonia, no, no;" said Annie. "Your beautiful hair--it would be a sin to put a pair of scissors near it."

"A promise is a promise," said Antonia. "Which is the best hairdresser?"

They stopped at one in Bond Street, and half an hour later Antonia left the shop, very stiff about the head and red about the face.

"The hairpins are sticking into me all over," she gasped, "and the weight of the fringe is like a furnace on my forehead; but never mind."

"It isn't at all becoming either," said Annie.

Antonia looked at her with large eyes of reproach.

"Do you think I *want* it to be becoming?" she said. "That would be the final straw."

The fashionable dress was not only bought, but put on, and Mrs. Bernard Temple scarcely knew her daughter when she saw her back again.

"I'm in misery," said Antonia; "but a promise is a promise. My dear mother, when you are married to Sir John, that dear, dear old man, you need not expect to see me often at the Grange."

"I really do not see, Antonia, why you should speak of your future father as so very old."

"He's old to me," said Antonia. "I always speak of people as I find them."

"You are a most extraordinary girl," remarked her mother.

But she made this remark so often that Antonia did not think it necessary to reply.

By a late train in the afternoon the whole party were conveyed back to the Grange, where Hester received them with rather a puzzled expression on her face. As soon as possible she drew Annie aside, and began to speak to her.

"I cannot imagine what is the matter," she said; "father is going on in a most extraordinary way. You won't mind my speaking frankly, Annie, but he seemed really quite relieved when you all went away. Then he got that telegram from Mrs. Bernard Temple, and rushed off to town in a hurry. He came back the following evening completely altered--very silent and absorbed, but with a kind of change over him which Nan and I could not help noticing. I asked him if he had seen anything of Squire Lorrimer, and he looked hard at me and said--'I wonder if you are in it, too.'"

"Oh, I know, I know," said Annie softly, rubbing her hands; "dear Antonia, dear Antonia."

"Oh, for pity's sake, Annie, don't you get mysterious," exclaimed Hester, almost fretfully. "What can Antonia have to say to Squire Lorrimer? Let me finish my story. I asked father if he had seen him, and he replied, 'I have heard and seen enough of Lorrimer to fill all my thoughts.' He would not tell me another word; but he went to town again the next morning, and came back absolutely excited in the evening. Fancy my father in a state of excitement! He was ever so nice to me; and when Nan said that she must go to school almost immediately, he said that Mrs. Willis should be invited to come back to the Grange, for he wanted us all to have a happy meeting before his wedding. And he has been telegraphing to all kinds of people all day, and I believe all the Lorrimers are coming here to-morrow. Father said he wanted to have a real, jolly time, and that everyone of the Lorrimers, even to little Phil, and, of course, Jane Macalister, were to be asked. I ventured to remind him that dear Molly and all of them were not just in the mood for festivities at present, but he would not listen to me for a moment. He said, that on such an auspicious occasion he must have his own way, and that he would engage that they would be jolly enough when the time came."

"So they will, I am sure," said Annie. "Did you say Mrs. Willis was here, Hester?"

"Yes, she came an hour ago. She is in her room. She says she will take you and Nan back with her to Lavender House the day after to-morrow."

Annie's face, which had been very bright a moment before, grew suddenly grave. She murmured something half aloud.

"I won't be outdone by Antonia," she said.

"Really, really, Annie," exclaimed Hester, "I shall get to hate Antonia, if you allude to her in that sphinx-like way any longer."

Annie looked hard at Hester with dilating eyes and paling cheeks.

"Do you remember," she said, suddenly coming up to her friend, "the old Annie of Lavender House?"

"How can I forget her," said Hester; "when she is my dearest friend?'

"Do you remember," continued Annie, "the heaps and heaps of scrapes she used to get into, and how there was no peace for her, and no way out of them at all except by confession?"

"Yes, I remember," said Hester, gravely.

"Well, I am going to confess now."

"To confess! But you have done nothing wrong, Annie darling."

"Oh, haven't I; I've been just at my old pranks--just as heedless, as impetuous, as mad, as I have ever been. Hester, I have done wrong, but as it does not concern you, I won't tell you, dear. Only before I go to Mrs. Willis, I should like to congratulate you."

"To congratulate me? On what?" asked poor Hester.

"On having the chance of such a girl as Antonia for your sister."

"Now, really, I wont listen to another word," said Hester. "I have quite made up my mind to **endure** Antonia, and to be patient with her, but if, in addition, I am to congratulate myself, I'm just afraid I can't rise to it. Run away if you want to, Annie, and when you cease to be mysterious I will talk to you again."

Annie left the room and went slowly upstairs to Mrs. Willis's bedroom. She knocked and was admitted. What she said--what words passed between the two were never known, but when Annie left that room there was a look on her face which reminded those who saw her of the best of Annie in the old days, and Mrs. Willis was more affectionate than ever to her dear pupil that evening.

The next day dawned bright and splendid. The trees were beginning to put on their autumn tints, but the air was still full of summer. The Lorrimers at the Towers were busy making preparations to come over to the Grange. They had been invited to the festival by no less a personage than Sir John Thornton himself, and he had couched his epistle in gay and pleasant words.

"As if we had any heart for it," murmured Molly to herself.

"It is over a week now since we have had even a line from father," whispered Nell to her own heart; "how can we care to go and laugh at the Grange?"

"We are going from the dear old place in a week," thought Guy. "I don't believe anyone can draw a smile out of me to-day."

But Boris was happy enough to go, for he was so young that any change was delightful; and as his pets were also leaving the Towers, and he and Kitty had just thought of a splendid way to prepare them for their journey, he felt quite light-hearted once again, and that he would be happy in his new home.

When Jane Macalister heard of the invitation, she flatly refused to accept it.

"Go, if you choose to," she said, with a wave of her hand to the assembled children; "you are young, and it's good for the young to forget. But I shall take the opportunity of sewing up the feather beds in their brown-holland cases. I vowed and declared that when this move had to be made no outsider should come in to pack, so my hands are full, and I have neither time nor heart for frivolity."

"But, Jane, you are specially asked; you are mentioned by name," said Kitty.

"By name, am I?" asked Jane. "Who invited me? That chit of a Hester?"

"No, indeed; the great, magnificent Sir John himself."

"Hoots!" exclaimed Jane; "he's cracked over his second marriage, or he wouldn't bother about an old body like me. I'll none of it. Go away children, and let me get on with my work."

The children withdrew, apparently discomfited, but they guessed that when the time came Jane would go with them, and it proved that they were right.

She made no remark as she joined the group, only at intervals as they all walked across the fields, the single expression, "Hoots!" passed her lips.

In due course they all crossed the stile and entered the grounds of the Grange. They had gone a little way, when Boris uttered a short, sharp cry.

"Why, there's father!" he exclaimed. The others all looked up at this, and then there was a rush and a helter-skelter, and Squire Lorrimer, looking just like the Squire of old, no longer bent nor bowed, nor broken hearted, was surrounded by his family.

Boris mounted on his father's shoulder, and Nell clasped the Squire's hand and looked into his face. Mrs. Lorrimer came close to her husband's side, and Molly stood behind him.

"Where's Guy?" said the Squire in a hoarse kind of voice. "Come here, my boy, I want to say something. It was Sir John's will that I should tell you the good news here, or you'd have all heard from me before I came down to meet you by this path, and we'll all go up and thank him presently."

"For what, father?" asked Molly.

"Why, the most wonderful thing," replied the Squire. "It seems that a girl called Antonia--a strange girl whom I have only met once--put a thought into my old friend's head, and he has acted on it in such a way that, without anything being done which I could not accept, I am enabled to continue as owner of the Towers."

"Oh, father!" said Guy, with a great gasp.

"Yes, my boy," continued the Squire, "I need not sell now. Sir John has lent me money to get over my difficulties, and on such easy terms that it will be possible to pay him back in the course of years without ruining any of us. Drummond was glad to be out of his bargain, so the whole thing was settled last night. We'll be poor enough still, but we need not leave the Towers; and if we are all careful, and I let my farms well--by the way, Sir John is going to take two of them--I have not the least doubt that the debt will be cleared away by the time you are of age, Guy. Anyhow, I feel like a new man. I can hold up my head once more, and all I can say is, God bless Antonia!"

"What's the matter, Jane?" exclaimed Boris.

"Hoots!" said Jane, whose face was nearly purple. "I felt this morning that I needn't go on sewing up those feather beds."

She turned her head aside, and, to the amazement of everyone, burst into tears.

Those tears of Jane's seemed to loosen all tongues. Eyes grew bright, eager voices flew, lips were wreathed in smiles. All the Lorrimers in a body went up to the Grange, where Sir John and his family came out to meet and welcome them.

"And where's Antonia?" asked the Squire.

Everyone else, even Mrs. Bernard Temple, was present, but Antonia was not to be found. Annie volunteered to go and look for her.

After a long search she found her at last busily painting some huge dock leaves, which she had found in her morning ramble, and pulled up by the roots.

"Come, Antonia, you are wanted," said Annie.

"What for?" said Antonia. "Pray don't stand in my light, Annie."

"But they're all waiting for you, every one of them--the Lorrimers, and Hester, and Sir John, and the rest. They want to thank you; it was your doing, you know."

"Of all things in the world," replied Antonia, "I hate being thanked most of all. I did nothing. It was all dear old Sir John. And look what he has given me, Annie.

This magnificent paint-box. Oh, the darling! the beauty! Oh, the rapture of possessing it! I'll go if I must when I have finished my dock leaves, but not before."

The Codes Of Hammurabi And Moses
W. W. Davies

The discovery of the Hammurabi Code is one of the greatest achievements of archaeology, and is of paramount interest, not only to the student of the Bible, but also to all those interested in ancient history...

Religion   ISBN: *1-59462-338-4*   Pages:132
MSRP $12.95

The Theory of Moral Sentiments
Adam Smith

This work from 1749. contains original theories of conscience amd moral judgment and it is the foundation for systemof morals.

Philosophy   ISBN: *1-59462-777-0*   Pages:536
MSRP $19.95

Jessica's First Prayer
Hesba Stretton

In a screened and secluded corner of one of the many railway-bridges which span the streets of London there could be seen a few years ago, from five o'clock every morning until half past eight, a tidily set-out coffee-stall, consisting of a trestle and board, upon which stood two large tin cans, with a small fire of charcoal burning under each so as to keep the coffee boiling during the early hours of the morning when the work-people were thronging into the city on their way to their daily toil...

Childrens   ISBN: *1-59462-373-2*   Pages:84
MSRP $9.95

My Life and Work
Henry Ford

Henry Ford revolutionized the world with his implementation of mass production for the Model T automobile. Gain valuable business insight into his life and work with his own auto-biography... "We have only started on our development of our country we have not as yet, with all our talk of wonderful progress, cone more than scratch the surface. The progress has been wonderful enough but..."

Biographies/   ISBN: *1-59462-198-5*   Pages:300
MSRP $21.95

The Art of Cross-Examination
Francis Wellman

I presume it is the experience of every author, after his first book is published upon an important subject, to be almost overwhelmed with a wealth of ideas and illustrations which could readily have been included in his book, and which to his own mind, at least, seem to make a second edition inevitable. Such certainly was the case with me; and when the first edition had reached its sixth impression in five months, I rejoiced to learn that it seemed to my publishers that the book had met with a sufficiently favorable reception to justify a second and considerably enlarged edition. ..

QTY

Pages:412

Reference   ISBN: *1-59462-647-2*   *MSRP $19.95*

On the Duty of Civil Disobedience
Henry David Thoreau

QTY

Thoreau wrote his famous essay, On the Duty of Civil Disobedience, as a protest against an unjust but popular war and the immoral but popular institution of slave-owning. He did more than write—he declined to pay his taxes, and was hauled off to gaol in consequence. Who can say how much this refusal of his hastened the end of the war and of slavery ?

Law   ISBN: *1-59462-747-9*   **Pages:48**
MSRP $7.45

Dream Psychology Psychoanalysis for Beginners
Sigmund Freud

QTY

Sigmund Freud, born Sigismund Schlomo Freud (May 6, 1856 - September 23, 1939), was a Jewish-Austrian neurologist and psychiatrist who co-founded the psychoanalytic school of psychology. Freud is best known for his theories of the unconscious mind, especially involving the mechanism of repression; his redefinition of sexual desire as mobile and directed towards a wide variety of objects; and his therapeutic techniques, especially his understanding of transference in the therapeutic relationship and the presumed value of dreams as sources of insight into unconscious desires.

Pages:196

Psychology   ISBN: *1-59462-905-6*   *MSRP $15.45*

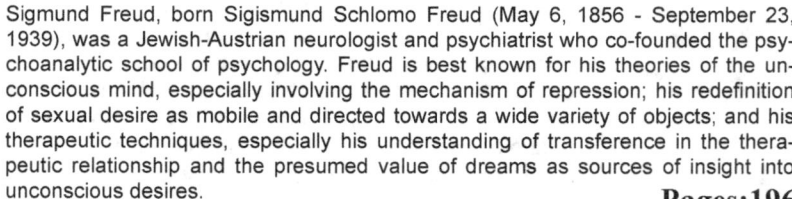

The Miracle of Right Thought
Orison Swett Marden

QTY

Believe with all of your heart that you will do what you were made to do. When the mind has once formed the habit of holding cheerful, happy, prosperous pictures, it will not be easy to form the opposite habit. It does not matter how improbable or how far away this realization may see, or how dark the prospects may be, if we visualize them as best we can, as vividly as possible, hold tenaciously to them and vigorously struggle to attain them, they will gradually become actualized, realized in the life. But a desire, a longing without endeavor, a yearning abandoned or held indifferently will vanish without realization.

Pages:360

Self Help   ISBN: *1-59462-644-8*   *MSRP $25.45*

www.bookjungle.com *email: sales@bookjungle.com fax. 630-214-0564 mail: Book Jungle PO Box 2226 Champaign, IL 61825*

QTY

The Rosicrucian Cosmo-Conception Mystic Christianity by *Max Heindel* ISBN: *1-59462-188-8* **$38.95**
The Rosicrucian Cosmo-conception is not dogmatic, neither does it appeal to any other authority than the reason of the student. It is not controversial, but is: sent forth in the, hope that it may help to clear... New Age/Religion Pages 646

Abandonment To Divine Providence by *Jean-Pierre de Caussade* ISBN: *1-59462-228-0* **$25.95**
"The Rev. Jean Pierre de Caussade was one of the most remarkable spiritual writers of the Society of Jesus in France in the 18th Century. His death took place at Toulouse in 1751. His works have gone through many editions and have been republished... Inspirational/Religion Pages 400

Mental Chemistry by *Charles Haanel* ISBN: *1-59462-192-6* **$23.95**
Mental Chemistry allows the change of material conditions by combining and appropriately utilizing the power of the mind. Much like applied chemistry creates something new and unique out of careful combinations of chemicals the mastery of mental chemistry... New Age Pages 354

The Letters of Robert Browning and Elizabeth Barret Barrett 1845-1846 vol II ISBN: *1-59462-193-4* **$35.95**
by *Robert Browning* and *Elizabeth Barrett* Biographies Pages 596

Gleanings In Genesis (volume I) by *Arthur W. Pink* ISBN: *1-59462-130-6* **$27.45**
Appropriately has Genesis been termed "the seed plot of the Bible" for in it we have, in germ form, almost all of the great doctrines which are afterwards fully developed in the books of Scripture which follow... Religion/Inspirational Pages 420

The Master Key by *L. W. de Laurence* ISBN: *1-59462-001-6* **$30.95**
In no branch of human knowledge has there been a more lively increase of the spirit of research during the past few years than in the study of Psychology, Concentration and Mental Discipline. The requests for authentic lessons in Thought Control, Mental Discipline and... New Age/Business Pages 422

The Lesser Key Of Solomon Goetia by *L. W. de Laurence* ISBN: *1-59462-092-X* **$9.95**
This translation of the first book of the "Lernegton" which is now for the first time made accessible to students of Talismanic Magic was done, after careful collation and edition, from numerous Ancient Manuscripts in Hebrew, Latin, and French... New Age/Occult Pages 92

Rubaiyat Of Omar Khayyam by *Edward Fitzgerald* ISBN: *1-59462-332-5* **$13.95**
Edward Fitzgerald, whom the world has already learned, in spite of his own efforts to remain within the shadow of anonymity, to look upon as one of the rarest poets of the century, was born at Bredfield, in Suffolk, on the 31st of March, 1809. He was the third son of John Purcell... Music Pages 172

Ancient Law by *Henry Maine* ISBN: *1-59462-128-4* **$29.95**
The chief object of the following pages is to indicate some of the earliest ideas of mankind, as they are reflected in Ancient Law, and to point out the relation of those ideas to modern thought. Religion/History Pages 452

Far-Away Stories by *William J. Locke* ISBN: *1-59462-129-2* **$19.45**
"Good wine needs no bush, but a collection of mixed vintages does. And this book is just such a collection. Some of the stories I do not want to remain buried for ever in the museum files of dead magazine-numbers an author's not unpardonable vanity..." Fiction Pages 272

Life of David Crockett by *David Crockett* ISBN: *1-59462-250-7* **$27.45**
"Colonel David Crockett was one of the most remarkable men of the times in which he lived. Born in humble life, but gifted with a strong will, an indomitable courage, and unremitting perseverance... Biographies/New Age Pages 424

Lip-Reading by *Edward Nitchie* ISBN: *1-59462-206-X* **$25.95**
Edward B. Nitchie, founder of the New York School for the Hard of Hearing, now the Nitchie School of Lip-Reading, Inc, wrote "LIP-READING Principles and Practice". The development and perfecting of this meritorious work on lip-reading was an undertaking... How-to Pages 400

A Handbook of Suggestive Therapeutics, Applied Hypnotism, Psychic Science ISBN: *1-59462-214-0* **$24.95**
by *Henry Munro* Health/New Age/Health/Self-help Pages 376

A Doll's House: and Two Other Plays by *Henrik Ibsen* ISBN: *1-59462-112-8* **$19.95**
Henrik Ibsen created this classic when in revolutionary 1848 Rome. Introducing some striking concepts in playwriting for the realist genre this play has been studied the world over. Fiction/Classics/Plays 308

The Light of Asia by *sir Edwin Arnold* ISBN: *1-59462-204-3* **$13.95**
In this poetic masterpiece, Edwin Arnold describes the life and teachings of Buddha. The man who was to become known as Buddha to the world was born as Prince Gautama of India but he rejected the worldly riches and abandoned the reigns of power when... Religion/History/Biographies Pages 170

The Complete Works of Guy de Maupassant by *Guy de Maupassant* ISBN: *1-59462-157-8* **$16.95**
"For days and days, nights and nights, I had dreamed of that first kiss which was to consecrate our engagement, and I knew not on what spot I should put my lips..." Fiction/Classics Pages 240

The Art of Cross-Examination by *Francis L. Wellman* ISBN: *1-59462-309-0* **$26.95**
Written by a renowned trial lawyer, Wellman imparts his experience and uses case studies to explain how to use psychology to extract desired information through questioning. How-to/Science/Reference Pages 408

Answered or Unanswered? by *Louisa Vaughan* ISBN: *1-59462-248-5* **$10.95**
Miracles of Faith in China Religion Pages 112

The Edinburgh Lectures on Mental Science (1909) by *Thomas* ISBN: *1-59462-008-3* **$11.95**
This book contains the substance of a course of lectures recently given by the writer in the Queen Street Hall, Edinburgh. Its purpose is to indicate the Natural Principles governing the relation between Mental Action and Material Conditions... New Age/Psychology Pages 148

Ayesha by *H. Rider Haggard* ISBN: *1-59462-301-5* **$24.95**
Verily and indeed it is the unexpected that happens! Probably if there was one person upon the earth from whom the Editor of this, and of a certain previous history, did not expect to hear again... Classics Pages 380

Ayala's Angel by *Anthony Trollope* ISBN: *1-59462-352-X* **$29.95**
The two girls were both pretty, but Lucy who was twenty-one who supposed to be simple and comparatively unattractive, whereas Ayala was credited, as her Bombwhat romantic name might show, with poetic charm and a taste for romance. Ayala when her father died was nineteen... Fiction Pages 484

The American Commonwealth by *James Bryce* ISBN: *1-59462-286-2* **$34.45**
An interpretation of American democratic political theory. It examines political mechanics and society from the perspective of Scotsman James Bryce Politics Pages 572

Stories of the Pilgrims by *Margaret P. Pumphrey* ISBN: *1-59462-116-0* **$17.95**
This book explores pilgrims religious oppression in England as well as their escape to Holland and eventual crossing to America on the Mayflower, and their early days in New England... History Pages 268

www.bookjungle.com *email: sales@bookjungle.com fax: 630-214-0564 mail: Book Jungle PO Box 2226 Champaign, IL 61825*

QTY

The Fasting Cure *by Sinclair Upton*   ISBN: *1-59462-222-1* **$13.95**
*In the Cosmopolitan Magazine for May, 1910, and in the Contemporary Review (London) for April, 1910, I published an article dealing with my experi-
ences in fasting. I have written a great many magazine articles, but never one which attracted so much attention...* New Age/Self Help/Health Pages 164

Hebrew Astrology *by Sepharial*   ISBN: *1-59462-308-2* **$13.45**
*In these days of advanced thinking it is a matter of common observation that we have left many of the old landmarks behind and that we are now pressing
forward to greater heights and to a wider horizon than that which represented the mind-content of our progenitors...*   Astrology Pages 144

Thought Vibration or The Law of Attraction in the Thought World   ISBN: *1-59462-127-6* **$12.95**
by William Walker Atkinson   Psychology/Religion Pages 144

Optimism *by Helen Keller*   ISBN: *1-59462-108-X* **$15.95**
*Helen Keller was blind, deaf, and mute since 19 months old, yet famously learned how to overcome these handicaps, communicate with the world, and
spread her lectures promoting optimism. An inspiring read for everyone...*   Biographies/Inspirational Pages 84

Sara Crewe *by Frances Burnett*   ISBN: *1-59462-360-0*   **$9.45**
*In the first place, Miss Minchin lived in London. Her home was a large, dull, tall one, in a large, dull square, where all the houses were alike, and all the
sparrows were alike, and where all the door-knockers made the same heavy sound...*   Childrens/Classic Pages 88

The Autobiography of Benjamin Franklin *by Benjamin Franklin*   ISBN: *1-59462-135-7* **$24.95**
*The Autobiography of Benjamin Franklin has probably been more extensively read than any other American historical work, and no other book of its kind
has had such ups and downs of fortune. Franklin lived for many years in England, where he was agent...*   Biographies/History Pages 332

Name	
Email	
Telephone	
Address	
City, State ZIP	

☐ **Credit Card**   ☐ **Check / Money Order**

Credit Card Number	
Expiration Date	
Signature	

*Please Mail to: Book Jungle
PO Box 2226
Champaign, IL 61825
or Fax to: 630-214-0564*

ORDERING INFORMATION

web*: www.bookjungle.com*
email*: sales@bookjungle.com*
fax*: 630-214-0564*
mail*: Book Jungle PO Box 2226 Champaign, IL 61825*
or PayPal *to sales@bookjungle.com*

Please contact us for bulk discounts

DIRECT-ORDER TERMS

**20% Discount if You Order
Two or More Books**
Free Domestic Shipping!
Accepted: Master Card, Visa,
Discover, American Express

www.ingramcontent.com/pod-product-compliance
Lightning Source LLC
Chambersburg PA
CBHW080902020726
47502CB00008B/2324